RAMAGE'S

MUTINY

Historical Fiction Published by McBooks Press

RAMAGE'S MUTINY

by

DUDLEY POPE

THE LORD RAMAGE NOVELS, NO. 8

McBOOKS PRESS, INC.
ITHACA, NEW YORK

Published by McBooks Press 2001
Copyright © 1977 by Dudley Pope
First published in the United Kingdom in 1997 by
The Alison Press/Martin Secker & Warburg Limited

Cover painting by Paul Wright.

Library of Congress Cataloging-in-Publication Data

Pope, Dudley.
  Ramage's mutiny / by Dudley Pope.
    p.   cm. — (Lord Ramage novels ; no. 8)
  ISBN 0-935526-90-0 (alk. paper)
    1. Ramage, Nicholas (Fictitious character)—Fiction. 2. Great
  Britain—History, Naval—19th century—Fiction. 3. Great
  Britain. Royal Navy—Officers—Fiction. 4. Napoleonic Wars,
  1800–1815—Fiction.   I. Title
PR6066.O5 R35 2001
823'.914—dc21   01-030316

Distributed to the trade by National Book Network, Inc.,
15200 NBN Way, Blue Ridge Summit, PA 17214
800-462-6420

Additional copies of this book may be ordered from any bookstore
or directly from McBooks Press, Inc., ID Booth Building, 520 North
Meadow St., Ithaca, NY 14850. Please include $4.00 postage and
handling with mail orders. New York State residents must add sales
tax. All McBooks Press publications can also be ordered
by calling toll-free 1-888-BOOKS11 (1-888-266-5711).
Please call to request a free catalog.

Visit the McBooks Press website at www.mcbooks.com.

Printed in the United States of America

9 8 7 6 5 4 3

To my cousin
Dorothy Pope
with love

A U T H O R ' S   N O T E

WITH one exception, all the places mentioned in this story exist. The traveller will, however, look in vain for Santa Cruz on the Spanish Main. The student of naval history will be reminded of the tragedy of the *Hermione* . . .

D. P.
Yacht Ramage
English Harbour, Antigua

THE WEST INDIES

VIRGIN ISLANDS

Atlantic Ocean

Anegada
Tortola
St John
St Thomas
Snake Island
(Culebra)

Anegada Passage

Virgin Gorda

PUERTO RICO

Crab Island
(Vieques)

St Croix

Anguilla

LEEWARD ISLANDS

St Kitts
Nevis
Montserrat

Barbuda

Antigua

Guadeloupe

Dominica

Martinque

St Lucia

WINDWARD ISLANDS

St Vincent

BARBADOS

Grenada

Isla de Margarita

Punta
Peñas

La Guaira

Santa
Cruz

Caracas

CHAPTER ONE

THE LITTLE dockyard at English Harbour was already bustling, although the sun was only just lifting over the rounded hills to the east. In the West Indies the day began at dawn so that men could do as much heavy work as possible before the sun began to scorch the energy from their bodies.

Ramage eased himself into the rattan chair on the balcony of the Commander-in-Chief's house, glancing down warily as protesting creaks warned that termites were busily and silently chewing their way through the legs to convert the springy wood into little piles of brown powder.

As he relaxed to wait for the Admiral he guessed that today Captain Ramage was far from popular with the dockyard staff. They were all well paid and provided with comfortable houses, and normally enjoyed a quiet life interrupted only twice or three times a year when a frigate came in for a self-refit, using her own seamen to do the work and relying on the dockyard staff for little more than interference.

Now, however, the master shipwright, master attendant, storekeeper and bosun suddenly found themselves responsible for two former French frigates, seven merchantmen and a schooner, all brought into Antigua as Captain Ramage's prizes.

They had orders from the Admiral to help commission one of the frigates within seven days, while the other—which needed careening for repair to her bottom—had to be ready within three weeks because she was to escort the merchant ships to England. Not only that, but the Admiral was here to make sure the work was completed on time.

Although the Admiral was harrying the dockyard staff without mercy, Ramage had little sympathy for them. They had settled into a way of life where rum was an important part of the day's ritual. While some heathens stopped work at sunrise and sunset and knelt facing the east to say prayers, these dockyard fellows rarely started work but frequently interrupted their leisure to reach for a bottle and top up their glasses.

Ramage had little doubt that a sudden inventory of the dockyard would reveal that they, in combination with the storekeeper, were running a prosperous but illicit business turning the King's stores into ready money, selling rope, sail canvas and paint to merchant ships calling at St John's, the main harbour on the north-western side of Antigua.

Few masters worried about breaking the law and having rope on board that had the "King's Yarn" in it, a coloured thread that showed it had been laid up in one of the Navy's ropewalks and issued only to Navy ships. Most of the rigging in a merchant ship took a coat of Stockholm tar to help preserve it, and that hid the "King's Yarn."

There was corruption in every dockyard and English Harbour was probably no worse than the rest. Because it was small, however, the flaws were more obvious. It comprised only a few stone buildings with grey slate roofs and reminded Ramage of a fifteen-horse stable on the fringe of Newmarket Heath. But what it lacked in size and honesty it made up for in sheer beauty.

It was built at the inner end of a narrow channel which twisted its way like a fjord between ridges of steep hills. The entrance was hard to find and most captains coming in for the first time were thankful for the fortifications on each side, Fort Barclay and the Horseshoe Battery, because the channel did a sharp turn and from seaward there was no hint that ten ships of the line and half a dozen frigates could be safely moored inside, sheltered by the hills from the brisk Trade winds and with cables from their sterns secured to permanent anchors dug in along the beach.

Ramage saw smoke across the channel, beyond the careening wharf, and a few minutes later smelled the sharp tang of hot pitch as seamen stoked up the fire under one of the big cast-iron pitch kettles standing waist-high on a small point, well clear of ships and buildings in case they became overheated and burst into flames. Nearby one of the French frigates, *La Comète,* was already hove-down at the Carénage Wharf, lying almost on her side like a stranded whale, with several sheets of copper sheathing missing along the rounded turn of the bilge and showing black stripes where carpenters and their mates were perched on a small raft, busy removing damaged planking.

Ramage reflected that barely two weeks ago off Martinique that frigate was doing her best to sink the *Juno* frigate, which he then commanded. Now she was a prize and instead of being dead or a prisoner he was sitting on the balcony of the Commander-in-Chief's house waiting for orders. These would concern the second French frigate, now anchored farther up the channel in Freeman's Bay. She was the *Surcouf,* which he had cut out of Fort Royal, and which would be his new command as soon as all the paperwork was completed; one of the fastest and most heavily armed frigates in the Caribbean, and certainly the loveliest: the French had a knack of building graceful ships.

But sitting here now, enjoying the first half an hour's peace and quiet since then, he felt chilled. He had taken terrible risks with his ship and his men, gambling with a recklessness that now appalled him. He had been lucky—the prizes were proof of that—but he had risked lives with less concern than some pallid gambler at Buck's watched a rolling die with a hundred guineas at stake. Had there been an alternative? Yes, if he cared for his men he would not have risked cutting out the *Surcouf*. Yet those same men would have marked him down as a coward if he had left her alone. Was success a justification?

As he considered the grim contradictions he watched two boats pulling away from the *Surcouf*. They were laden with casks and bound for Tank Bay at the head of the channel, where there was a fresh-water spring. The frigate's sails were hanging down like enormous creased curtains: old Southwick, her new Master, was seizing the opportunity of airing them before the wind came up, part of the everlasting fight against the mildew that needed only a day or two of hot and humid weather to speckle the cloth with black mould and rot the stitching, however much the thread was waxed.

A whiff of mildew as he moved slightly told him that his steward had not aired the coat he was wearing, but it was pleasant sitting here, breeches newly pressed, silk stockings uncreased, shoes shining, sword scabbard polished . . . One thing he missed afloat was sitting comfortably in the fresh air: one was always standing or pacing up and down like an animal in a cage.

The sun was rising quickly now and bringing colour to hills which had been dark with shadow, but all its early pinkness could not disguise the fact that no rain had fallen on Antigua for several weeks. The earth which Nature had spread thinly on the hills was now arid, streaked with brown scars where the coarse grass had withered and grey where jagged rocks jutted out like enormous teeth. This was the time of day, for perhaps five minutes, that always reminded Ramage of a summer sunrise tinting the heather in the Scottish Highlands.

As the sun climbed higher the colours changed, growing harsher. Soon one would notice only the vivid blue of the sky, the hard brown of the hills and the dark green of the mangroves growing in a thick band along the water's edge, the thin red roots twisting like predatory claws. Now the light and shadow caught the cacti scattered over the hills like outrageous artichokes and, every ten yards or so, he could see the single trunk of a century plant sprouting ten or twelve feet high, the yellow blossoms now withering, golden foxgloves past their prime.

Ramage's eye caught the flash of red on Fort Barclay as a sentry turned in the sunlight beside the small stone magazine built on the inland side of the battlements. Now he could see the breeches of the guns gleaming black as the sun lifted the shadows. Twenty-six guns, with a dozen more in the Horseshoe Battery on the other side of the entrance. Ramage wondered if any of them had ever fired against an enemy. It would be a brave Frenchman who tried to force his way in, because there was also the masked battery just at the back of the beach facing the entrance, twenty more guns concealed by sand dunes and shaded by palm trees, poised like a cat waiting in front of a mouse hole in the wainscoting.

At the moment the masked battery covered Admiral Davis's flagship, the 74-gun *Invincible*, which was lying with her anchors towards the entrance and her stern held by a cable which ran to the beach and was secured to another anchor half buried in the sand, left there permanently for the big ships.

Footsteps behind him brought Ramage to his feet and he turned to find the Admiral and Captain Edwards, who commanded the *Invincible*, blinking in the sunlight as they came out on to the balcony. The Admiral nodded cheerfully.

"Ha, mornin', Ramage; sittin' here admirin' your prizes, eh? Can't see the cordage for the guineas, no doubt!"

Henry Davis, Rear-Admiral and "Commander-in-Chief of His Majesty's Ships and Vessels upon the Windward and Leeward Islands Station," was in a cheerful mood; a condition which Ramage guessed had been brought about by an equally calculating look at the prizes—and the knowledge that a commander-in-chief took an eighth share in the prize-money. A young captain might find glory in the gunfire, Ramage thought sourly, but all too often promotion depended on his contribution to his admiral's prize account.

The Admiral gestured to Ramage and Captain Edwards to sit down and lowered himself into a rattan chair with the usual care of anyone who had spent much time in the Tropics and knew of the sabotage which termites wreaked. He passed a bundle of papers to Ramage: "The inventory of the *Surcouf* and the valuation. I'll buy her in, of course. She's three years old, so £14 a ton is a fair price. Seven hundred tons, which means £9800 for hull, masts, yards, rigging and fixed furniture. I think the Admiralty and Navy Board will approve that."

"And the rest of her equipment, sir?" Ramage asked.

"Normal valuation based on prices at Jamaica dockyard," the Admiral said briskly. "That's the valuation in England plus sixty per cent—the price they charge merchant ships." He pointed to the papers he had just given Ramage. "The figure is there—about £7500, I think. A total of just over £17,000 for the whole ship. It'll work out less for *La Comète*," he added, waving towards the careened frigate. "She's three years older and damaged. Then you have the schooner and the seven merchantmen. A tidy sum for you and your men. The two frigates bring you nearly £10,000, with £5000 shared between the lieutenants, Master and Surgeon . . . Why, the seamen will get £50 each—the equivalent of four years' pay!"

"They earned it," Captain Edwards commented. "And that doesn't include the merchant ships and head-money."

"I know they earned it," the Admiral said crossly, "and they'll earn it twice over by the time they've carried out the orders I'm preparing for Ramage. Now," he said impatiently, indicating that the subject of the prize-money was closed, "how long before you'll have that *Surcouf* commissioned?"

Although Ramage had guessed this was the real reason why he had been ordered to report to the Admiral, it was a difficult question to answer. The Admiral had originally promised to shift the ship's company of his last command, the *Juno*, to his new one, but the *Juno* had not yet arrived in English Harbour. No doubt Aitken, the First Lieutenant who had been left in command off Martinique when Ramage transferred to the *Surcouf* with a prize crew, had a perfectly good reason for the delay in reaching Antigua, but in the meantime Ramage was left with only forty men.

So far he had met with nothing but obstruction from the dockyard's master attendant, bosun and storekeeper—who were probably scared stiff in case this sudden influx of work resulted in demands for stores which would reveal their peculations—but this was usual, not worth even mentioning to the Admiral.

"About a week, once I get all my Junos. That's providing we use the French guns, sir. If we shift them and have to get out all the shot—" he broke off as Admiral Davis waved aside the idea. The two navies used different sized shot, but providing the *Surcouf* carried enough for her next operation it did not matter.

"Provisions?" demanded the Admiral.

"Three months on the French scale, sir, and three months' water."

"Very well. The *Juno* should be in within a day or two—I can't think what's delayed that young fellow: hope he's not going to be a disappointment. Anyway, a week from the time she arrives, eh?"

His round face was lined, and the thick black eyebrows which jutted out of his brow like small brushes were drawn down, giving him a quaintly fierce appearance, like a truculent shoe-black.

"Now, her name. I don't like *Surcouf;* no need for us to celebrate a dam' French pirate."

"Calypso!" Ramage was startled to find he had spoken the word aloud and hurriedly added: "Perhaps you would consider renaming her 'Calypso,' sir."

"Sounds all right, but I've forgotten my mythology. What does it mean, eh?"

Captain Edwards stretched out his legs with the air of a man whose subject had just been reached on the agenda. "When Odysseus was wrecked he was cast up on the island of Ogyvia, where Calypso lived. She was a sea nymph, sir. They—er, they lived together for several years, and when Odysseus eventually wanted to leave and go home, she promised him immortality and eternal youth if he stayed."

"But he refused, wise fellow," the Admiral commented. "Can think of nothing worse than living forever. Anyway, that's the woman you had in mind, eh Ramage?"

"Yes, sir—"

"Why?" the Admiral interrupted bluntly. "You seemed to have the name ready on the tip of your tongue."

"No sir, I didn't know you intended renaming her. I was thinking yesterday that the *Jocasta* frigate was rather like Odysseus, only she's held by the Spanish in a port on the Main—"

"Very fanciful," sniffed Admiral Davis, "but your job will be to get her out."

Edwards grinned. "Zeus ordered Calypso to release Odysseus, sir. Perhaps Ramage had you in mind as Zeus: you give the *Calypso* frigate orders to release Odysseus—or, rather, the *Jocasta* frigate."

"It all sounds just as vague and confusin' as Greek mythology always was when I was a boy," the Admiral grumbled, "but the name sounds right enough. Better than that damned French pirate. Very well, *Calypso* she is."

"Thank you, sir," Ramage said politely, turning slightly so that the sun was not in his eyes. It was getting hot now; the heat was soaking through his coat and he had tied his stock too tight: his neck would be raw in places before he could leave the Admiral's house and loosen it.

Admiral Davis was frowning at the back of his sleeve, as though suspicious that the gold braid and lace was really pinchbeck. He seemed almost embarrassed. But Ramage knew that admirals were never embarrassed by anything they had to say to a junior post captain—in his own case one of the most junior in the Navy List. When he left England a few months ago his name had been the last on the List. Since then perhaps a dozen more lieutenants had been made post and their names would now follow his. Promotion was by seniority, which meant being pushed up from below, helped by a high mortality among the names above you on the List: there was nothing like a bloody war to hoist you up the ladder.

Yet Ramage could see that the Admiral was certainly at a loss for words. He now inspected the nails of his left hand, tugged at his chin and finally gestured angrily at his burly flag captain. Edwards had obviously anticipated that this would happen, and he turned to Ramage. "The *Jocasta*," he said. "You know how she fell into Spanish hands?"

"I've heard only gossip," Ramage said carefully, guessing this would be his only opportunity of finding out what really happened and realizing that the Admiral could hardly bear to talk about it.

Captain Edwards caught the Admiral's eye, noted the approving nod, and said: "She left Cape Nicolas Mole—that's at the western end of Hispaniola, as you probably know—some two years ago. Captain Wallis commanded her and had orders from Sir Hyde Parker at Jamaica to patrol the Mona Passage for seven weeks with the *Alert* and *Reliance* in company.

"After three weeks the *Alert* sprang a leak and Captain
Wallis ordered her back to the Mole. A fortnight later, on a night
when the *Reliance* had been sent off in chase of a suspected privateer, the *Jocasta's* ship's company mutinied. They murdered
Wallis and all his officers and sailed the ship to La Guaira, on
the Main. There they handed her over to the Spanish, who refit-
ted her but, as far as we know, never sent her to sea. At present
she's in Santa Cruz."

"Did all the ship's company mutiny?"

Edwards shook his head. "She had a complement of some
150 men. We think about a third of them were active mutineers."

"And the rest?" Ramage asked, curious about their fate.

Admiral Davis snorted and slapped his knee. "They're mutineers too! All right, Edwards, I know you don't agree with me,
but they did nothing to stop the mutiny, nor did they try to
recover the ship, so they're just as guilty."

"Santa Cruz," Ramage said hurriedly, noticing Edwards's face
reddening with suppressed anger, "is it well defended?"

"Well enough," Edwards said grimly. "The harbour is a large
lagoon. The entrance is more than half a mile long and too narrow for a ship to tack. It's a case of 'out boats and tow' if the
wind is foul. Forts on each side of the entrance and a third one
at the lagoon end of the channel. I have a rough chart ready for
you," he added quickly, as if dismissing the forts.

"How many guns in the forts?" Ramage asked warily.

Edwards shrugged his shoulders. "We can't be sure. Perhaps
thirty or forty."

"Altogether?"

"No," Edwards said uncomfortably, "in each fort."

More than a hundred guns, plunging fire at point-blank range,
and the target a frigate being towed past them by men rowing

in boats . . . Ramage felt the heat going out of the sun. Most of those guns would be twenty-four- or thirty-six-pounders, against the *Calypso*'s twelve-pounders.

"And the *Jocasta*'s in commission, so there'd be her guns as well," he said, then suddenly realized he was thinking aloud.

"And more than three hundred men on board her," the Admiral said, his voice carefully neutral. "We—the Admiralty, rather —have received word that she's to sail for Cuba in the middle of July. In four weeks' time."

Ramage now found himself puzzled as well as worried. Captain Edwards's point about Santa Cruz's entrance being narrow and strongly defended had made him think that the *Calypso* was intended to make a direct attack, which would be another way of committing suicide. But now the Admiral was talking about the *Jocasta* sailing for Cuba. He almost sighed with relief: his imagination was making him overly nervous; Edwards was being offhand about the forts simply because there was no need to go into Santa Cruz! He looked at the Admiral, who avoided his eyes, finding something of interest at the harbour entrance. "You want me to take her as soon as she sails, sir?"

Admiral Davis shook his head, still looking away. "The Admiralty have ordered her to be cut out of Santa Cruz," he said tonelessly. "Want to teach the Dons a lesson, I suppose, and they won't risk her slipping through our fingers and reaching Cuba."

Ramage felt the chilly ripple of fear tightening his skin: again he pictured the forts firing at the *Calypso* as she was towed in, and at both frigates as they sailed out. Was the fear showing in his face? He was thankful that neither the Admiral nor Edwards was looking at him. The perspiration on his brow and upper lip owed nothing to the sun; it was cold, and he wiped it away with what he hoped would seem a casual movement of his hand.

Then he caught a glance exchanged between the two men,

and although he could not interpret it he knew there was something strange and underhand about the whole business. It had begun several months ago, when he was on leave in London, a lieutenant enjoying a rest. Then suddenly he had been summoned to the Admiralty, unexpectedly made post and given command of the *Juno* frigate.

All that had been very flattering; orders were addressed to "Captain Ramage" and it did not matter that his name was at the bottom of the post captains in the Navy List, the most junior of them all. Then he had been sent off to the West Indies in the *Juno* with urgent instructions for Admiral Davis and orders to put himself under the Admiral's command. He had known nothing about the Admiralty's instructions, except that they concerned some "special service." They had nothing to do with Captain Ramage; he was merely the Admiralty's messenger.

He had since discovered that the "special service" was the recapture of the *Jocasta,* and that Admiral Davis had chosen his favourite for it, a Captain Eames, and despatched him to Santa Cruz. The newly arrived Captain Ramage had been given orders appropriate for the most junior captain on the station—to blockade the French port of Fort Royal, Martinique.

From then on, Ramage thought wryly, the Admiral's plans had gone awry. The junior captain had caused the capture of two French frigates, sunk three others, and seized seven merchantmen. The favourite captain, as far as Ramage could make out, had come back from Santa Cruz to report complete failure. Well, war was a massive game of chance; he was prepared to admit that good luck had brought the French convoy into the trap he had set off Fort Royal, and bad luck might have prevented Eames from cutting out the *Jocasta.* That being so, why was he now sitting on the Admiral's balcony at English Harbour being given orders which were—not to put too fine a point on it—the ones that Eames had already failed to carry out? Eames was a very senior captain; he was sufficiently high in the Navy List that within a year or two he could reasonably expect to be given command of a 74-gun ship.

The reason, he decided coldly, was that Eames had failed. He had failed miserably and the Admiral was hurriedly whitewashing him. He wasn't sending Eames back to try again, nor was he risking any of his other captains; no, he was sending out the newcomer, Captain Nicholas Ramage. A man whose name was the lowest on the post list was supposed to succeed where someone halfway up the list had failed. And failed so badly, Ramage guessed, that everyone on the station was remaining tactfully silent about it.

Suddenly he realized that Captain Ramage was not expected to succeed; he was expected to fail. He saw it as though he had just walked from darkness into a well-lit room. Admiral Davis was protecting one of his favourites and yet, in his own curious way, he was trying to be fair. He felt guilty about it; that explained why he had left Edwards to explain the situation.

A despatch would soon be on its way to the Admiralty in the next Post Office packet brig describing how Captain Ramage had attacked and seized the convoy off Martinique, and their Lordships would be pleased that he had captured two frigates. The despatch would be printed in the *Gazette* and Captain Ramage's stock would be high.

Admiral Davis's next despatch would tell their Lordships how Captain Ramage had tried to cut out the *Jocasta* from Santa Cruz, and how he had failed. There would be no mention of Eames's earlier attempt; as far as their Lordships would know, Ramage had been the only one sent on the "special service." Ramage would be the Admiral's scapegoat: it was as simple as that. And, he realized, the one person who would not care would be himself; he would be dead. There could be few survivors from a determined attempt to cut out the *Jocasta*.

Not only had Eames failed, Ramage reflected bitterly, but he had raised the alarm at Santa Cruz. For the past couple of years, and probably longer, the Spanish garrison had dozed happily in the heat of the sun; the enemy was never sighted and no doubt round shot rusted in the torrential tropical showers and the carriages of the guns rotted. Then Eames had appeared off the coast and roused the Dons as surely as a prodding stick stirred up a beehive. Sentries would now be alert, rust would be hammered from the shot, and gun carriages repaired. For the next few weeks the Spaniards would be full of bustle and zeal; they would be more than ready for the *Calypso* frigate . . .

It was unfair, of course, but it was also the Navy. No doubt in the past lieutenants and captains had complained that the First Lord of the Admiralty had favoured young Ramage, giving him orders that allowed him to cut a dash and get his name in the *London Gazette* with almost monotonous regularity. Still, perhaps he had enough credit at the Admiralty by now so that if he survived a complete failure at Santa Cruz—a big "if"—it would not have a disastrous effect on his career.

What had Admiral Davis just said? The Admiralty wanted to teach the Dons a lesson? Yes, it made good sense; cut out the *Jocasta* from under their very noses (and hope to find some of the original mutineers still on board, so that they could be hanged for treason as well as mutiny). It would be a warning for any British seaman who might have the thought of mutiny flash across his mind on a wet and windy night; a warning to the Dons for having welcomed a mutinous ship. They seemed not to realize that the spirit of mutiny was like fire—it did not respect flags or frontiers.

Why had Eames failed, Ramage wondered. Driven off by the guns of the forts? Went aground in the channel? Sailed down to the lagoon but found the *Jocasta* too strongly manned to be able to board her? The Admiral had mentioned three hundred men, twice her normal complement under British command.

He looked up to find both the Admiral and Edwards watching him closely, as if trying to read his thoughts. Or, he suddenly realized, more like fishermen trying to see if the fish had taken the bait.

"Captain Eames," Ramage said diffidently, "he—er, he met with some difficulty?"

The Admiral grunted, as though the question had given him a sharp and unexpected prod under the ribs. "Completely misunderstood his orders, unfortunately. Came back with valuable intelligence, though. Had to send him straight off on another operation, otherwise he'd be on his way back to Santa Cruz."

Ramage smiled politely and the Admiral smiled back, and then Edwards smiled, and all three of them knew that each understood Eames's role. The failure at Santa Cruz was now Eames's raddled mistress, a shrill harridan who for the rest of his life in the Navy would occasionally look over his shoulder and nag him. Officially no one would talk about her—there would probably be the occasional captain who would gossip, but that couldn't be helped, because Admiral Davis could not hope to keep it a secret forever—but Eames would always be ashamed, always worried in case someone broke the rules and spoke.

"Yes, we owe Captain Eames a lot for providing valuable information about the entrance," Admiral Davis said as Edwards unfolded a piece of paper and began smoothing it out. "Edwards has a copy of the chart. Plenty of soundings on it—to seaward, anyway. And the guns—the exact number are marked in. On the two forts at the entrance, anyway . . ." His voice trailed off as he realized that his praise was damning Eames.

"Neutrals," Edwards said suddenly, obviously intending to break the silence that followed. "Eames said one or two neutral ships go in and out of Santa Cruz every week. Mostly American. These dam' Jonathans seem to get in everywhere with their cargoes of 'notions' and salt fish."

He finished smoothing the sheet of paper and gave it to Ramage. "It's rather a small scale, I'm afraid; Eames's Master didn't have time to re-draw it. No need to return it, though: I have a copy."

Ramage nodded. The sketch was small but it was neat and, judging by the distance from the forts at the entrance to the nearest sounding, it damned Eames for a cowardly poltroon. Ramage glanced up and saw that Edwards had read his thoughts on this occasion, but instead of causing embarrassment it seemed to hint at a friendly understanding. In the dim future Edwards might prove to be an ally—or, at least, not an enemy.

"A week," Admiral Davis said absently. "A week after the *Juno* comes in. If the *Calypso* is delayed much longer, I'll have to send you men from the flagship. The *Jocasta*'s due to sail from Santa Cruz in four weeks—not a lot of time, even though the Dons are always late."

CHAPTER TWO

BACK ON BOARD the frigate, Ramage settled down at his desk to read through the *Calypso*'s inventory. On the deck above his head he could hear carpenter's mates getting ready to rig a stage over the transom to remove the board with the name *Surcouf* carved on it, and the carpenter was already over in the dockyard searching for a suitable piece of straight-grained wood on which to carve the new name of *Calypso*. No doubt he was cursing the choice because it included four curved letters. Carpenters preferred names like "Vixen" or "Kite" which, in capitals, meant the chisels or gouges had to cut only straight lines.

The inventory ran to dozens of pages, each signed by the four dockyard men, and beside each item was their valuation. The first few pages covered the hull, masts and spars. Then came all the sails, blocks and cordage, as well as the spares. He noted that the French followed the Royal Navy in allowing four anchors and six cables, although at one hundred fathoms each the cables were shorter.

He turned the pages of the rest of the inventory, the first full one he had ever seen, and although he saw many of them every day he found himself surprised at the number of items needed for a ship as small as a frigate. The reason was simple enough, of course; she was the home of more than two hundred men as well as a fighting ship which had to be sailed and navigated.

He glanced at random at the descriptions. Three large copper kettles in which the ship's company's food was cooked were valued at £12 each. There were two-minute, half-hour and one-hour glasses ("with sand running free") which cost less than he would have expected—the two-minute glasses were valued at twopence each.

Then came the spare sails: a new main-topgallant was valued at £12 5s 4d. The list of purser's stores had a note that the clothing was new "but of poor quality." Well, that would have to be taken on shore; the storekeeper must get rid of it as best he could. Ramage was not having poor-quality clothing sold to his men.

Perishable stores—the French must have gone to a lot of trouble in Fort Royal to provision the ship. He noted that, by Royal Navy standards, there was an enormous quantity of various cheeses which the dockyard surveyors had not tried to name, merely contenting themselves with the comment that they were in good condition "and strong in flavour."

There were dozens of defective casks, which meant plenty of work for the dockyard coopers, making and fitting new staves. The master shipwright had made a deduction of £4 10s for repairs, based on the cost of employing three coopers for six days at 5s a day per man.

How he hated all this paperwork. Now he had to check and sign the requisitions for all the remaining items needed for the *Calypso* to sail as one of the King's ships. He reached across the desk for several pages held down by a paperweight.

The Surgeon's requirements were on top. Bowen needed a sick book, journal and various forms for his daily reports to the Captain. Then came a string of abbreviated Latin representing the medicines and nostrums needed to keep the seamen fit and sound in wind and limb.

The purser needed a ton of forms, judging from his list. Tables for casting up allowances of food for the ship's company, bed lists, tobacco lists, forms for reporting surveys on casks of salt beef and pork which held fewer pieces than the total stencilled on the outside, forms for reporting the leakage of beer . . . Ramage felt his patience ebbing as he continued reading: the King's ships carried so much paper that he was sometimes surprised they remained afloat. The sheer quantity only became apparent when a ship was commissioned. Bounty list, conduct list, muster table, captain's journal, master's log, account of impressed men, daily report of this, daily report of that . . .

He could guess the dockyard storekeeper's answer to such a requisition: a large packet of blank paper, a box of powder for making ink, a couple of dozen quills and a few straight-edges, and the suggestion that the *Calypso* make use of the *Seaman's Vade Mecum* (which gave specimens of just about every form, voucher, list and report in the Navy) and draw her own.

He heard someone clattering down the ladder and a moment later the Marine sentry at the cabin door called out: "Mr South-wick, sir!"

"Send him in."

The old Master looked tired: his eyes were rimmed with red, his shoulders sagged and his white hair, usually flowing like a dried mop, was dank with perspiration and plastered down on his head. Although they had served together for several years, this was one of the few occasions when Ramage had seen South-wick showing his years.

Ramage stood up from the desk and gestured to Southwick to sit with him on the settee which ran athwart the cabin.

"The carpenter tells me we have a new name, sir," Southwick said wearily. "It's about the only thing we can get without hav-ing to hoist it on board."

"The *Juno* will be in shortly," Ramage reassured him, "then we'll have all our men. The Admiral can't spare anyone, so we'll have to make do for the time being."

"Aye, forty men aren't enough to commission a ship of this size. The guns," Southwick added anxiously, "I hope we aren't going to have to shift them?"

"No," Ramage assured him, "the Admiral reckons we have enough shot on board."

Southwick gave a sigh of relief. "Thank goodness for that. I can't think why the Frogs have to use a different measure any-way. And the Dons—all foreigners, in fact."

"How is the work going?" Ramage asked hurriedly, hoping to head off a tirade against foreigners and their wicked, devious and wilful ways, particularly with weights and measures.

"Well, now we've got those dockyard fellows out of the way I can tidy up the ship. Every blessed thing had to be stretched out and measured or lined up and counted. Cables, blocks, pots and pans, sails, candles . . . Now everything has to be stowed again. Is the Admiral buying her in?"

Ramage nodded. "At a valuation of about £17,000."

Southwick's eyes lit up for a moment, then he said gloomily: "I don't expect the Admiralty and Navy Board will approve that price."

"Don't worry about that; the Admiral knows he'll get his knuckles rapped if he pitches it too high. Anyway, you'll do well enough. At that price you share £5000 with three lieutenants and Bowen. Even at half that you'd still get a tidy sum to invest in the Funds. And that's only for the *Calypso*."

"Aye," Southwick admitted, cheering up slightly. "There should be another thousand Pounds in it, if those thieving prize agents don't take it all."

"More than that: seven merchant ships fully laden. The Admiral is sending them to England with *La Comète* as soon as she's repaired."

The Master shrugged his shoulders. "It's as broad as it's long. Out here the cargoes fetch more and the ships less; in England it's t'other way round."

But the old Master's depression was lifting. He had been under a heavy strain for the past few days and was driving himself and his few men to get the *Calypso* ready for sea. Nor did English Harbour help: it was hot and humid because the very characteristics that made it a sheltered anchorage also meant there was precious little breeze to cool a ship. Although awnings kept the worst of the sun's heat from the decks, there was no draught through the ship herself. Days were bad but nights were worse; the heat stayed locked below and made sleeping difficult. The seamen were luckier—Ramage had given permission for them to sling their hammocks on deck at night. However the Captain, for the sake of discipline, had to sleep in his own cot and curse the Tropics.

"We're still going after the *Jocasta,* sir?" Southwick's tone made it clear that he was more interested in attacking enemy harbours than sitting in British dockyards.

"Yes, we sail as soon as we're ready. Find out all you can about Santa Cruz. I've a rough chart for you—one drawn up by Captain Eames, or his Master."

Southwick gave one of the prodigious sniffs for which he was famous; a perfect combination of contempt and distaste but, if he was ever challenged about it, still just a sniff. "I'll be interested to see it. I've already had the sight of a very small-scale one of that part of the coast—the Master of the *Invincible* has it; captured from a Spanish prize it was—and that Santa Cruz is a rare hole in the wall."

Ramage went over to the desk, found Captain Eames's small chart, and gave it to Southwick, who looked at it as though it had just hit him in the face. "Wha—wha—just look at it!" he gasped. "The *Invincible*'s scrap of paper covering the whole coast tells us more than this does!"

Ramage patted Southwick on the shoulder. "Let's be honest: the only chart that'd do us any good is one that gives us the soundings all the way down the entrance channel and the whole of the lagoon. I doubt if even the Spanish have an accurate one! They probably rely on a pilot. You know the sort of thing—thump, 'That's a rock!'—'Yes, Captain sir, I'll remember it next time!'"

Southwick continued looking at the chart and, using his finger and thumb, measured a distance against the latitude scale. "They never went within two miles of the entrance—look, sir, their nearest sounding gives 'em away!"

"Lots of guns in the two forts," Ramage said mildly. "Hot work running a line of soundings under fire."

Southwick stared at him and Ramage flushed: he was so contemptuous of Eames that he now found himself making excuses
for the wretched man, and Southwick was not only puzzled by
what Ramage had said but angry with Eames on his own account.

"Under fire, sir? What's to stop 'em going in closer after dark?
Or if that doesn't suit 'em, send a boat in. The Dons weren't rowing guard across that entrance!"

"Well, at least the *Jocasta* is fitted out," Ramage said. "We
won't have any work to do before we sail her back."

"The first word came from the Admiralty, didn't it, sir? Well,
they've probably got it all wrong. I'll bet the Dons have only just
started fitting her out, and she's not due to sail until this time
next year. You wait and see if I'm not right, sir."

Southwick was cheering up; there was no doubt about that
—he was grumbling with more relish. "This was reliable information," Ramage said. "It came from Madrid, apparently. It seems
the Spanish are trying to assemble a big convoy in Cuba and
need a powerful escort: our frigates from Jamaica have been rattling the bars right off the entrance to Havana."

Southwick nodded in the doubting manner of a gamekeeper
listening to a garrulous poacher explaining away the three pheas-
ant in his bag. In Southwick's view no information from the
Admiralty was ever to be relied on. Solid facts came only from
other masters; it was the result of experience and observation
carefully noted down in log books or on charts, and all else was
illusion, the eternal Cape Flyaway that many people talked about
but no one ever rounded.

"Well, the *Jocasta* is in there, and whether she's ready or not
we have to find a way of winkling her out." Ramage was curious to hear what Southwick, a firm devotee of board-'em-in-the-
smoke tactics, might propose.

The Master scratched his head, using the same motion that a seaman might employ to ruffle the head of a mop before wetting it in a bucket. "You always set a lot o' store by surprise, sir, but I can't see how we can surprise 'em at Santa Cruz. Why, that Captain Eames went just close enough to make them as jumpy as a shepherd hearing a fox barking at lambing time.

"No chance of making an accurate landfall in the dark and sending in boarding parties by boat—the current along the coast is too strong for that," he added. "But if we arrive off the coast in daylight we'll be spotted, wherever we are, and the word will be passed to Santa Cruz. If the wind's fair for sailing in through the entrance channel, it's foul coming out. Towing out two frigates one way or the other past those forts—well, that doesn't bear thinking about. Even cavalrymen galloping along the beach on either side could use us for target practice. So that leaves us with . . ."

Ramage waited several moments, and then prompted him: "Leaves us with what?"

Southwick tugged a large lock of hair in frustration. "To tell you the honest truth, I'm damned if I know. In fact I'm beginning to have some sympathy for Captain Eames. What have you in mind, sir?"

"First, you'd better save some sympathy for me. Second, don't get fixed ideas. The chart shows the whole thing is impossible, and I think that's what defeated Eames: he kept thinking about the chart, so he was beaten before Santa Cruz hove in sight."

There was a sudden shouting on deck and both men hurriedly moved to the skylight to listen. Ramage caught some of the words and heard someone running down the companionway to report. "The *Juno*'s in sight," he said. "We'll have our men on board by nightfall."

CHAPTER THREE

THE SUN had dipped below the ridge of hills that ended in Fort Barclay and twilight was beginning to fade the colours when a boat from the *Invincible* came alongside with a midshipman carrying a message from Admiral Davis. It was a brief one, telling Ramage that the *Calypso* had been given the number 132 in the List of the Navy. From now on any flag signal made to her would be prefixed with the number 132, and she would also use it to identify herself—after enough time had elapsed for other ships to be notified, of course. As he wrote her name in the signal book, Ramage saw that she fitted in a blank space (previously filled by a ship sunk, captured or sold out of the Navy for scrap) between the 110-gun *Caledonia* and the 80-gun *Cambridge*.

The second part of the Admiral's message ordered him to report on board the flagship, and Ramage guessed that it was not until the Admiral gave the order to make a signal for the *Calypso*'s Captain to come on board that it was realized that she had no number to go with her new name.

Ramage took the sword from his steward and buckled it on while Southwick bellowed for the Captain's coxswain and had a boat brought to the gangway. Why on earth did the Admiral want to see him now? The mosquitoes came out in thick clouds just as the sun set and usually vanished an hour later. It was in the nature of admirals, Ramage thought angrily, to want to see junior captains at mosquito hour. By the time he arrived on board the *Invincible* he would be itching from a couple of dozen bites.

Southwick was waiting at the gangway. "The quartermaster says that Mr Aitken is still on board the flagship, sir." He lowered his voice and murmured: "He tells me—why he didn't report it before I don't know—that one of the *Invincible*'s boats filled with Marines went over to the *Juno* and came back with four men in irons . . ."

The tone of the Master's voice made it clear that he knew Ramage would draw the same conclusion: Aitken had trouble on board, and armed Marines taking away men in irons was most likely to mean a mutiny. Yet the *Juno* had anchored well away from the *Invincible*. If there was a threat of further mutiny on board surely the Admiral would have re-anchored her within range of the flagship's guns?

Mutiny among the Junos? The thought left him numbed. It couldn't happen; those men would never mutiny. Yet four men taken to the flagship in irons spoke for itself. Had Aitken turned out to be a petty tyrant the minute he was given temporary command? It was just as unthinkable that the crew of a frigate should mutiny and murder the captain and officers and hand the ship over to the enemy—yet the *Jocasta* was in Santa Cruz at this very moment, proving that the unthinkable was not impossible.

"The Admiral probably wants to question you about them," Southwick said miserably, echoing Ramage's thoughts. Four men. Who were they? He could not guess the name of even one of them. He climbed into the boat and nodded to his coxswain to cast off.

Thomas Jackson was an American who, like Southwick and the boat's crew, had served with Ramage for several years. Sandy-haired and lean, the coxswain was usually a cheery man. Now his shoulders were hunched and he avoided Ramage's eye. The normally happy Italian Alberto Rossi, the irreverent Cockney Will Stafford—all the men in the boat looked as though they were rowing off to the flagship to be flogged round the fleet. They too had seen the *Invincible*'s Marines and drawn their own conclusions.

As he sat in the sternsheets slapping at mosquitoes landing

on his wrists and face, Ramage turned to Jackson. "Did you recognize the prisoners?"

"No, sir," the American said. "The light was going. I had a look with the bring-'em-near but they were in leg-irons and that made 'em crouch down a bit. The Marines were shovin' them, too."

By now the boat was leaping through the water and Ramage felt very close to the men. They had been carefully chosen over a long period and all of them had been in action with him many times. He found he had to think carefully to remember just how many times and was glad of the distraction. Jackson had been with him when the *Sibella* frigate sank under them in the Mediterranean; he had helped rescue the Marchesa from Bonaparte's cavalry, and had regarded himself as Cupid's assistant ever since; with him again in the *Kathleen* cutter (when Southwick had joined) while they captured the dismasted Spanish frigate; a survivor when the Spanish ship of the line rammed them at Cape St Vincent . . . it went on and on.

Suddenly Ramage shivered: Paolo was on board the *Juno!* Had he been hurt in the mutiny? He had recently survived three bitter actions in a week; but he was an impetuous boy, yet to celebrate his fourteenth birthday. "The Marcheezer's nevvy," that was how most of the Junos described Paolo Orsini, and he had become a favourite, not only because he was the Marchesa's nephew but because he was quick, willing, cheerful and fearless. None of the men knew that he was the heir to the kingdom of Volterra and would become its ruler if the Marchesa died without having children.

If the Marchesa died . . . England was four hours ahead of Antigua, so by now she would be in bed and asleep. She was living with his parents, but would they be down in Cornwall or at the London house? If his father had anything to do with it they would be at St Kew; the old Admiral had little liking for London life.

Gianna, too, preferred the country: it was as if all her memories of the life she had led in that great pile of a palace at Volterra had vanished. There a dozen servants came running at her slightest gesture and her ministers listened with grave faces to whatever decision she made concerning the citizens of her kingdom. It was potentially heady stuff for a young girl, but she was born to it. She had ruled—and successfully—from the time her father and mother had died within weeks of each other. When Bonaparte's Army of Italy had swept south she had fled— into the arms of Lieutenant Lord Ramage who, with Jackson, had just survived the sinking of the *Sibella,* the frigate sent from Corsica to rescue her.

So much had happened since then. More actions and pro- motion for him; a certain amount of happiness for her. She had learnt to accept her exile from Volterra and she had fallen in love with him. She could not understand why he did not resign from the Navy, pointing out with cold logic that there were dozens of captains and scores of lieutenants who were on half-pay because there were no ships for them, nor likely to be.

Then young Paolo had arrived in England, having managed to escape from the French and determined to go to sea with the Royal Navy. Ramage had been reluctant to take him. He was a thoroughly pleasant lad who spoke English perfectly, but Ram- age had a vivid imagination and could picture himself trying to find words to tell Gianna that Paolo had been killed, or badly wounded. So far his letters had told her of the good progress the boy was making, but now . . .?

Captain Edwards met him on the *Invincible*'s gangway, unsmil- ing and, apart from a brief apology for possibly interrupting Ramage's supper, uncommunicative as he led the way to Admi- ral Davis's cabin.

Aitken was sitting opposite the Admiral, his boyish face lit by a lantern hanging from the deckhead. He seemed relaxed—as relaxed as any lieutenant given temporary command of a frigate was ever likely to be in the presence of his commander-in-chief. The Admiral looked the same as usual, his round face glistening with perspiration from the heat of the cabin, his bushy eyebrows lifting as Ramage came into the cabin and lowering as he gestured to a chair.

"Sit down, sit down," he said impatiently. "A drink? No? Suit yourself."

Ramage saw that all three men were now looking in front of them. Without turning the Admiral said irritably: "You didn't remind me to give the *Calypso* a pendant number. Couldn't make a signal so had to wait for a boat to get over to you. It'll make me late for supper and I have guests." He added, as if talking to himself: "Damned dull crowd they are, too. Tradesmen and parsons, and all of 'em up to their necks in smuggling with the Jonathans."

He turned suddenly to Ramage: "Young Aitken here has just brought in four mutineers from the *Jocasta*. Found 'em on board a Jonathan off Guadeloupe."

Ramage almost sighed with relief. That explained the Marines, and the four men in leg-irons. He felt guilty of disloyalty to his Junos for thinking that any of them would have mutinied. His Calypsos, he corrected himself; Aitken would be ferrying them over within the next few hours.

"Have to bring 'em to trial," Admiral Davis said, "and I need you to make up the number for the court. You won't be able to sail until they're sentenced, but you might get some useful information. Question 'em about Santa Cruz."

There were only five post captains in English Harbour at the moment—six if you included the lieutenant whom Admiral Davis had just promoted and put in command of *La Comète*. A minimum of five captains was needed to form a court martial, and

Ramage was not sure if the new man could sit before the Admiralty confirmed the promotion. Obviously the Admiral thought he could not.

The Admiral could not preside at a court martial—by regulation that was a job for his second-in-command, in this case Captain Edwards. And they had to find someone to act as deputy judge advocate—the *Invincible's* purser, probably, or the Admiral's secretary. A court martial provoked a shower of paperwork.

The Devil take it: he did not want to spend days sitting on a court martial when he should be busy getting the *Calypso* ready for sea. Yet the chance to examine the four British seamen about the *Jocasta's* position at Santa Cruz would . . .

"I'm doubtful if Ramage can question the prisoners before the trial if he is to be a member of the court, sir," Captain Edwards said quietly.

"Hmm, must admit I can't think of a precedent, but what difference does it make if he questions them before the trial instead of during it? As a member of the court he can ask all the questions he wants."

"There's no apparent difference, sir," Edwards said patiently, "but we've no judge advocate to consult, and there'd be trouble if we hanged the men and the Admiralty later ruled the trial invalid because a member of the court was involved before the hearing."

"Oh, very well. No questions before the trial, Ramage."

Ramage realized that, with every ship in the Navy carrying a list of the names and descriptions of all the mutineers, several must have been captured and tried by now, and the evidence given at their trials would be available.

"Nine of them so far," the Admiral said in reply to Ramage's question. "The first four were brought into Barbados a year ago. One turned King's evidence so we could convict the other three, and they were hanged. The fourth hadn't been a mutineer, or so he claimed. Then three more were found serving in a Spanish privateer and taken to Jamaica. The man who turned King's evidence was sent to Port Royal to give evidence against them and they were hanged, too. Mutiny and treason. Then a pair of them were taken off Brest, and the man was sent to England to give evidence."

"So there is no one over here to give evidence against these men, sir?"

"No," Admiral Davis said crossly. "It would take too long to send to England for the witness."

Ramage realized that it was going to be a difficult trial. If all four men kept silent—remained loyal to each other, in fact—he did not see how they could be convicted. One of them must be persuaded to turn King's evidence. Or Admiral Davis should send all four men to England so that they could be tried there. That was the surest way of seeing that justice was done.

The Admiral obviously guessed Ramage's thoughts. "We need a trial out here as an example. I've been hearing some disturbing reports from some of our ships. A few hotheads here, a few there. Easy to stir up a ship's company, especially during the hurricane season when the heat makes everyone edgy.

"We still don't know *why* the Jocastas mutinied," he added crossly. "Three trials, and all we know is that there were half a dozen ringleaders and the rest of the men followed them. And some loose talk that Wallis was a bit free with the cat-o'-nine-tails. Mind you, he had to be, after the Nore and Spithead."

Captain Edwards was shaking his head, and Ramage knew he too had compared the dates. "The *Jocasta* affair was a month before we had news out here that the Fleet had mutinied at Spithead, sir."

"Same kind of hotheads, though," the Admiral growled. "Irishmen, members of that damned London Corresponding Society—traitors, the whole bunch of them."

Edwards said nothing. Perhaps, Ramage thought, he too had reservations about the late Captain Wallis, who had sailed from Jamaica, where he had been one of Vice-Admiral Sir Hyde Parker's favourites. He had been sailing under Sir Hyde's orders at the time of the mutiny, and Sir Hyde would have made sure that no information detrimental to Wallis reached the Admiralty from Jamaica—even though, he reflected bitterly, the only way of preventing mutiny in other ships was to find out exactly why it had happened in the *Jocasta*. Obviously that was what angered Admiral Davis. He would know better than anyone else in the West Indies if Sir Hyde was covering up for Wallis.

"The men you captured," Ramage asked Aitken, "what were their ratings in the *Jocasta*?"

"Two topmen, a quartermaster and a steward, sir—or so they claim. They were rated ordinary seamen in the American ship."

"Where did they join the American?"

"La Guaira and Barcelona. They left the *Jocasta*—she has a Spanish name now, of course—several months ago. A year or more, in fact."

The Admiral grunted and took the glass of punch that a steward was offering him. "Very well, then. I've told Aitken to transfer the Junos to the *Calypso* tomorrow in the forenoon, so you get your men and your First Lieutenant back again. I can't see the trial starting for a couple of days." He took out a large watch and grunted yet again. "My guests will be getting impatient: I must go back to the Dockyard. Tell you the truth, staying on shore is a mixed blessing. All those people—and twice as many mosquitoes. Don't know which are more irritating."

CHAPTER FOUR

ON BOARD the *Calypso* next day everyone's temper frayed. More than 150 men had been brought over from the *Juno* and the purser had to enter details of each one of them in the muster book. There, in 27 columns, were recorded all the details that the Admiralty, Navy Board and Sick and Hurt Board would ever want to know about a man—including whether he was a volunteer or "prest," where he was born and his age, his full name and rank, and what clothing, bedding and tobacco had been issued. The last column on that page, headed "D., D.D., or R.," would not be filled in by one of those abbreviations until the man left the ship by one of only three possible ways: Discharged (to another ship or to a hospital), Discharged Dead (death from battle, accident or illness) or Run, the Navy's phrase for deserting.

Ramage paced round the deck, pausing occasionally at the table set up by the purser in the shade of the awning. The men were filing past fairly quickly and the list of names in the muster book was lengthening. Looking over the purser's shoulder at the first few names, Ramage was once again reminded of the cosmopolitan nature of the Navy in wartime. The first five names in the book, filled in several days earlier, were of men from various parts of Britain, the sixth was Thomas Jackson, an American volunteer from Charleston, the seventh Alberto Rossi from Genoa, the eighth the Londoner Will Stafford, who served as apprentice to a locksmith and then became a burglar until a press-gang swept him into the Navy. The ninth was a Dane, the tenth an Irishman.

All the men seemed to be glad to be on board: at the table and as he walked round the ship he saw grinning men who were hoping that the Captain would give them a nod. After telling Jackson how much prize-money each man was likely to get, he had the impression that the word went round the ship faster than if he had mustered them all aft and announced it. Prize-money did not make such men fight any better; they needed no inducement. But it was a satisfying bonus after the battle. Many of them would spend the money in a few days' carousing, cutting a dash with whichever fortunate doxies first hooked a grapnel when they went on shore. Others would save it towards the day when they gave up a seaman's life. When would that be? The war had gone on for years, and there was no end in sight. Politicians in London talked loudly, and listeners to the voices booming with such authority could choose between forecasts of defeat for Bonaparte in one year or fifteen. Pitt was a fool or a genius; Fox a hero or a traitor.

Whatever their politics, Ramage thought bitterly, they all cheered when one or other of these spice islands of the West Indies was captured, yet the value was only the cheers it brought in Parliament because the cost in garrisoning the islands was enormous. Regiments came out and within a few months half the men were dead from the black vomit. Such losses in battle would start a row in Parliament . . .

The Devil take the gloomy thoughts. He walked away from the purser's table. So far—and this was the second time he had commanded a ship in the West Indies—he had managed to keep his men fit, but he knew he had been lucky; stories of half a ship's company dying of fever in a couple of weeks were legion. He was doubly lucky, because Bowen was a fine Surgeon.

In fact, he reflected, a captain was no better than the men serving him. Southwick was a fine Master; he had good lieutenants, particularly Aitken, the First Lieutenant. Aitken had dumbfounded the Admiral who, because of the young Scot's distinguished behaviour in the recent action off Martinique, had proposed making Aitken post and giving him command of the *Juno*, but Aitken had asked permission to continue sailing as First Lieutenant with Ramage. Both Admiral Davis and Ramage had been puzzled—it was the first time either of them had come across a man not wanting to be made post.

The obvious explanation had been that Aitken was scared of the responsibility, yet he had fought well while commanding a prize frigate. And the obvious explanation had proved wrong: Aitken had explained—much to Ramage's embarrassment—that he still had much to learn and wanted to continue serving with Captain Ramage.

Bowen was perhaps the best example of Ramage's luck. Bowen had been a doctor in Wimpole Street, one of London's most fashionable physicians. Then he had started drinking heavily and soon, a gin-sodden wreck, was reduced to serving in the Navy as a surgeon.

His first ship had been commanded by Ramage. The prospect of having the health of his men in the hands of a drunkard— and concern about what might happen if any of them were wounded in battle—had led to Ramage and Southwick effecting a ruthless cure of Bowen's drink problem. Now, a couple of years later, Bowen was one of his most valued officers—a fiendish chess player, stimulating company, and a man devoted to the health of the ship's company. He never touched a drop of liquor. He had since been back to London, where he could have returned to treating wealthy dowagers for non-existent complaints, but instead he had asked only that Ramage allow him to continue serving as his ship's Surgeon. Well, better one volunteer than three pressed men.

Ramage reached the fo'c's'le, paused by the belfry and looked aft. What a mess! There was not a square foot of clear deck: sails were stretched out like collapsed tents with men busy at work on them with needles and palms. Southwick was prowling round looking for worn canvas and marking out where he wanted extra patches sewn on to take care of chafe.

The bosun and his mates were working on a pile of blocks, with a carpenter's mate driving out the pins so that they could be greased. As soon as men left the purser's table and stowed their sea bags they were being given jobs. The decks were dirty, the brasswork green with verdigris, but a morning's work would see all that cleaned up, though it would need a week to get it sparkling. It was important now that running rigging should rend freely through blocks, that sails should not chafe holes on rigging or spars.

The gunner had the locks of all the guns up on deck, spread out on a sheet of canvas, and was checking them one by one. He had a large box of flints and a seaman was sorting through them, putting aside any that did not have a sharp edge that would ensure a good spark.

Three men who had not been on board more than half an hour were manhandling the big grindstone into position while others were collecting the cutlasses—more than two hundred of them—ready to give them all a sharp edge. More men were taking boarding-pikes from their racks round the masts—the heads, exposed to the spray, were rusty. Once they had been sharpened they would be given a coat of blacking and the wood of the staffs would be oiled to stop it splitting in the heat of the sun. All small jobs and all tedious, requiring a lot of men, but vital if the *Calypso* was to be an efficient ship.

There should be another ten men coming on board from the *Invincible* this afternoon to make up the *Calypso*'s ship's company to two hundred, and more Marines had just arrived. Few frigates ever had more than three-quarters of their official complement, and Ramage knew it was an indication of how the Admiral viewed the *Jocasta* operation that he was making sure that the *Calypso* had more than her complement.

He could see that Aitken, who had been on board only long enough to change into an old uniform, was busy with a group of men at a stay-tackle, hoisting up a heavy awning from below. There would soon be fifteen minutes of chaos as they stretched out the awning and tried to work out how the French secured it, but the sun was scorching and the men needed some shade.

Wagstaffe should soon be back on board and no doubt telling a story of the insolence of the storekeeper. The Second Lieutenant had a long list of the *Calypso*'s requirements and Ramage was determined he was not going to be fobbed off. If the *Calypso* did not get them now, while commissioning, she never would, and with the Admiral anxious to have the frigate ready, Ramage knew he would have a sympathetic ear for any complaints about a storekeeper's shortcomings.

Jackson came up to him and saluted. "A boat from the flagship is coming to us, sir. She's been to the other ships in the anchorage. There's a lieutenant on board."

Ramage nodded. More orders, no doubt. The Marine Lieutenant, Rennick, approached and, coming smartly to attention, reported that all his Marines were now on board. "One lieutenant, one sergeant, two corporals and forty private Marines, sir!" he said like a priest reciting a liturgy.

"Forty-three men, eh? Quite a force you have now!"

"Yes, sir," Rennick said cheerfully. "It'll take a few days to lick the new men from the flagship into some sort o' shape, but the sergeant's a good man: served with me in another ship when he was a corporal."

"Very well," Ramage said solemnly, half wishing Captain Edwards could have heard Rennick's patronizing comment on the extra men sent over from the *Invincible*. Yet Rennick was probably right. He was plump, the tropical heat made him perspire like a leaking head pump, but he was a very efficient officer. He was a strict disciplinarian—but he knew when to crack a joke with his men, who were proud of him. And men proud of an officer would follow him into action whatever the odds.

"These extra men from the flagship," Ramage said quietly, "if you're doubtful about any of them, send them back."

Rennick grinned and shook his head. "I know, sir, the one rotten apple! But the sergeant picked 'em. Every man wanted to serve in the *Calypso*. Seems they've all heard about you, sir."

The Marine Lieutenant had all the subtlety of a caulker's maul; he made the statement in his usual direct manner and Ramage knew it was not in him to flatter his Captain. For all that, Ramage found it hard to understand why Marines should want to leave the comparative comfort of a ship of the line and transfer to a cramped frigate—particularly as by now most of them would know the *Calypso* was bound for Santa Cruz. Even if a miracle occurred and the *Calypso* managed to cut out the *Jocasta*, at least half the seamen and half the Marines would be buried at sea the following morning; the most purblind optimist could see that.

"I'm glad to hear it, and I can rely on you to polish them," Ramage said. "Tell me when you want me to inspect them; I'll breathe fire down their necks."

"I've already warned 'em, sir; I said all that easy living in the flagship is a thing of the past."

Ramage gestured towards the grindstone, which was just beginning to spin and shower sparks as it put an edge on the first of the cutlasses. "The men are attending to the cutlery. Your Marines had better start on the muskets; we have 250 on board. And check the flints, too. We have ten boxes, I believe, with two hundred flints in each. Make sure they are marked musket or pistol size—it'd be just like the French to mix them up. And the pistols: check them over, too. The French equivalent of a Sea Service pistol is not too reliable, if my memory serves me."

"Yes, sir. What about tomahawks?"

Ramage pointed to the pile beside the cutlasses. "All we need is a tinker mending kettles."

Jackson came back to report that the boat from the *Invincible* had two lieutenants on board.

"Very well," Ramage said. "Tell Mr Aitken that our new Fourth Lieutenant is probably about to arrive."

The *Calypso* had all her men on board: four lieutenants, Master, Surgeon, and 203 warrant, petty officers and seamen, as well as Rennick and 43 Marines—a total of 253 officers and men, the most Ramage had ever commanded.

In front of him on the desk were the first letters concerning the trial of the *Jocasta's* four mutineers—and the news that Aitken would be needed, too. He had not thought of that, but apparently the machinery of a trial needed someone to start it off.

"Whereas Lieutenant James Aitken, for the time being commanding His Majesty's ship *Juno*, has represented to me that he did take four men from the American schooner *Sarasota Pride* on suspicion that they were formerly of His Majesty's frigate *Jocasta*," said Admiral Davis's letter, he was ordering a court martial to try the four men for mutiny.

The letter, addressed to "The Captains of His Majesty's vessels, &c, at English Harbour, Antigua," had to cite at length all the various acts of Parliament and amendments relating to courts martial, and finally concluded, after giving the men's alleged names and aliases: "I do hereby assemble a court martial composed of the captains and commanders of the squadron under my command, for the trial of the said four men for the offences of which they stand charged, and to try them for the same accordingly."

With that came a memorandum which said, in language which Ramage was thankful to see had not been mangled by lawyers: "You are to attend a court martial which is to be assembled by Captain Herbert Edwards, on board His Majesty's ship *Invincible* in English Harbour, Antigua, on Monday next, the fourteenth instant, at eight o'clock in the morning in order to sit as member of the same." That was also signed by Admiral Davis, but the third, from Captain Edwards, said that Ramage was "desired to attend a court martial," giving the place and time, and adding the time-honoured injunction: "It is expected you will attend in your uniform frock." Sword, clean stock and stockings, polished boots, white breeches and frock coat—no one brought before a naval court martial could complain that his judges were not well dressed.

Ramage pictured the four prisoners. It was unlikely all of them could read or write. They would be receiving copies of the charge and formal requests from whoever had been appointed the deputy judge advocate (probably the *Invincible*'s purser, at eight shillings a day) for lists of witnesses they wished to call in their defence. Ramage felt sorry for them—until he remembered that Captain Wallis, four lieutenants, master, midshipman, surgeon and a lieutenant of Marines had been murdered and one of the King's ships handed over to the enemy . . .

The new Fourth Lieutenant seemed a lively youngster, he thought, in a deliberate attempt to cast off thoughts of the mutiny and the trial. Peter Kenton was twenty-one years old and the son of a half-pay captain. He was only four or five inches over five feet tall and had flaming red hair. His face was heavily freckled and peeling—his skin was obviously sensitive to the sun. More important than his appearance was Southwick's first report on him.

The Master had decided the fore-topsail had too many patches to withstand the brisk winds they would find off the coast of the Main, and Kenton was given a few men and orders to get the new one up from the sailroom and stow the old. The young Lieutenant had started off well by saying he could make do with fewer men and, with the new sail on deck, went ahead preparing everything to hoist it up to the yard.

So even though the lad had not been on board three hours, Kenton's stock stood high with Southwick, and Ramage knew it was no passing whim, because over the years the old Master had seen dozens of lieutenants come and go—old ones and young, experienced and inexperienced, quiet and noisy. Lieutenants had commissions, so even the most junior in the ship were senior to Southwick: masters were warrant, not commission officers. For all that, it was a rash lieutenant that ran foul of a master, who was usually a fine seaman and often worth any brace of lieutenants that chance or influence brought on board a ship of war.

On the deck below, James Aitken had stripped off his uniform and was washing, using a quart of water in a small basin perched precariously on his wooden trunk. His cabin was eight feet square with only five feet of headroom, and the lantern contributed more heat than light.

No cooling draughts ever penetrated this part of the ship. Aft on the lower deck, just clear of the tiller, was the gunroom with three cabins opening off to one side and four on the other, the accommodation of the four lieutenants, Bowen, Southwick and Rennick. They ate their meals at the long table running almost the length of the gunroom, and a square scuttle beside the table reminded them that they were separated from several tons of gunpowder only by the thickness of the deck, because it covered the hatch leading to the magazine.

Just forward of the gunroom there were two cabins to larboard, belonging to the Captain's clerk and bosun, and two to starboard, occupied by the gunner and carpenter. A larger cabin formed the midshipmen's berth, normally crowded but now occupied only by Paolo Orsini and a master's mate. Forward of them, abreast the mainmast, the Marines slung their hammocks while the seamen had the rest of the deck forward.

Aitken began towelling his bony body. He knew the effort would leave him dripping with perspiration, but he was happy to be back with Captain Ramage, Southwick, Wagstaffe and Bowen, despite the discomfort. He had enjoyed his brief command of the *Juno* and her captain's quarters were spacious: the great cabin running the width of the ship, the smaller one called the coach, and a third which was the bed place.

Spacious (by comparison with his present cabin) and even luxurious, with sideboard, wine-cooler, chairs, settee and desk, but lonely. That was what had hit him the moment he was given the temporary command. The captain's accommodation formed the after end of the main deck; everyone else, officers, petty officers, seamen and marines lived on the next deck below. That alone increased the sense of isolation: the knowledge that he was alone and above all the others, like a spinster occupying the top floor of a house, with all the other residents on the ground floor.

Yet that was only part of it: most of the isolation came from the fact that the man living in that accommodation was the captain; he made the decisions and gave the orders. He had to be right the first time, and for the sake of discipline (and perhaps pride) he could not ask for second opinions.

The captain ate alone, unless he invited some of his officers to dinner; when he was not walking the quarterdeck he was alone in his cabin, reading, thinking, brooding or sleeping. To someone who had never experienced this almost terrifying isolation, a captain's life seemed easy: he never stood a watch (although he left orders that he was to be called when land was sighted, if the course could not be laid because of a wind shift, or for a dozen other reasons) and really did not work, apart from signing papers prepared by his clerk, writing up his journal (usually borrowing the master's log and copying it) and generally making sure that the officers did their jobs properly.

Aitken now knew from experience what envious young lieutenants, dreaming of the day they would be made post, never considered. The captain had the final responsibility for *everything* in the ship. If she sprang a leak and sank because the pumps became blocked with rubbish, ran on a reef after the master made a mistake or the current ran faster or slower than expected, lost a mast when rigging failed or wood rotted, was sunk after attacking an enemy too powerful, or ran away when admirals considered she should have stayed and fought—all these were the captain's responsibility: he was the person court-martialled even though the real fault could lie with dozens of other men, ranging from the officers of the deck to a seaman heaving the lead and calling out a wrong sounding.

The safety of the ship, in good weather and bad, on passage or in battle, was only part of it. The surgeon's job was to cure the men's illnesses, but a good captain did his best to make sure the men did not become ill in the first place. Captain Ramage, for instance, was fanatical in going to any length to make sure there were fruit and fresh vegetables for the men whenever possible, and many a time the cook's mate's hands had been raw and stinging, crushing fresh limes to provide the juice issued to the men daily to ward off scurvy.

Yet, Aitken reflected as he began dressing, the physical health of the ship's company was also only part of the story: there was always trouble among two hundred seamen. Hot weather shortened tempers; fights occurred in a few seconds, men who had been friends for months had bitter quarrels and applied to change their mess, deciding they wanted to try their luck with a group of another six or eight men. A man received a letter from home relating some tragedy or crisis; another began hoarding his tot so that he could get blind drunk every few days. A man sulking over an actual or imagined injustice at the hands of a petty officer would slack. One man merited promotion while another ought to be demoted . . .

These were the normal problems in a well-run ship, and in each case the captain had to decide what to do: he had to be a judge one minute and a father the next; a medical man and a navigator. Yet not every ship was well commanded. The pleasure—yes, that was the right word—of serving with Captain Ramage was not that he was always right (the whole ship's company knew how uncertain his temper was before breakfast) but that he *cared*. If he was wrong then it was not likely anyone else would have been right. He treated his men as though they were his sons, though many were his age and the majority much older. Southwick, for instance, could have been his father.

It showed in many ways. He watched their diet to keep them fit; but like a true father he made damned sure they did their work properly. He rarely flogged a man (none in Aitken's time, and according to Southwick only twice in his whole career), but Aitken had seen seamen who would have preferred the lash of the cat to the lash of the Captain's tongue.

As he pulled on his stockings, smoothing out the wrinkles, Aitken realized that he was in effect assessing Captain Ramage because he had been thinking a lot about Captain Wallis and the

Jocasta. Something had gone dreadfully wrong on board that ship, and although no one yet knew exactly what it was, Aitken was becoming more and more certain that if any one man was to blame it was Captain Wallis.

Which is where his gloomy thoughts started: in a ship *everything* depended on the captain. Aitken knew that Admiral Davis had been surprised when he asked to be allowed to remain with Captain Ramage instead of being made post and given command of a frigate, but the reason had been simple enough: he did not think he was yet fit for command. Not that he couldn't handle a frigate—that was easy enough—but he wanted to learn more about keeping a ship's company well disciplined but happy. It boiled down to having a seaman call you "sir" because he regarded you as the captain, not because you were the man put in as captain and backed up by the Articles of War.

Aitken suspected that Captain Wallis had commanded his ship by waving his commission in one hand and the Articles in the other, forever charging men with breaking an article and setting the bosun's mates to work with the cat. With Captain Ramage the only time the men heard of the Articles of War was every fourth Sunday when, by regulation, they had to be read aloud.

If the Navy suddenly turned republican, he thought, the men would elect Lord Ramage as their captain. Lord Ramage—it was hard to remember he was a lord and, when his father died, would become the Earl of Blazey. How many men in the Navy had a title but refused to use it? Perhaps he would now that he was a captain. According to Southwick it had started when he was a midshipman, when a twelve-year-old with a title might find himself in difficulties on shore when he ranked above his captain socially, and often his admiral as well.

Aitken tried to picture Captain Ramage as a young midshipman. He must be about twenty-five now. No doubt as a youngster he would have been in constant trouble with his mathematics:

even now he knew just enough to make him a good navigator, but no more, and would often make jokes at his own expense about his poor mathematics, or tease Southwick, who had an uncanny knack for adding up rows of figures in his head. What he lacked in mathematics he made up for in seamanship: Aitken had watched him handling the ship on scores of occasions and he did it quite instinctively. As a good rider seems part of his horse, so Captain Ramage seemed to be part of the ship. The way he handled the *Juno* when he put her alongside this very ship, for example . . .

Twenty-five was Aitken's age as well, but Ramage had had half a dozen or more *Gazettes* almost to himself. Wounded three times, sunk twice: it was a remarkable record. Would his luck hold? Luck did not come into the tactics Captain Ramage used. He was lucky only because so far he had not been cut down by a cannon ball or hit by a musket shot.

Perhaps the most remarkable thing about him was that he had earned every bit of promotion. Having a father who was both an admiral and the holder of one of the oldest earldoms in the country would normally have ensured rapid promotion; but for much of his career the Admiral had been out of favour with the government—the scapegoat, Southwick said, for some mistake the government of the day had made many years ago.

Aitken tucked in his shirt and sat down to cool off. From an officer's point of view, the worst thing about the Captain was that his face gave nothing away—unless you watched his eyes. He could be in a fury or he could be making a joke (he had a dry wit) but his face revealed nothing, except for the eyes. They were set deep, like the muzzles of guns in the ports before they were run out, but when he was angry they fixed on you; you could no more avoid them than if they were a pair of pistols aimed at your head.

Those alarming eyes were going to have plenty of work to

do: the *Calypso* was a fine-looking ship, and from all accounts sailed like a witch, but she would need a broomstick to get into Santa Cruz to cut out the *Jocasta*. Luckily, most of the ship's company had been in action together several times.

He heard the steward clattering plates and cutlery as he set the table outside in the gunroom. This was what he had missed while commanding the *Juno*, the company of men like Bowen and Southwick and Wagstaffe. Phew, he was tired—as indeed every man on board must be, after today's work. The ship still looked a mess to the untrained eye, but she would be ready long before the court martial reached a verdict on the mutineers. In a strange way he wished he had never sighted that Jonathan and taken them off. It was one thing to kill four men with a round shot fired at an enemy in battle; it was another to cause four men to be hanged from the yardarms.

He found he was dreading the sound of the signal gun calling the captains to the flagship for the trial.

CHAPTER FIVE

AT PRECISELY seven o'clock on Monday morning the muffled thud of a signal gun echoed up the channel and across the dockyard, bouncing off the hills and finally losing itself among the valleys. Pelicans paddling lazily round the *Calypso* suddenly took off, frantically launching themselves with clumsy thrusts from their webbed feet; tiny green herons squawked off into the shelter of the mangrove roots.

Ramage watched the smoke from the *Invincible*'s gun drift

away to leeward and saw high at her mizenmasthead a Union flag break out and flutter lazily in a gentle breeze. Four men now in irons on board the flagship would have heard that gun—it would be only a few feet from where they were under guard— and they would know they were soon to stand trial for their lives over something that happened more than two years ago.

Will Stafford put down the telescope, picked up the slate and wrote: "7 o'clock, flagship fired one gun and hoisted Union at mizenm'head." He glanced up but decided to wait before adding the rest of the entry: "Captain & First Lieutenant left ship to attend court martial."

He saw that both officers looked drawn: the skin on the Captain's face was taut, and the light from the sun, still low, emphasized his high cheekbones and deep-sunk eyes. He was tanned, but Stafford saw the strain was there. And the First Lieutenant—Mr Aitken never took a tan, and now he was even more pale, and nervous too, fiddling with his sword, his eyes glancing round the ship. Anyone would think they were on trial, Stafford thought, instead of the two pair o' murderers.

Ramage saw that the boat was waiting at the starboard gangway, the painter being held forward and the sternfast aft. He patted his pocket to make sure he was carrying his commission and saw Southwick had noticed the gesture and knew what it meant. The Master obviously had in mind discreetly checking that he had not forgotten it.

The *Calypso* was the farthest from the *Invincible,* yet already a boat was on its way from one of the other frigates. Southwick raised an eyebrow and Ramage nodded, whereupon the Master bellowed: "Man the side!" Two seamen ran to the gangway and swung over the side to hold out the manropes for the two officers to grasp as they climbed down the ship's side, treading carefully on the battens that formed narrow steps. Ramage gestured to Aitken, who swung his sword round, jammed his hat firmly on his head and went over the side into the boat. Ramage followed, and when they went alongside the *Invincible* the sequence would be reversed: the senior officer was the last in and first out of a boat.

Jackson soon had the men rowing briskly, but Ramage told him to slow down. The court martial began at eight, and within the limits of obeying orders—which meant obeying the seven o'clock gun—he had no wish to waste time on board the flagship in idle chat with the other captains. The Admiral, for once, could sleep in late at his house in the dockyard: he would not appear on board the flagship until the trial was over, because no doubt his great cabin would be used, with refreshments served in the coach.

The boat was a pistol-shot from the *Invincible* when a Marine sentry shouted "Boat ahoy!" and Jackson bellowed back *"Calypso!"* —the traditional way of indicating that the boat carried the captain of the ship named. Ramage heard shouted orders and sidesmen appeared to hold out the two manropes.

Edwards was on deck to greet him, bulky and cheerful, sword-hilt gleaming in the early sunlight, the picture of a competent and confident flagship captain. He gestured to two captains standing behind him. Like Ramage, both were wearing epaulets only on their right shoulders, showing that they had less than three years' seniority.

"You've all met?" Edwards asked. They had not and Edwards introduced them: Edward Teal of the *Anita*, a thin man of perhaps forty, sad-faced and probably embittered that it had taken him so many years to be made post, and John Banks of the *Nereus*, plump and red-faced, and four or five years older than Ramage, a man as cheerful as Teal was melancholy. Ramage then introduced Aitken.

A Marine sentry hailed again and a third captain came on board and was introduced to Ramage. John Marden wore epaulets on both shoulders and, Ramage was told, had commanded the *Wasp* frigate in the West Indies for more than two years. Marden was barely five feet tall and lean, his face tanned and lined. His eyes were sharp and his ears curiously pointed, reminding Ramage of a pixie.

Edwards took out his watch. "Twenty minutes to go. I trust you all have your commissions?" With that he led the way to his cabin and offered them tea.

Precisely at eight o'clock another gun fired in the *Invincible* to signal the beginning of the trial and Captain Edwards led the way to the Admiral's great cabin. The long dining table had been put athwartships at the after end of the cabin with five chairs placed along one side, so that the captains would sit facing forwards, their backs to the big sternlights.

A rotund, bespectacled man already sat at a chair at one end, a pile of papers, inkwell, pen and several books in front of him. Edwards introduced the *Invincible*'s purser, Eric Gowers, who had been appointed deputy judge advocate.

There were two rows of chairs at the forward end of the cabin—Ramage guessed they came from the wardroom and that the ship's officers would be eating their meals sitting on forms until the trial ended—with a single chair in front of the table ready for the witness. Between the table and the first row of chairs was an open space: there the prisoners would stand, guarded by Marines and with the provost marshal to one side.

As if to underline the fact that the *Invincible* was primarily a fighting ship, there were two guns on each side in the cabin, their train tackles neatly coiled, the barrels shining black and the carriages and trucks freshly painted. The gun ports were open to keep the cabin cool. Against the forward bulkhead there was a well-polished mahogany sideboard with a matching wine-cooler beside it, shaped like a Greek urn. Over the sideboard was an oil painting of a plump and pleasant-looking woman, probably the Admiral's wife. She looked amiable enough, Ramage noted.

Edwards went to the centre chair at the after side of the table and sat down. In front of him was a small gavel, and he looked at the four captains. "We might as well begin. Please read your commissions—you start," he said, gesturing to Marden.

Ramage saw that Gowers, the deputy judge advocate, noted down the date of the commission: Marden had been made post six years ago. As soon as all the commissions had been read, establishing their seniority, Edwards told them to take their seats. Marden, as the senior, sat on Edwards's right, with Teal on his left, Banks beyond Marden and Ramage, as the junior, next to Teal, on Captain Edwards's extreme left.

By now a Marine lieutenant had come into the cabin: he must be acting as the provost marshal (at an extra four shillings a day, Ramage thought inconsequentially).

Edwards gestured towards Gowers. "Very well, we will make a start."

The deputy judge advocate turned to the provost marshal. "Bring in the prisoners and all the witnesses. The prisoners first."

Two Marines with drawn cutlasses marched into the cabin, the white pipeclay on their crossbelts a startling contrast to their polished black boots. Behind them, shuffling in single file, came four seamen, unshaven, their faces shiny with perspiration and their wrists in irons. Two more Marines followed.

The Marine lieutenant walked round to line up the men in front of the table but Edwards, seeing the pistol in his hand, snapped: "We don't need pistols. Leave that thing outside!"

As the provost marshal hurried out the seamen took up their

positions and Ramage saw that none of them looked up at the five captains facing them. Mutineers? Perhaps, but they looked like any seamen chosen at random—or, for that matter, any four men picked off the streets of a country town on market day. The only difference was that they were frightened; awed and overwhelmed at finding themselves standing in an admiral's cabin, facing five captains, flanked by armed Marines, and on trial for their lives.

Ramage rubbed a scar over his right eyebrow. He could imagine what each of the men was thinking. Each was trying to relate this moment with the time two years ago when a yelling horde of their shipmates seized the *Jocasta* and murdered the Captain and officers. Had these men been terrified onlookers, active mutineers, or the men who had actually committed murders? And how was the court to discover the truth?

Would one of the men stand as witness against the other three—turn "King's evidence" as it was usually called? Captain Edwards had just explained, over their cups of tea, that there seemed some doubt whether an offer could be made to a prisoner before the trial began—that he would be allowed a free pardon if he gave evidence against the other accused men. Edwards had roundly cursed the fact that there was no judge advocate in the fleet. He and the purser had read through the only available books on naval courts martial, and there was a reference to a famous judge saying that if a man was promised a reward for giving his evidence before he actually gave it, this "disables his testimony." All five captains knew of cases where one of the accused had "turned King's evidence" but none of them had been a member of the court when it happened. And Edwards, anxious that there should be no mistakes, had decided to wait and see how the trial proceeded.

Finally the provost marshal was back, looking harassed but

without his pistol, and followed by several officers, including Aitken. Only the Scot was a witness; the rest were onlookers. The moment they were all seated Edwards tapped the table gently with the gavel, obviously careful not to damage the polished wood.

"The court is in session. Gowers, read the orders."

The purser selected several sheets of paper, stood up, adjusted his spectacles and read out the Admiral's order for assembling the court martial.

Devon, Ramage thought to himself; the purser is a Devon man. Shrewd, alert, probably a very competent purser. But, like the rest of the court, his knowledge of law extended no further than the pages of the two or three reference books in front of him—and upon whose pages the lives of these four men might well depend. Not even that, because the facts and points of law the books contained were only as relevant as the court's ability to find them . . .

Gowers finally read the warrant appointing him, put down the papers and picked up a Bible. He then walked round to the front of the table, stopping in front of Captain Edwards. He handed him a card as Edwards put his hand on the Bible. Edwards began reading the oath written on the card, and Ramage saw all four prisoners look up.

"I, James Edwards, do swear that I will duly administer justice according to the Articles of War and orders established by an act passed in the twenty-second year of the reign of His Majesty King George II . . . without partiality or favour or affection; and if any case shall arise which is not particularly mentioned in the said Articles and orders, I will duly administer justice according to my conscience, the best of my understanding, and the custom of the Navy in like cases . . ."

Gowers then administered the oath to the other captains in order of seniority, and then himself took an oath that he would never "disclose or discover the vote or opinion of any particular member of this court unless thereunto required by act of Parliament."

Now the court was legally in existence, and Gowers sorted through his papers once more, found what he wanted and, when he glanced across at Captain Edwards, received an approving nod. He half turned towards the four prisoners and as if guessing what was coming, three of them stared down at the deck; the fourth, standing at the far end of the line and the oldest among them, almost bald with the round face of a village grocer, kept his eyes on the deputy judge advocate.

It was not the stare of defiance, Ramage was certain of that. The other three now seemed to be shrinking, as though fear was slowly wilting them, but the fourth man appeared to be gaining confidence as the others were losing it.

Gowers began reading out the charge. It was brief. After naming the four men and saying they had been part of the *Jocasta's* ship's company on the day of the mutiny, it first accused them of taking part in the mutiny and "aiding and assisting" in the murder of Captain Wallis, four lieutenants, Master, midshipman, Surgeon and the Lieutenant of Marines. It then went on to accuse them of "aiding and assisting" in running away with the ship and handing her over to the enemy, deserting, "holding intelligence with the enemy," and "concealing mutinous designs." All, the charge concluded, in breach of the third, fifteenth, sixteenth, nineteenth, twenty-eighth and thirty-sixth Articles of War.

That death was the penalty in all but one case the men well knew, having heard the Articles read to them at least once a month. Ramage had watched the four closely while Gowers was reading, and the deputy judge advocate had, probably without realizing it, given a slight emphasis to each key word—mutiny, murder, deserting—like a carpenter hammering home the nails of a box. Three men had gone pale; perspiration was now running down their faces. The fourth man was calm, as though his conscience was clear or, perhaps, because he knew he had a cast-iron defence.

It was getting hot in the great cabin: the ship being moored with her stern towards the beach presented her broad transom to the east, and the sun was beating through the sternlights on to their backs. As soon as Gowers finished reading the charges, Captain Edwards signalled the provost marshal to have the curtains drawn. The material was thick—it had to stop light escaping at night when the Admiral was at sea and wanted lanterns in his cabin—and the cabin was soon only dimly lit by sunlight sparkling on the water and reflecting through the four gun ports.

Captain Edwards tapped the table with his gavel: "All witnesses save the first will withdraw." He said it with a curious intonation which made Ramage glance up: as far as he knew Aitken was the only witness, yet three officers rose from the chairs behind the prisoners and left the cabin. They left noisily, scraping the chairs, and all the prisoners glanced behind them, alarmed and curious, obviously puzzled over who they could be.

Captain Edwards was obviously going to be a good president of the court: his voice was authoritative but not abrupt, his orders brief without being curt. "Call the first witness," he said.

"Lieutenant James Aitken," Gowers said, picking up the Bible and selecting a card, which he handed Aitken. "Place your right hand on the Bible and make the oath written here."

Aitken took the oath and then went to the chair facing the president and only six or eight feet from Ramage.

"You are James Aitken, a lieutenant of the Royal Navy, and formerly the acting commanding officer of the *Juno* frigate on the fifth of June this year?"

"I am," Aitken replied, only the broadness of his Scottish burr betraying his nervousness.

Edwards leaned forward, indicating that he was about to take over the questioning: "Relate to the court what happened on the fifth day of June."

"The *Juno* was on passage from off Martinique to Antigua and we were four leagues west of the north-western tip of Guadeloupe. We sighted a brig to the east of us and gave chase."

"What colours was she flying?"

"None at first, but she soon hoisted an American flag."

"Did she try to avoid you?"

"No, sir. We came up to her and I ordered her to heave-to."

"What was your purpose in doing that?"

"I wanted to see if she had any British subjects in her ship's company, sir."

"Very well, then what happened?"

"I boarded her with ten men. I was short of officers," he explained. "I took the list of the *Jocasta*'s ship's company and inspected the American brig's papers."

"Did you find any of the *Jocasta*'s men on board?"

"At first I found one name, Albert Summers. I told the American master that this man was a mutineer from the *Jocasta* and demanded that he be produced."

"Was he produced?"

"Yes, sir, and at the same time—or, rather a few minutes before, because he was waiting nearby—another man came up to me and said he was from the *Jocasta* and wanted to give himself up."

"What was his name?"

"He said it was George Weaver."

"Did that name appear on your list?"

"No, sir."

"Point him out."

Aitken indicated the round-faced man at the other end of the line.

"What did you do then?"

"When Albert Summers was brought before me I accused him of being one of the Jocastas and told him I was putting him under an arrest."

"Then what happened?" Edwards asked quietly.

"He became very excited. He admitted he had served in the *Jocasta* but said he wasn't the only one."

"What did you understand by that?"

"It was a slip of the tongue but I assumed from his manner and gestures that there were others on board the brig using false names. I told him to identify them, but he refused."

"How did you discover them?"

"I asked the American master where his men had been signed on. Weaver and Summers were among the last names in the ship's articles, so I suspected they had been signed on while the ship had been in La Guaira or Barcelona—the log showed they were her last ports."

"What did you do then?"

"I instructed the American master to muster all the men he had signed on in any port on the Main."

"And he did so?"

"He did not agree readily," Aitken said dryly, "but Weaver offered to point them out—the former Jocastas."

"Did he do so?"

"After a few minutes. He was most savagely attacked by Summers, who tried to strangle him and called him a traitor."

"Point out the prisoner Summers."

Aitken indicated the man nearest to him. Ramage had been speculating which of the men he was, and had finally guessed he was this man who had an air of evil and viciousness about him. Thin-faced with thinning black hair, his eyes too close together and his nose long and thin, the skin over the bridge stretched tight, he was the man that any officer would watch. Shifty, lazy, troublesome, he was typically the worst in a press-gang's harvest. Indeed, Ramage thought, he was probably a jailbird, released from prison into the custody of the press-gang.

Edwards nodded and Aitken resumed his evidence. "We secured Summers and tended Weaver. He then pointed out two more men—the other prisoners," he said, gesturing to the two standing in the middle of the line. "I asked the American master if he had signed those men on in La Guaira, and he admitted taking on two there and two at Barcelona. That agreed with what was written in the ship's articles."

"Only these four, then?"

"So he said, and Weaver confirmed it, sir. The master signed a document to that effect, and his mate witnessed the signature."

As Aitken produced a paper from his pocket Gowers interrupted: "The witness must speak more slowly. I have to write down every word, and . . ."

The paper was handed over the table to the president, who read it and passed it to Gowers. "This is an exhibit, so keep it safely." Gowers gave a sniff, as though the instruction was a slur on his competence.

"What did you do then?" Edwards asked Aitken.

"I took the four men in custody. The American master demanded a receipt for them, saying he would protest to the American government. I gave him one—and warned him of the dangers of signing on mutineers."

"Very sound advice," Edwards commented dryly. "That completes your evidence?" When Aitken nodded, Edwards looked up at the prisoners. "Have you any questions to ask this witness?"

Weaver shuffled forward a pace—a move which made one of the Marine sentries swing round to watch him.

"By your leave, sir, I do."

"Carry on, then, but speak slowly so the deputy judge advocate can write it all down."

"I came up to you the moment you boarded, didn't I, sir?" Weaver asked Aitken.

"I think you did," Aitken answered. "I can't be sure because I was looking for the master. But you were waiting to speak to me, that was obvious."

"Was my name on your list, sir?"

"The name George Weaver was not."

"Did you—" the man paused. The careful way that the president, Gowers and Aitken had been speaking, lapsing from time to time into the jargon of courts martial, was obviously bothering him, and the president said quickly: "Just phrase your questions clearly, as though you were talking to a shipmate."

"Aye, thank'ee, sir. Did you ask any of the others—these three here—who I was?"

"Yes, they all said they knew you only as George Weaver, and you were the Captain's steward."

"Did you ask them when I joined the ship, sir?"

Aitken nodded. "Yes I did, because of your claim."

Edwards leaned forward and looked directly at Aitken. "What claim was this?"

"Well, sir, he claimed he had nothing to do with the mutiny and that no one else—no one not serving in the *Jocasta* at the time that is—could have known he was on board."

"That's it, sir," Weaver said excitedly, taking another step forward and being pushed back by a Marine.

Ramage guessed that Edwards knew all about the claim, but what he knew from Aitken's original report was not evidence: the truth of the affair was, legally, what appeared in the court martial minutes that Gowers was keeping, and this laborious question-and-answer procedure was the only way of recording it.

"Wait a moment, Weaver; I am questioning Mr Aitken," Edwards said. "Now, tell the court about this matter, and remember the rule about hearsay evidence: what Weaver told you *is* evidence, but what Weaver said someone else told him is not."

"Quite, sir. Well, Weaver said that after the *Jocasta* sailed from Jamaica, and before the mutiny, she fell in with a British merchant ship and pressed five men. Among them was Weaver."

Aitken paused as Gowers waved his quill frantically, warning him to speak slowly, and Ramage suddenly realized the point Weaver was trying to make. As far as the Admiralty was concerned, Weaver did not exist—at least, not as a Jocasta.

"Weaver claimed that because the mutineers destroyed the *Jocasta*'s latest muster book, the Navy did not know that he was on board. The Navy only knew the men who were on board when the ship was in Jamaica, when the previous muster book was sent in."

The five captains understood exactly what Weaver meant, but it had to be explained more fully for the minutes. "Did Weaver know that muster books are sent to the Admiralty from time to time?" the president asked.

"Yes, sir. He told me that a new muster book had been started a week before the *Jocasta* sailed from Jamaica, so that the only record the Admiralty had of the men on board during the mutiny came from the previous muster book."

"Did he know of any men who had left the ship *after* the new muster book was started but before the ship left Jamaica?"

That was a shrewd question, Ramage noted; Captain Edwards was as concerned with the truth of the whole mutiny as he was with trying these four men. His question could avoid a man being wrongly accused of being on board the ship.

"Yes, sir. He mentioned three men who had been discharged dead just before the mutiny."

"He gave the names?"

"Yes, sir."

"Were these dead men's names on the list of mutineers you had in your possession?"

"Yes, sir."

"Very well. Now, Weaver, have you any more questions to ask this witness?"

"Yes, sir." He turned towards Aitken. "Did I say to you that I was giving myself up, sir?"

"You did."

"And wasn't you taken aback, like, and didn't you go right through your list and ask me if the name 'George Weaver' was an alias?"

"I was puzzled at first, yes, and I did check the list again."

"Why, sir?"

There was a sudden silence in the cabin: Gower's pen stopped squeaking and every man's eye was on Aitken. Even the Marine sentries realized how much depended on the Scots officer's reply.

"Because you'd have been left in the American brig if you had kept silent. At least, unless one of the other prisoners gave you away."

Captain Edwards held up his hand. "Summers refused to denounce the other two. Do you think he would have denounced you?"

"Yes, sir, providing he was asked direct; we'd had a falling out," Weaver said simply, obviously realizing that the question and answer did much to destroy his defence. "But, sir, I went up to this gentleman to give myself up the minute he boarded. I didn't know why he was coming on board. No one did. It just seemed routine. No one knew he was looking for Jocastas— why, all that happened two years ago. I didn't know he'd find Summers."

Ramage leaned forward to catch the president's eye and Edwards nodded, giving permission for him to ask a question.

"Why did you sign on board the American brig?" Ramage asked.

"T'was the only way I could get away from the Main, sir."

"Why did you want to get away from the Main?"

Weaver looked puzzled and went to scratch his head, but his hands were manacled. "Well, sir, I was trying to get back to my own folk."

That was what Ramage had expected, but Weaver was taking too much for granted; he was expecting the court to understand instinctively why he had done certain things. More questions were needed so that Weaver's answers filled in the story.

"But you were in an American ship, bound for an American port."

"Aye, sir, I were; but the Jonathans are the only ones what come into ports on the Main. I was reckoning on getting to England from Charleston, or maybe back down to Jamaica."

"Supposing you reached England or Jamaica—what did you intend to do?"

"Do, sir? Why, report to the authorities—just like I did when this gentleman came on board the brig."

"Why did you think the lieutenant boarded the brig?"

"I dunno, sir. Mebbe to press some men, like when I was pressed into the *Jocasta*. But the minute I saw the *Juno* was a British ship I told my mate I was going to try to get on board."

"Your mate?"

"The friend of mine I met in Barcelona: the one what got me signed on."

"Was he an American or one of these prisoners?"

Weaver looked dumbfounded. "An American, sir. Why, if

these fellers—" he nodded towards the other three men "—if they'd known what I was going to do they'd 'ave done me in. Why, you saw that Summers tried to throttle me. Well, you didn't, sir, but the lieutenant did."

Edwards tapped the table lightly with his gavel.

"Are you prepared to give evidence against the other prisoners?" he demanded.

"Why, yes, sir, of course."

"Clear the court," Edwards said briskly.

CHAPTER SIX

THE FOUR prisoners were marched out, the onlookers left the cabin and the provost marshal shut the door with a flourish as he ushered the last man out. Captain Edwards gave a sigh of relief. "Well, we've got our witness!"

"What was all that business earlier on?" Marden asked. "Those three lieutenants going out when you ordered all but the first witness to leave the court?"

Edwards grinned and confessed: "That was in case none of the prisoners turned King's evidence. If they thought Aitken was the only witness against them, they'd know that if they kept their mouths shut they'd be safe. The fact that three officers left at that moment was a fortunate coincidence."

"Indeed it was," Marden said. "I'm glad they could take a hint!"

"Ah well," Edwards said, "we now have to consider what to do next. Are we agreed that Weaver should be allowed to turn King's evidence?"

The four captains agreed, and Edwards asked Gowers: "Are we following the correct procedure?"

"I think so, sir," the deputy judge advocate said. "We haven't made him any promises."

"Indeed not!" Marden exclaimed. "As far as he knows he'll be strung up from the foreyardarm as soon as he's told his story."

Captain Teal coughed. "His story might be quite detailed if he gives enough evidence to convict those men."

Edwards shrugged his shoulders and, to Ramage's relief, said flatly: "As president of this court I intend to give these men a fair trial. I'm not concerned with whitewashing anyone. Anyone at all," he added heavily, and the four captains knew that he included the unfortunate Wallis and his Commander-in-Chief, Vice-Admiral Sir Hyde Parker. Did Admiral Davis and Edwards consider that Sir Hyde should have put a restraining hand on Wallis's shoulder? Ramage was not sure.

Edwards looked left and right at his fellow captains. "Very well, since we're all agreed about this man Weaver, we'll call him as our next witness. Gowers, is one witness sufficient to convict on a capital charge?"

The purser opened a book in front of him, looked up the index and turned to a page. "Ah, here we are, sir—'As a prisoner . . . by the rules of common law may be found guilty on the uncorroborated evidence of a single witness, so, if the court or jury believe the testimony of an accomplice—' that word is in italic type, sir '—though such testimony stand totally uncorroborated, a prisoner may be found guilty of a capital crime.'"

"That's clear enough," Edwards commented. "Now, you remember that passage I marked about King's evidence: read it out to the court."

Gowers turned back a page. "It begins with a discussion of whether accomplices can be witnesses—they can, of course—and then says that if the court agrees to them being so admitted, it is 'upon an implied confidence which the judges of courts of law have usually countenanced and adopted; that, if such accomplice make a full and complete discovery of that, and of all other crimes or offences . . . and afterwards give his evidence without prevarication or fraud, he shall not be prosecuted for that . . . Were not this to be the case, the greatest offenders would frequently escape unpunished, from want of sufficient evidence.'"

"Very sound," Marden commented.

"I agree," Ramage said cautiously, "but in fact aren't we deciding before we hear any evidence that Weaver is guilty although we'll let him off if he turns King's evidence?"

"Hmm, that's a point," Edwards admitted.

"Excuse me, sir," Gowers said. "If the evidence warrants it, I think the court would simply return a verdict of not guilty in his case."

Marden nodded in agreement. "There's no other way of clearing a man once he's charged. I can see what Ramage means, though: that even if Weaver was guilty of every one of the crimes, he'd be 'not guilty' because he's turned King's evidence, but the same applies if he is completely innocent and turns King's evidence."

"But, sir," Gowers said patiently, "the court can make that clear in its verdict. It can find a man guilty but 'because of mitigating circumstances' let him go free: that makes it clear he is being released in return for giving evidence. Or he can be found not guilty. That is—with respect, sir," he told the president, "a very dear difference."

"Of course, of course," Edwards said, "but you were right to raise the point, Ramage. Very well, Gowers, let 'em in!"

The prisoners marched in, led by Summers, and as Ramage watched him he knew he would have to be careful to judge him only on the evidence. Nature had given Summers an appearance which could make honest men condemn him without a word being spoken.

The president told Gowers: "Call the next witness."

"George Weaver," Gowers said, and waved back the Marine sentry who was obviously going to escort him to the witness's chair. "Go over there," he added, because Weaver obviously had not grasped what was happening.

Gowers then asked: "You are George Weaver, and on the fifth of June last you were serving in the *Sarasota Pride,* an American vessel?"

"I were."

Gowers paused and then wrote down "Yes." He was uncertain what the next question should be and glanced over at the president, who coughed and asked: "Have you ever served in one of the King's ships?"

"Aye, sir, the *Jocasta*—for three weeks."

"How came you to be serving in her?"

"You know that already, sir!" Weaver protested.

"You are giving evidence now," Edwards explained patiently. "The court has to hear the whole story, and in the proper sequence."

"Very well, sir. I were steward in the *Three Brothers* out of Plymouth. Bound from Port Royal, Jamaica, to Antigua, she was, when somewhere orf Navassa Island the *Jocasta* sent over a boarding party and pressed five men, including me."

"How were you rated in the *Jocasta?*"

"Well, Captain Wallis gave us the chance of volunteering, so we'd get the bounty, and we took it. Seems his steward had just died—'e was one of them what you've still got on that list of mutineers, by the way—and so I got made 'is steward."

"Do you remember the date you boarded the *Jocasta?*"

"Aye, the fifth of November, it were, an' a lot of fireworks there were a few days later."

"Quite," Edwards said calmly, "but just answer without any additions. Now, how soon did you become aware that some of the ship's company might be discontented?"

"Soon as I went on board, sir: twelve men was flogged that afternoon."

Ramage glanced at Summers and the other two men. "Why had Captain Wallis awarded that punishment?" Edwards asked.

Weaver paused, and Ramage thought it was an unwise question for Edwards to have asked at this stage; but the words were spoken.

"Well, sir, seems they was furling the foretopsail the day before, and Captain Wallis said he'd flog the last man down orf the yard, and a man fell and was killed—"

"Stop," Edwards ordered. "That is hearsay evidence and—"

"T'isn't hearsay, sir, beggin' yer pardon, an' I heard you explaining what hearsay was. No, sir: I heard Captain Wallis say it with his own voice."

"But you were not on board."

"Not the day it happened, sir, but before he had those dozen men flogged he did some speechifying, an' he said they hadn't learned the lesson."

Edwards was silent but Marden asked: "What lesson, and how did it tell you about the threat?"

"The lesson was that they was too slow furling the topsail," Weaver said patiently.

"But Captain Wallis said only one man, yet you say twelve were flogged."

"Yes, sir. He never did flog the last man because he was the one what fell and killed hisself. 'Murmuring,' that's what the

Captain flogged the twelve for. He said they was murmuring after the man was killed."

Ramage saw that Captain Teal, sitting next to him, had clenched his hands as they rested on the table top. Threatening to flog the last man down—that could only create panic. Flogging a dozen men for "murmuring" when they saw a frightened shipmate fall from the yard in his rush to avoid punishment . . . The Navy, Ramage thought bitterly, was better off without men like Wallis. Edwards was still silent. Was he being tactful, leaving the junior members of the court the task of questioning Weaver? The minutes would make uncomfortable reading at the Admiralty, but there were other captains at sea, not as bad as Wallis perhaps but likely to become so; the story should come out, if only to warn them.

"What punishment was awarded the twelve men?" Ramage asked.

"Three dozen each, sir, and he had a left-handed bosun's mate who laid on the last dozen and so crossed the cuts."

"What happened on the lower deck that night?" Ramage knew he asked the question only to compare the answer with what he guessed his own reactions would have been if he was a seaman.

"Some of them decided to take the ship, sir."

"How many men decided?"

"About a dozen."

"Were any of these prisoners among the dozen?"

"Yes, sir. Summers, him what tried to strangle me in the *Sarasota Pride*."

"Why did he try to strangle you?"

"Because I never did join the mutiny, sir."

Ramage watched Summers. No reaction; the man's eyes remained staring at the deck. He seemed remote from the trial—

perhaps he was at this moment back on board the *Jocasta*, reliving that time two years ago . . .

"Did the ship's company mutiny the next day?"

"No, sir, not for several days."

"Why was there a delay?"

"The floggings, sir."

"What floggings—the dozen the day you joined the ship?"

"Oh no, sir!" Weaver exclaimed, surprised at Ramage's question. "Eight men was flogged the next day, two dozen each, an' four of the men was among the ringleaders, an' by the time the bosun's mates had finished with them their backs was so cut up they could 'ardly move, let alone mutiny."

"Why were they flogged?"

"No one was quite sure, sir. Cap'n Wallis said it was the thirty-sixth Article."

Again Ramage sensed the tension among the captains sitting at the table: they were seeing a grim picture of Wallis emerging, not because Weaver was trying to blacken him but because the simple answers gave away more than the man realized. The thirty-sixth Article covered "All other crimes . . . which are not mentioned in this Act." An unscrupulous captain could use it to have a man flogged because he sneezed; indeed the Article was usually called "The Captain's Cloak," because it covered everything. But one had to try to be fair to Captain Wallis: that bare answer in the minutes could be misleading.

"You must have some idea of what these men did."

"No, sir. Not then, nor the next day."

Edwards interrupted and asked harshly: "What happened the next day—the third day, in fact?"

"The Captain picked 22 more men an' charged 'em under the thirty-sixth. They was all put in irons—that's what set it orf."

"Set what off?" Edwards asked, obviously trying hard to remain patient.

"The mutiny, sir. It started off with men freeing the 22 prisoners, so they shouldn't be flogged. Most of them still had bloody backs from floggings they'd got earlier."

Edwards obviously decided that he had heard enough about the mutiny generally because he said abruptly: "I am going to ask you about the activities of these prisoners, but first tell the court what you were doing immediately before the mutiny."

"Well, sir, Cap'n Wallis was an impatient man, like, and when he called for his steward—that was me, o' course—he didn't like no delay. So he made me sling me 'ammock just outside his door, right by where the Marine sentry stood.

"That night there was a lot of talk on the lower deck, but I don't know what it was all about—though I could guess—because I kept away from it."

"Did you know they were plotting a mutiny?"

Weaver waited a full half-minute before answering and then, taking a deep breath, said: "I know what Article Twenty says—' If any person in the Fleet shall conceal any traitorous or mutinous practice or design . . .'—but I've got to confess I knew but I didn't say nothing."

"Why did you not report it?"

"Because they said they'd cut my throat if I did."

"How could they do that, once you warned the officers?"

"They would take the ship anyway, sir," Weaver said simply, "even if the officers were ready."

"How do you know that?" Edwards demanded sharply. "There were the Marines."

"Most of them—all except the lieutenant and sergeant—were in it."

Edwards knew it was impossible for the sergeant to have been unaware of groups of men gathering on the lower deck and whispering together, but he did not pursue the point; the man had been murdered anyway.

"How and when did the mutiny start?" Edwards asked.

"About ten o'clock at night, sir. The men rushed up from the lower deck. Some seized the quarterdeck, others went to the gunroom, and some went to the Captain's cabin."

"What about the Marine sentry at the Captain's door?"

"He was in the group that murdered the Captain—leastways, I think he was, sir."

"Why don't you know? You must have been in your hammock, which you said was slung by the door."

"As soon as the men came rushing up I started to get out of me 'ammock, sir, but the sentry fetched me a clip with the butt o' his musket and knocked me out, sir."

"Very well, let's consider the activities of these other prisoners. What do you know of Summers?"

"He was one of the leaders, sir. He was the one that threatened to cut me throat if I warned the officers."

"Did he take part in any of the murders?"

"The Captain, sir. I was just getting up after the sentry knocked me out—this was after they'd finished in the cabin—and Summers came out and kicked me in the side, an' he said: 'I've just done in your bloody Captain.'"

"You are sure of the words?"

"Yes, sir, but Perry—'im that's standing there next to 'im—said: 'No, I gave 'im the cut that did for 'im,' and the two of them started quarrelling about it."

"Why should they quarrel about it?"

"They was all in liquor, sir, and later on, when they was trying to get the votes, each of them said they should be the leader because they'd killed the Captain."

"And who was—er, elected captain?"

"Summers, sir, because Perry stood down."

"Why did Perry stand down?"

"Because of Summers and that knife of his. He suddenly

grabbed Perry and knocked him down and held a knife at 'is throat and said he would kill him too, rather than let him command the ship."

"And Perry agreed?"

"Yes, sir, he didn't 'ave no choice, really, but they elected him mate. Summers captain and Perry mate, just like a merchant ship."

"What about the other people necessary to work the ship—were they elected too?"

"Yes, sir."

"Harris, the third prisoner there," Edwards said, "what do you know of him?"

"He wasn't a ringleader, not at first, sir. But after the mutiny he finished off some of them."

Edwards was so puzzled he could only repeat Weaver's words: "Finished off some of them?"

"The wounded officers—the First and Third Lieutenants and the Lieutenant of Marines: they was still alive after the ship was taken."

"How was Harris concerned in their murder?"

"The mutineers were voting on everything, and they were told to make a show of hands whether the living officers should be put to death or kept alive and handed over to the Dons, but Harris swore they should all die."

"He simply made that statement?" Edwards demanded.

"Oh no, sir: he shouted that as he ran below, and he stabbed them where they was lying."

"What did the mutineers think of that, then?"

"Most of them abused him when he came back to the quarterdeck and said what he had done, but that was all."

Ramage leaned forward to catch the president's eye and received a nod of approval.

"Were you the only man who did not take part in the mutiny?"

"No, sir, there was forty or fifty of us."

"What happened to you?"

"We was given all the unpleasant work until we got to La Guaira. Swabbing the blood off the decks, and things like that, sir."

"So there were about 125 mutineers?"

"About that, sir. I think there was 182 in the ship's company."

"So the prisoner Summers was elected leader by more than 125 mutineers, and Perry the second-in-command, that is correct?"

"Yes, sir."

"And Harris—what did he do?"

"Well, sir, he was always in liquor, and not many of the mutineers would have anything to do with him after he killed the wounded. He used to stay close to Summers and run errands for him: fetch him a mug of rum or a chaw of tobacco," Weaver said contemptuously. "He was trying to make up for being a Johnnie-come-lately, that's what the rest of us reckoned."

Ramage made a mental note that Weaver's evidence had so far condemned the other three prisoners for conspiracy, concealing mutinous designs, mutiny and murder. It remained to cover running away with the ship, deserting and "holding intelligence with the enemy." Yet every question that was asked merely underlined the other question that none of them would ever ask out loud: what private hell had Wallis established on board the *Jocasta* that made more than five score seamen rise against him? Ramage was certain the mutiny had been directed entirely at Wallis: the murder of the officers had been incidental. Indeed, the fact that most of the mutineers later wanted to keep alive the wounded survivors bore that out.

More than twenty seamen had been put in irons ready for a flogging next day for—at best—some frivolous charge contrived by Wallis. Part of the mutiny had been to free those men. Part? It was probably the whole reason, but releasing the men meant disposing of the officers and the Captain. Would the men have spared Wallis and the officers if they could have freed the prisoners without bloodshed? Idle speculation: no one would ever know . . .

Beside him Captain Teal cleared his throat. "After the mutiny was over and the new captain had been elected, how did the men decide where to take the ship?"

"They argued almost the whole day, sir. Some was for taking her back to Jamaica, and some was for the Main."

"*Jamaica?*" Teal asked incredulously.

"Aye, sir. They wanted to draw up a document which everyone on board signed, a round robin, they said, and give it to the Commander-in-Chief when they arrived there."

Edwards lifted his hand to stop Teal. "This document," he said brusquely, "what would it have said?"

"Well, sir, they all agreed what it would say; what they didn't agree about was whether it would do any good. Them as thought it wouldn't eventually won on a show of hands."

"But what would it have *said?* What did they want to tell the Commander-in-Chief?"

"Why, sir," Weaver said, as though it should have been obvious to everyone, "to tell the Admiral that they meant no harm by what they'd done, that they was loyal to the King but was in mortal fear that Captain Wallis would flog 'em all to death. An' give the Admiral the figures, of course."

"What figures?" Edwards was obviously fascinated, but Ramage had already guessed what was coming.

"The figures for the floggings, sir: the Captain had flogged 109 men in seven weeks, a total of 2616 lashes . . ."

"That's *your* story!" Edwards exclaimed, clearly shocked.

"No, sir," Weaver said firmly, "they was the figures taken from the *Captain's* journal. Summers showed it to the Spanish officers when they came on board at La Guaira. Captain's own figures, they was."

There was a complete silence for two or three minutes. Ramage did some hurried sums. That averaged fifteen floggings a week with each man getting two dozen lashes. Captain Marden then asked: "The mutineers finally voted to take the ship to the Main?"

"Yes, sir. Summers and a few of the others made speeches and said if they went to Jamaica they'd all be hanged, signed letter or not, because the Admiral wouldn't listen to them, Captain Wallis being his favourite, so they voted for La Guaira."

"Summers made such a speech," said Captain Teal. "What of the other prisoners, Harris and Perry?"

"Perry followed Summers and spoke for La Guaira. Some of the others said the same thing, and then Harris made a long speech. He just repeated what Summers said and the men soon got tired of listening to him and called for a vote."

"What happened when the ship arrived off La Guaira?"

"The Spanish came out. One of the officers spoke English."

Ramage gave Teal a nudge to indicate he had some questions and asked: "Did you anchor off the entrance or what?"

"No, sir. Summers hoisted white flags—flags of truce, he called 'em—front the fore, main and mizen, and then hove-to off the anchorage. After about an hour a Spanish boat came out full of soldiers. And lots of officers, of course."

"Who did the negotiating?"

"Summers, sir, but there was a committee of six mutineers he had to report to. They had to agree to everything."

"Had the committee decided on the terms—on the price they were going to ask the Spanish for handing over the ship?"

"Price, sir?" Weaver was genuinely shocked. "Oh no, sir, they weren't a selling of her! No, all the terms they asked was to be allowed to live on the Main and start a new life."

"That was for the mutineers. What about those of you who did not mutiny?"

"That depended on Summers, sir. He had three lists. One was the men to be handed over to the Spanish as prisoners; the second was men who should be allowed to go free; the third them as should get rewards."

"Were those to be handed over to the Spanish, the men in the first list, those who had not taken part in the mutiny?"

"Not all of them, sir. There was about 25. The cook, some seamen and myself."

"What about the second list? Were they men who had not been in the mutiny?"

"Yes, sir. You see some of us had upset Summers or Perry, and as a sort of punishment we were put on the first list. They used to go round threatening people. As bad as Captain Wallis, they was. Them as hadn't took part in the mutiny and hadn't fallen foul of Summers went on the second list."

"The Spanish authorities agreed to all this?"

"They did eventually, sir, but at first they thought it was some sort of trap. They insisted on taking nearly everyone on shore in the boat, twenty at a time. They brought out more Spanish seamen each time they came back. Then they tried to sail her into the anchorage."

"Tried?"

"Yes, sir; they got her in irons, and eventually Summers took the conn and brought her in."

"How do you know that—surely you had been taken off as prisoners?"

"No, sir, the prisoners were put in irons with a guard of Spaniards. We got worried once when the ship touched a rock and we was all trussed up, but she came off all right."

Edwards tapped with his gavel. "The court will adjourn until eight o'clock tomorrow." Only then did Ramage, glancing at his watch, realize they had been listening to evidence for more than five hours.

CHAPTER SEVEN

WHEN THE court sat again next morning Weaver was back at the end of the line of prisoners while Gowers read aloud the minutes of the previous day's hearing. Although all five captains had avoided discussing the trial, either when the previous day's session ended or before today's began, they knew that the pile of papers covered with Gowers's spidery writing formed the worst condemnation of a captain in the history of the Navy.

"Breadfruit Bligh" had been sent off the *Bounty* by her mutineers, but he was still alive—indeed, the last Ramage heard of him he was commanding a 74, as unpopular with the Admiralty as with his ship's company. Bligh had been too free with the cat-o'-nine-tails in the *Bounty* but compared with Wallis—Ramage did not doubt Weaver's story and knew that his fellow captains agreed—Bligh was no more violent than one of Mr Wesley's preachers.

Gowers's voice droned on, but he had made a good job of the minutes: it must be hard to concentrate for hours on end. Finally he finished and told Weaver: "You are still on oath: take up your position again as a witness."

Captain Edwards had several slips of paper in front of him, and Ramage realized that on each was written a question. It made it easier for the deputy judge advocate if he was given a written question immediately it was asked: he simply numbered it and wrote down the number and corresponding reply in his rough copy of the minutes.

"You described yesterday how the *Jocasta* arrived at La Guaira. Relate what happened to you after the ship came to an anchor."

"We prisoners was kept on board two days and then taken on shore under guard and lodged in the town jail. Five days later we were told we would have to work for our keep, and if we didn't we'd starve."

"What work was this?"

"Helping build fortifications at La Guaira, sir. Breaking up rocks and carrying them to the masons."

"For how long did you do this work?"

"Until the fortresses was completed. Fourteen months, sir."

Breaking up rocks under a scorching tropical sun: for weeks the sun would be directly overhead at noon. It said much for Weaver that he had survived.

"You received pay?"

"They called it subsistence money, sir, and we never actually received it. They used to set up a table every Saturday evening, at the end of the week's work, count out the money due to each man and call out 'is name and tell 'im 'ow much it was. Then they tipped all the money back in the bag and said it was being taken to buy our food. I s'pose the paymaster took it; they're a sticky-fingered lot, those Dons."

"When the fortifications were finished, at the end of the fourteen months, what happened to you then?"

"They freed us all. Them that survived, anyway: eight had died. They said we could live in La Guaira or we could leave if we wished."

"What did you do?"

"I 'ad to go into the 'ospital for four months. I 'ad such sores on me 'ands from 'andling the rocks, and they spread over me back when the sun burned cracks into the skin. After that I tried to find work but there weren't none. I tried to find some of the others what was in the prison with me, but by then they'd all gorn to other places to look for work."

"What about the mutineers?"

"Some of them was still in La Guaira with jobs. A few of the committee was still there, and these three," he pointed to the prisoners. "The Spanish had paid them a reward so they didn't have to work, but by the time I saw them they'd just about spent all their money."

"Did you stay in La Guaira?"

"No, sir. I signed on in a Spanish coasting vessel what was going to Barcelona, down the coast. Just that one voyage. I was still there in Barcelona when the *Sarasota Pride* came in, and I met one of her men who got me signed on. Then I found out that Summers, Perry and Harris was on board. They'd joined at La Guaira. But I was desperate to get away, so I just swallowed all their insults."

"What happened to the *Jocasta?*"

"They kept her at La Guaira for several weeks—I don't recall exactly how long, sir. Then they took her along the coast to a place called Santa Cruz, leastways that's what Summers told me. They gave her some Spanish name."

"Is there anything else concerning this affair that you should tell the court?"

"I don't believe so, sir."

"Very well," Edwards said. He looked across at Summers.

"Do you have any questions to ask the witness?"

Summers shook his head but Edwards snapped: "Say 'Yes' or 'No'; it has to be recorded in the minutes."

"No, sir."

"Did you have any questions to ask the previous witness, Lieutenant Aitken?"

"No, sir."

Edwards asked the other two men the same questions, but neither had anything to say.

"You may stand down, Weaver. The court has some questions to ask the other prisoners."

He pointed to Summers: "Do you deny you were a ringleader in the mutiny, and later elected captain of the ship?"

"No, sir," Summers mumbled. He had his hands clasped tightly and he lifted them from time to time, as if in an obeisance, to wipe away the perspiration streaming down his forehead and into his eyes, making him blink as though surprised by a bright light.

"You were the man who suggested it and planned it," Edwards said. "Do you deny that?"

"No, sir." He suddenly straightened himself up and said simply: "T'was my idea and my plan, sir."

The confession—though Ramage sensed that the man was in fact making a claim—took Edwards by surprise. "You alone?"

"At first, sir. Then I persuaded some of the others. Soon there was forty or fifty—more than Weaver knew about."

"Why did you want to murder all the officers and run away with one of the King's ships and hand her over to the enemy?" Edwards asked the question quietly, speaking slowly and distinctly. "Now, think carefully before you answer."

"I did all the thinking two years ago, sir. You see, sir, he had us trapped, the Captain did. He weren't quite right in the head. He reckoned every man's hand was against him, officers and seamen and Marines, all in a big conspiracy. Conspiracy, that's what he always called it. If a tiny bit of grease dripped out of the sheave of a block—it's bound to 'appen in the 'eat of the sun—and made a spot on the deck, he reckoned someone did it a'purpose to upset him."

Summers was speaking slowly, watching Gowers to make sure he wrote down his words. Ramage saw the man was changing as he told his story; he was like a wilting plant recovering after a refreshing shower of rain. The shifty look was going; the narrow face was flushed and Ramage wondered if in fact the man was normally plumper, reduced now to a skinny wreck by two years of living in the shadow of a noose.

"He was doing us all in, one after the other: we was livin' like animals in a trap, sir. Nothing pleased 'im; he attended all sail-handling with a watch in 'is 'and. Officers were punished, too. Many a time one of the lieutenants was put on eight-hour watches —eight on and four off, so half the time there'd be two of 'em on watch, 'cos the rest stood their normal watches. They was like ghosts from being so short of sleep."

Edwards held up his hand: clearly he regarded this as having nothing to do with Summers's guilt—that had already been established by Weaver's evidence—and despite his earlier determination that no one, captain or admiral, would be whitewashed, he was alarmed by Summers's revelations. But the seaman would not be silenced; he was reliving those months—Ramage realized it might have been years—on board the *Jocasta*, and this was the first time he could tell the story to someone he regarded as "authority."

"He had us trapped, sir—you've got to understand that. We was always ready an' willing to fight the French and the Dons—he knew that. But when the last man fell and was killed because the Captain always said he'd flog the last man down, we knew we had to kill him or he'd kill us. T'wasn't the first time a man had died like that, sir; he'd been doin' it for six months and three men had already fallen. We dreaded seeing a squall come up, sir:

putting in a reef, letting fall or furling sail—every time it meant a flogging for someone. You know how many times a day there's sail-handling of some sort.

"In Port Royal we daren't do nothing about protesting in case he charged us with 'mutinous assembly'—if he saw more'n a couple of men talking together he'd flog 'em because he reckoned they was plotting. We couldn't think of no way of escaping from him without taking the ship, sir."

"But you killed all the officers!" Edwards interrupted harshly.

"As God's my witness, sir, we didn't intend to. We was going to release the twenty-three seamen in irons and lock the Captain in his cabin, but someone raised the alarm and the officers came out with swords and pistols an' started fighting, even though we told them we'd spare 'em."

"The Captain," Edwards said coldly. "You murdered him."

"Yes, sir. An' it happened like this. I led the party what was going to secure him—we had a pair of irons all ready—but by the time we got to the door of his cabin there was so much shoutin' and yellin' all over the ship that he was roused out and waitin' for us, a sword in 'is hand. A long thin sword, like you use for duelling."

"So you murdered him."

"He wouldn't listen to us," Summers said stubbornly. "The minute I opened the door I told him to submit and his life would be safe, but 'e just rushed at me with 'is sword. I was holding a lantern—lit me up but not 'im o' course—and he nearly spitted me. I struck at him in self-defence, sir."

Ramage leaned forward and turned to the president. "Could we recall Weaver and ask him about the mutineers' intentions, sir?"

"Good idea. Weaver, step forward. You are still on oath, remember. Carry on, Ramage."

"Weaver, you have just heard Summers say they did not

intend to kill the Captain and officers. What do you have to say about that?"

"I can only speak of what I heard and saw, sir. The talk I heard was just to take the ship and lock up the Captain. When they went and killed everyone I thought they'd changed their minds."

"Do you know that they *did* change their minds?"

"No, sir. Now I come to think of it, maybe that was why they was angry with Harris for killing the wounded officers after it was all over."

"But when they broke into the Captain's cabin, didn't you hear what was said?"

"I was unconcherous at the time, sir."

"You think Summers's story that they intended to take the ship without killing anyone might be true?"

"I do, sir. Summers is right that Captain Wallis thought everyone's 'and was plotting against him. The First Lieutenant was so frightened he never dared answer the Captain but with an 'aye aye, sir.' None of the officers ever had enough sleep from having to stand extra watches."

"Why didn't you mention all this when you first gave evidence?"

"I never thought you gentlemen would believe me, sir," he said simply. "I never 'eard tell of any captain like the *Jocasta*'s. He was a tyrant, sir, an' that's a fact, and I thank you for hearing us out."

Us. Weaver was not a mutineer, that was clear enough, and he obviously hated Summers and his cronies, but at that moment, as he described life on board the *Jocasta* under Wallis, it was "us." The officers, warrant and petty officers, seamen and Marines; they had all been in the trap, all fighting to stay alive. Eight hours on and four off for the lieutenants; sixteen hours on watch out of the twenty-four, and even the total of eight off interrupted by the need to be on deck to witness the floggings. Us—yes, Ramage thought, Weaver's evidence is true; he's an honest man.

Weaver stepped back into the line and Edwards pointed at Perry.

"Do you deny taking part in murdering Captain Wallis?"

"No, sir." Perry was not defiant nor, as far as Ramage could see, was he frightened. If anything he now seemed relieved that the whole story was out; as if Summers's evidence had been a confession for the three of them.

"Evidence has been given that you argued with Summers as to which of you gave Captain Wallis his death wound."

"That's what Weaver said, sir, and he's part right. Only he was recovering from the bang on the head, and he didn't understand the meaning behind what I said. What we was arguing about, rather. Not that it matters now," he added with a shrug.

"What *were* you arguing about?"

"Well, sir, I'd just told Summers I'd saved his life, and he wouldn't admit it. You see, sir, I was carrying the irons we was going to use to secure the Captain: irons in one hand and cutlass in the other. Summers had the lantern and went in first and shouted to the Captain, but he came straight at us with a sword. He'd have done for Summers but I knocked the sword away and that gave Summers a chance to 'ave a chop at 'im. Caught his left shoulder, and 'e staggered, but 'e came back at us, an' that's 'ow 'e got killed."

Perry had ended up in a rush of words, the aitches dropping in the excitement, and again the cabin was silent but for the squeaking of Gowers's pen, hurrying to catch up.

Then Captain Edwards said: "Summers, does that agree with your recollection?"

"Yes, sir, except that I gave the Captain his death wound. Perry was trying to save me."

The man was obviously hoping to take all the blame; there was no question of taking credit now.

"Perry, do you question any of Weaver's evidence?"

"No, sir, not now. Not after Summers put you right about not planning to kill the Captain an' officers in cold blood. We was just trying to save our backs—aye, an' our lives, too."

In a sudden movement he pulled up his shirt and turned his back to the seated officers. "Look!" he said loudly. "More'n two hundred lashes—an' not one of 'em for a real offence." He turned again before the sentries had time to move. "I never committed a real offence in all me days at sea. Four ships I served in a'fore the *Jocasta,* an' never a lash. More'n two hundred lashes Cap'n Wallis give me."

Edwards nodded and pointed to Harris.

"Evidence has been given that you ran below after the ship was taken and murdered the wounded officers. Do you deny it?"

"No, sir. I was beastly drunk at the time. I was mortal ashamed of meself afterwards."

"Of being drunk or murdering wounded men?" Edwards exclaimed angrily.

"Of the murdering, sir. But by the time I was sober again, t'was too late . . ."

"Do you disagree with any of the evidence against you?"

"Only that bit about me fetchin' an' carryin' for Summers, sir. I never did none of that. I was 'is aidy-dee-camp."

For the next fifteen minutes Edwards questioned the three of them about their activities after the ship had been handed over to the Spanish, and their stories agreed. The Spaniards had given them rewards. Summers, Perry and the six members of the committee received the most, enough money to live on for eighteen months. The rest of the mutineers received enough to last for six months, providing they were careful. Summers estimated that seventy-five or more of the mutineers were trying to make a living at various ports along the Main: most were fishing or serving in coasting vessels. Others had learned some Spanish and managed to find jobs. The rest had signed on neutral ships. Perry had reckoned that he and Summers were the only two ringleaders to leave the Main.

"Why did you try to leave?" Edwards had asked.

"We couldn't stand the Dons no longer," Perry had said contemptuously. "A lot o' 'eathens they are, what with all this burning incense and saints' days an' '*Caramba* this,' and '*Caramba* that.' Got so's we couldn't abide it no longer, an' all the streets like dungheaps. An' the priests always on at us, tryin' to make us into Catholics."

Finally Edwards had called on each man in turn to make his defence against the charges. None of them had anything more to say. Summers, the first to be asked, had said he was guilty as charged, and that he now realized that no matter how tyrannical Captain Wallis had been, it was no excuse for mutiny and murder, but it was done . . .

The court was cleared and as the provost marshal shut the door Edwards gave a deep sigh and pushed his chair back. "Well, that's goodbye to me ever getting my flag, but no one can say we haven't given the beggars a fair trial."

Marden stood up and Ramage watched him pace round the cabin, his hands clasped behind his back and small enough to be able to walk without bending his head to avoid hitting the beams. "How much do we believe?" Marden demanded and, gesturing at Gowers's pile of paper, added: "And how much do we record in the minutes?"

Edwards sighed and said: "I wish I knew. How much to record, that is. I'll have a word with the Admiral before Gowers writes his fair copy."

The cabin seemed enormous to Ramage now that the prisoners and their escort had left. Its size was exaggerated by the few men left at the table. Five captains, he reflected, who have been looking back two years in time, using the uncertain telescope of men's memories. The minutes should give a detailed picture of the mutiny in the *Jocasta* and its causes—as detailed and true as question and honest answer could make it.

The answers, particularly from Summers, had been honest; he was sure of that, although far from certain why he was so sure. He believed Weaver, too. That use of "us" was very significant: the Jocastas were united in their terror of Wallis even though they disagreed over how to do anything about it.

Now Edwards stood up and walked round to the front of the table, to where he could look at the other captains. He turned the witness's chair and sat down in it, crossing his legs and tapping his fingers on the hilt of his sword. He waited until Marden resumed his seat and then asked him flatly: "What do you make of it all?"

Marden said violently: "I'll stand trial for saying it, but Sir Hyde Parker ought to be in the dock, not these men. As Commander-in-Chief he should have warned Wallis long ago. Sent him home, in fact."

"If he knew," Edwards said.

"He knew all right." Marden's voice was harsh now and his face drawn by strong emotion. "Most of us who've been out here a few years had heard enough stories about Wallis. Now we know they were true. Not only true, but worse than we suspected. Far worse. And Sir Hyde knew; he's seen Wallis's journals with the figures for flogging. I only wish we had the latest one."

"Well, everything we say here is secret," Edwards said, "and just as well. However," he added quietly, "we should guard our tongues."

He looked across at Gowers. "We'll consider our verdicts in a moment, but don't write your fair copy of the minutes until I give you the word." Then he asked the captains: "Have you any questions? Do you want Gowers to read the minutes of today's evidence? How about you, Teal?"

"I wish I was away on a cruise," Teal muttered, as though the words forced their way from his mouth. "I wish I'd never heard a word of all this. I'll never trust a ship's company again!"

"Steady now!" Marden said. "Do you flog your men like Wallis did?"

"Of course not. A dozen lashes a month at most, and that's the same man who always gets regularly drunk: hoards his tot, knows he'll get a dozen if he's discovered, and regularly swills it down and then sits on the fo'c's'le in the lee of the belfry and sings bawdy songs at the bosun."

"Nothing wrong with a man who sings bawdy songs at a bosun," Edwards muttered. "Now, Banks, we haven't heard much from you. Any legal questions?"

Banks, junior of all the captains except for Ramage, shook his head. He was a shy man and not a little overawed by Edwards. "I'm like Teal: it's hard to believe what we've just been hearing."

"You, Ramage," Edwards said. "If you'd had any you'd have spoken up, eh?"

"Yes, sir. Some of my questions were aimed at helping me with the next operation."

"I noticed that. You'll have a copy of the minutes, though, and the Admiral's going to let you see the minutes of the other trials. We thought it wiser not to let you see them until we've reached a verdict on this one. Now, gentlemen, are you all ready to deliver your votes?"

A naval court martial was like the trial of a peer before the House of Lords, or the decision of the Privy Council: the junior voted first, followed by the rest in order of seniority, so that Edwards's vote would come last. The court's verdict would represent the majority of votes, and the system, so long a tradition, was intended to avoid a junior officer being influenced by a senior.

The four captains agreed they were ready.

"Read the charges again, Gowers," Edwards said.

As soon as the deputy judge advocate had finished, the president said: "I shall first name the accused man and then you give your vote. This will be on all the charges, unless you choose to divide them up. Now, Ramage, I'll start with you. Do you find George Weaver guilty or not guilty?"

"Not guilty, sir."

"Do you find Albert Summers guilty or not guilty?"

"Guilty on all the charges." Guilty, Ramage thought, but not entirely responsible. Wallis had murdered himself; he had baited the men beyond endurance. He had killed some; the survivors had killed him. Yet the verdict provided only two choices, guilty or not guilty . . .

"Henry Perry?"

"Guilty on all the charges."

"Henry Harris?"

"Guilty on all the charges."

Gowers noted down Ramage's vote, and the next to be asked was Captain Teal, who hesitated over the first name. "Weaver admits he was guilty of 'concealing a mutinous design.'"

Edwards shrugged his shoulders. "You are one of the judges," he said. "Vote as your conscience tells you."

Ramage had already given a lot of thought to that single charge, but Weaver had turned King's evidence anyway. In a strict court of law the man was guilty of concealment, but he had no choice; Ramage believed him when he said his throat would have been cut if he raised the alarm.

"Not guilty, sir," Teal said.

"Not guilty on all the charges, you mean."

"Not guilty on all the charges, sir."

The other captains voted in the same way—Weaver not guilty and the other three guilty—and after Captain Edwards had cast his vote he said formally: "The sentences for the three guilty men are covered by the Articles of War. They are mandatory and we can't change them. We all know the wording but Gowers had better read them out." He glanced at a paper in front of him. "They are Articles number Three, Fifteen, Sixteen, Nineteen, Twenty-eight and Thirty-six."

Gowers picked up a slim volume containing the Articles and began reading: "Article number three. If any officer, Marine, soldier or other person of the Fleet shall give, hold, or entertain intelligence with any enemy or rebel without leave from the King's Majesty . . . or his commanding officer, every such person . . . shall be punished with death.

"Article number fifteen. Every person . . . who shall desert to the enemy, pirate or rebel, or run away with any of His Majesty's ships . . . or any ordnance, ammunition, stores or provisions . . . or yield up the same cowardly or treacherously . . . shall suffer death . . .

"Sixteen. Every person . . . who shall desert or entice others so to do, shall suffer death or such other punishment as the circumstances . . . shall deserve . . . Nineteen. If any person . . . shall make . . . any mutinous assembly . . . and being convicted . . . shall suffer death . . .

"Twenty-eight. All murders committed by any person in the Fleet shall be punished with death . . . Thirty-six. All other crimes not capital . . . which are not mentioned in this Act . . . shall be punished according to the laws and customs in such cases used at sea."

As Gowers had read the Articles, Ramage had been making some notes. Four of the six Articles gave the court no choice: anyone found guilty had to be sentenced to death. The fifth gave death "or such other punishment;" the sixth, the Captain's Cloak, left it to the court. The five captains had found three of the men guilty; the law said, four times, that the sole penalty was death. There was no alternative.

"Bring in the prisoners," Edwards said. "We need not prolong things, although all of them, except Weaver, know what to expect."

C H A P T E R   E I G H T

NEXT MORNING Ramage was rowed over to the *Invincible.* He had no stomach for questioning three men who, within a day or two, would be hoisted by the neck to the foreyardarm of the flagship, but it might eventually save lives on board the *Calypso.*

He was taken to Captain Edwards and found him gloomy, his face as dark as his cabin was light from the early sun. "Sit down, Ramage. I have the minutes of the other *Jocasta* trials here and you can read 'em before you talk to the prisoners. Are you feeling all right?" he asked suddenly.

"I don't enjoy this sort of thing very much, sir," Ramage admitted.

Edwards glanced up, startled. "What do you mean—cutting out the *Jocasta?*"

"No, sir! Courts martial and questioning condemned men."

"That's reasonable enough. Nastiest trial I've ever seen—

although I'd warned the Admiral, he was badly shaken when he read the minutes. Badly shaken," he repeated. "He's worried in case we might have taken the questioning too far, where Wallis was concerned. I must admit he has a point. It didn't seem so at the time, but when you read the minutes . . ."

"I'd have thought it was unavoidable, sir."

Edwards shrugged his shoulders. "A case like this isn't straightforward, you know. Anyone reading those minutes—their Lordships, for instance—are going to ask why Wallis wasn't warned to ease up . . ."

"Perhaps Sir Hyde didn't know."

Edwards stared at Ramage. "What do you really think, eh? Man to man . . ."

"I think he knew well enough," Ramage said frankly. "He must have: he saw Wallis's journals and every flogging was recorded. He looked the other way. It could happen in someone else's fleet but not in one of his frigates."

"Exactly. He knew, and it was common gossip. Mind you, no one else knew just how bad it was."

"But why is Admiral Davis worried?"

"Because none of this evidence about Wallis came out in the other trials."

"A question of Sir Hyde's seniority, I suppose," Ramage mused.

"Precisely. Sir Hyde is nearly at the top of the flag list and Admiral Davis is near the bottom . . . Sir Hyde will probably protest to their Lordships the moment he hears. He'll claim that Admiral Davis did it deliberately; that the court's questioning was intended to discredit him. He's a touchy sort of man, always looking for insults."

"But Admiral Davis wasn't responsible!" Ramage protested. "We asked the questions!"

"Don't worry," Edwards said. "Our Admiral doesn't lack

courage. Anyway, none of this helps you with Santa Cruz—but you realize what bringing the *Jocasta* back here would mean?"

Ramage grinned because Edwards was being perfectly frank now. "That Admiral Davis wouldn't have to worry overly about the effect of those minutes on their Lordships." When Edwards nodded, Ramage could not help adding bitterly: "And Captain Eames would have nothing more to worry about, either."

Edwards inspected his fingernails for several moments. "Quite obviously I could never make any comment about a fellow officer serving on this station, but you are free to draw any conclusions you like. However, it would be unfortunate for all concerned," he said quietly, looking directly at Ramage, "if a second attempt failed."

In other words, Ramage knew, Edwards was just repeating the gentle warning. Eames had already established that it was quite impossible to carry out the Admiralty's order to cut out the *Jocasta*, but another captain had to be saddled with the failure: Admiral Davis was protecting his favourite frigate captain.

But why pick on me? Ramage thought to himself. He had made the Admiral several thousand pounds richer from prize-money, thanks to the captures off Martinique. Yet to be fair to the Admiral (however reluctantly), he had been picked because he was the newest arrival; someone to whom the Admiral owed no patronage or loyalty. Davis was shrewd enough to know that Ramage's stock would be high at the Admiralty once their Lordships heard about the Martinique affair, and if the next report they received told them that Ramage had failed at Santa Cruz, perhaps it would balance out.

"You realize what else bringing back the *Jocasta* would mean?" Captain Edwards asked, and Ramage sensed he had guessed his thoughts.

"Glory for everyone," he said sourly, and then added quickly as the thought had just struck him: "It would also make Eames look a fool."

Edwards nodded and then said: "That possibility hasn't yet occurred to the Admiral."

So Edwards had no time for Eames! "But has it occurred to Eames?" Ramage asked.

"No, nor will it. He'll be only too glad that you now have the job. It's a curious situation," Edwards said. "You'll have to make the best of it. If you succeed—and I'm not flattering you when I say if anyone can, it's you—you'll have a patron for life in the Admiral. And me, too, if I ever reach a position where I can do you a service. Now, you realize this conversation hasn't taken place. I've behaved most improperly as the Admiral's flag captain; you've said things that are best left unsaid. And I hope the air is a lot clearer! I'll leave you to go through those minutes. A copy of our trial minutes is on the top."

With that he left the cabin and Ramage started reading. Out of curiosity he began with the minutes of the trial completed yesterday.

"At a court martial, held on board His Majesty's ship *Invincible* in English Harbour, Antigua . . . the fourteenth of June and held by one adjournment the fifteenth of June . . . Present, Herbert Edwards, esquire, commanding officer of His Majesty's ship *Invincible* and second-in-command of His Majesty's ships and vessels upon the Windward and Leeward Islands station, president, and Captains J. Marden, E. Teal, J. Banks, N. Ramage . . ."

The first time he had ever been a member of a court martial, his name was on a document which concluded: ". . . the said Albert Summers, Henry Perry and Henry Harris, to be hanged by their necks until they are dead, at the yardarms of His Majesty's ship *Invincible*, and at such time as the Commander-in-Chief shall direct."

Many men had been killed in the past because he had given the orders which took his ship into action; many of the enemy were dead because of his orders to open fire; he had killed men himself with pistol and sword; but all of that was in the heat of battle with the knowledge that it was "Kill or be killed." This was so cold-blooded. Yet, as Southwick had said this morning before he left the *Calypso*: "Don't take on so: they knew that if they murdered they risked being stabbed with a Bridport dagger . . ." That was true enough, and it was a case where the slang was appropriate. The Navy's tribute to the Dorset town of Bridport which made such fine-quality hemp rope was to make "a Bridport dagger" another phrase for the hangman's noose.

Ramage picked up the minutes of the Barbados trial of *Jocasta* mutineers. It told him only what the accused men did; there was no hint of why. Nor did it mention any details that might help him off Santa Cruz. There was a mutiny, and the witness deposed that A did this and B did that and C did the other. No mention that some officers had survived and then been murdered by Harris. Ramage picked up the next set, from Jamaica, and they told the same scanty story: enough evidence to convict the accused— more than enough, there was no question of that—but no hint that the frigate was sailing in limbo and manned by seamen who felt themselves doomed at the hands of a mad captain.

Was Wallis really mad? Madness seemed remote, sitting in Edwards's neat cabin on board the *Invincible* in English Harbour, but how had it been on board Wallis's frigate? Did it give him pleasure to flog men, or did he genuinely think everyone on board, officers, Marines and seamen, was plotting against him? Either way he must have been mad: no sane man enjoyed ordering a flogging. Ramage put down the last of the minutes under a heavy paperweight. He had wasted half an hour and learned nothing from them. Or, rather, he had learned there was nothing to be learned, except that, however convincing the minutes of a court martial might seem, they were unlikely to give even a hint of the real problem . . .

Ten minutes later he was down in the perpetual gloom of the lower deck where the three condemned men were secured, their wrists in irons and each of them sitting on the deck with his ankles secured by another set of irons, the bar of which went through a ringbolt in the planking. Three Marines guarded them, and Ramage told the lieutenant who had escorted him to tell them to stand back out of earshot.

He knelt on one knee beside Summers. "You recognize me, Summers?"

"Indeed I do, sir, you saved my life once."

For a moment Ramage, more than conscious that he was one of the five judges who had condemned the three prisoners to death, thought Summers was making a bitter joke; but the man was grinning and he meant it seriously. Ramage stared at him, trying to recall the face, knowing that for two days he had watched those features to see what they might reveal by a passing expression.

"I don't recall you, Summers; I'm sorry." It seemed right to apologize to a condemned seaman but—

"The *Belette,* sir: I was one of an 'undred men and we was only on board your *Kathleen* for a few hours. I been telling me mates about it but they don't believe me. Nah then," he said happily, twisting to face Perry and Harris, "'ere's the gennelman himself and he can put me right if I tell a lie!"

With that he took a deep breath and launched off on his story: "There was the *Belette* up on the rocks under a cliff on the coast of Corsica and we'd all climbed on shore and taken over an empty castle—well, a big lookout tower—and barred it against the Frenchies when they arrived.

"Problem though, for Captain Ramage—he was a l'tenant then—is how he rescues us with his little cutter. Well, 'e gets up to all sorts of tricks and we bolt down the cliff, back on the wreck, and step on board the cutter like she was the Gosport Ferry, 'cos Mr Ramage has laid her alongside the wreck and is waiting for us, with the Frenchies blazing away from the top of the cliff like madmen! There, that's 'ow it was, wasn't it, sir?"

Ramage nodded, his thoughts in a whirl as memories of that desperate hour or two—carrying out his first orders in his first command—came swirling in. Southwick had been there, and Jackson, and . . . so many. And among the hundred or so Belettes who swarmed on board and were taken down to Bastia had been Summers, not even a face in the crowd, and years later chance had put Summers on board the *Jocasta* . . .

"Yes, that's what happened, Summers."

Perry and Harris were clearly impressed, but Ramage suddenly wanted to get up on deck again, into the sunshine. Down here, where they needed lanterns, the darkness and the humid heat, the occasional clank of the men's irons—yes, this was the final stages of justice, but it was hateful.

"Summers and you, Perry and Harris, I need your help—"

"O' course, sir!" Summers said eagerly, "just—"

"I have to cut out the *Jocasta*."

Summers's eyes dropped and Perry exclaimed: "Gawd."

Then Summers looked directly at Ramage. "It can't be done, sir: I swear it can't. Not even you, sir—an' I bin 'earing of some of the things you've done since the *Belette*. I was in Santa Cruz two months ago, maybe more. They got three 'undred or more soldiers on board, besides seamen."

"But, sir, that 'arbour. It's a cross-grained place; if the wind'll let you sail in, you can't get out again without towing. And t'other way about. A fort each side of the entrance and one at the far end, and their guns would smash you into so much driftwood. The channel's very narrow so that daylight or dark won't make no odds: the channel ain't more'n a hundred yards wide and the forts set back maybe fifty yards. The range—the most it'll be is a hundred yards . . . Gawd," he said, shuddering as his imagination put him in Ramage's place.

When Ramage said nothing Summers reached up with both hands, as if pleading: "Sir, believe me. I 'ate the Dons and I wish the *Jocasta* was 'ere in English Harbour. If I could 'elp you get her out—well, they're tying the 'angman's knots in the nooses ready for us now, and I'd go feeling better if I could do something to get 'er back, but yer can't do it, sir; that's why the Dons took 'er there to fit her out."

He paused a moment, deep in thought. "Ah! That's it, sir. Wait for her to come out. She's going to Havana. They'll have 'er ready in a few weeks, and it don't matter how many soldiers they've got—that's what most of 'em are—you could take 'er at sea. But to cut her out—no, sir."

Ramage shrugged his shoulders and shifted his cramped knee. "I have my orders, Summers, so describe the harbour to me as best you can. Do you know any depths?"

"I know the channel, sir: I bin in twice. First was with a *guarda costa,* then they made me take the *Jocasta* round—they're mortal feared of handling her, sir."

"Could you draw me a chart?"

"O' course, sir, if I 'ad pencil and paper."

An hour later Ramage went up on deck, Summers's chart folded carefully in his pocket. The three condemned men had asked to be allowed to shake him by the hand as he left, and then he was up in the bright sunshine. Death was illness, gunshot and sword thrust. It was old age, a fall from a yardarm or a ship sinking in a hurricane. But it was also the concluding words of an Article of War or a court martial sentence. He felt dazed, dizzy with a sense of unreality, and saw that Edwards was looking at him.

"It couldn't have been easy," Edwards said sympathetically, "that sort of thing never is. But just remember—the Navy is bound together by discipline. That's why we always beat the Dons: we have it, they don't. And discipline," he added bitterly, "means not murdering your officers . . ."

CHAPTER NINE

FIVE DAYS LATER the *Calypso* was reaching fast to the south-west and just beginning to pitch lazily as she came clear of the lee of Grenada, the southernmost of the Windward Islands. The coast of the Spanish Main was a hundred miles ahead, across the wide channel separating South America from the end of the chain of islands, and soon the frigate would be in the strong west-going current set up by the Atlantic flowing into the Caribbean.

The sun was scorching and the sea a deep yet dazzling blue, but to an untrained eye the only signs that the *Calypso* was a ship of war were the guns lining her sides: most of her men were sitting or lying in whatever shade they could find while aft four or five of them perched on the taffrail were juggling with fishing lines.

Because it was Sunday all the men were newly shaven with their hair tied in neat queues. This was the day when the ship's company was mustered and the captain had the men singing some hymns and, once a month, read the Articles of War to them. The order for the afternoon—apart from the men on watch—was "make and mend," a few hours when shirts and trousers could be patched by those energetic with needle and thread. Two men were helping each other cut out a shirt from a piece of cloth, one trying to hold the material flat on the deck while the other snipped away with scissors. Another man was whittling away at a carving of a horse, careful that the shavings fell into a piece of canvas.

Jackson, Rossi and Stafford were on the fo'c's'le, squatting in the shade of the flying jib with their backs against the carriage of a six-pounder. Three other seamen sprawled on the deck near them and apparently asleep were in fact listening to the conversation.

Stafford, the Cockney locksmith swept up by the press-gang— "a good man lost to the burglin' profession" as he often boasted —had been comparing the beauty of Spanish and Italian women with the English, more especially those from London. Rossi had been putting forward the claims of the ladies of Genoa, while Thomas Jackson, the only American on board, delivered a verdict that the women of southern Europe were usually too fat while those from the north were too thin.

"The Marchesa's an exception," he declared.

"She's the loveliest lady I ever saw," Stafford admitted. "Don't know why the Captain don't marry 'er."

"Ah, it hardly seems yesterday when we rescued her," Jackson said nostalgically.

One of the seamen sat up. "When you what?"

"Ah, you Invincibles, you don't know nothing," Stafford jeered. "You mean to say you've never 'eard 'ow, Jacko rescued a queen from under the 'ooves of Boney's cavalry?"

With that the other two sat up. "No," said one of them, "a real queen? Don't believe it!"

"She's not called a queen but she rules her own country," Jackson said. "Volterra's the place, in Italy. We were sent in a frigate to rescue her as Boney's troops marched south, only we were sunk and we ended up fetching her off in a boat."

"And she and the Captain—he was only a lieutenant then—went and fell in love," Stafford added.

"And very nice too," said one of the new men from the *Invincible*. "But like you was saying, why ain't they got married?"

"*Accidente!*" Rossi exclaimed indignantly. "If I marry all the women I love, I have a hundred wives!"

"Where's this lady now, then?" the seaman asked.

"Staying with the Captain's family," Jackson explained. "His father's got a big estate down in Cornwall."

"I pity her, then," the seaman commented. "That Cornish lingo: I can't never understand what they'm saying."

"Yorkshire, that's where you come from," Stafford said accusingly. "An' *you* talk about a lingo!"

"Lancashire," the man replied triumphantly. "Shows how much *you* know!"

"You'd better be learning Spanish," Jackson said. "We'll need it soon, from what I hear."

"Why we have to go an' chase out a lot o' murderin' mutineers I don't know," Stafford grumbled.

"Aye, there's a lot you don't know," the Lancashire seaman said. "There ain't a mutineer left on board the *Jocasta*; she's full of Spaniards. Three 'oondred or more; that was the scuttlebutt when we left the *Invincible*, and a narrow entrance to Santa Cruz with three forts an 'oondreds of guns."

"You people measure everything by the . . . ''oondred,'" Jackson said dryly. "Mr Ramage always divides the opposition by ten . . ."

"Your Mr Ramage is goin' to be the scapegoat; that's what I

'eard," another seaman said. "That there Captain Eames is the Admiral's favourite and he made a mess of it without even trying. But your chap is going to be the one that'll be put on the beach with half-pay when the Admiralty hears he's failed. Leastways, that's what I heard," he added hurriedly. "Seems unfair but there's no tellin' with officers."

"Speakin' of officers," one of the other seamen said, "the First Lieutenant seems all right."

"One o' the best," Stafford said emphatically. "Same goes for Wagstaffe and Baker. The new Fourth Lieutenant, Kenton—don't know about 'im, 'e's only been on board a few days."

"This little midshipman—he's a foreigner, ain't he?"

"Foreigner?" Rossi exclaimed. "*Accidente*, he's Italian. And so am I!"

"I couldn't have guessed," the seaman said with a grin.

"Mr Orsini—he's the Marchesa's nephew," Jackson explained. "A good lad. We're proud of him," he added, giving a gentle warning. "He's a proper terror when we go into action . . ."

"He'll need to be, and the rest of us."

"Sounds to me as though you Invincibles are scared of Santa Cruz," Stafford said.

"Aye—and rightly so. You'll see."

The Cockney shrugged his shoulders. "Would you attack a Spanish ship of the line wiv a cutter?"

"Course not!"

"We did," Stafford said flatly. "Leastways, Mr Ramage did and we was on board."

"You're joking!"

"I 'aint—ask Jacko and Rosey."

"What 'appened?"

"We was sunk."

"There you are! Must be barmy, your Mr Ramage."

Stafford sighed, as if losing patience with men of such feeble understanding. "The Spaniard was captured—and another ship of the line, too. All because of us. Mr Ramage, rather."

The seaman flopped back on the deck. "Maybe so, but your Mr Ramage is going to 'ave to work miracles at Santa Cruz."

"Look," Jackson said sternly, "you can stop this 'your Mr Ramage' talk. He's your Captain as well, now. Don't forget the Jocastas mutinied because their Captain flogged 'em by the score. I've been with Mr Ramage since afore he got his first command, and he's only ever flogged two men . . ."

"All right, all right. Just wait until you see Santa Cruz, Jacko. It'll make yer blood run cold."

The first sight of the Spanish Main was a distant view of the grey-blue hump of Punta Peñas, a hundred miles to the east of Santa Cruz and one of the entrances of the great Gulf of Paria, which separated the island of Trinidad from the mainland.

Southwick shut his telescope with a snap. "A long time since I last clapped eyes on the Dragon's Mouth," he commented to Ramage. "A good name for it, too: the currents in there are bad, and you can lose the wind in the lee of the island."

Ramage, preoccupied, said sourly: "Well, it doesn't concern us. I think we'll reverse our course until dusk—we don't want to be sighted yet."

Southwick had long since given up trying to guess his Captain's plans: when he was good and ready Mr Ramage would tell him how he proposed cutting out the *Jocasta* and expect any criticisms or suggestions to be made without hesitation. As he turned away to give the orders to wear the ship and steer back towards Grenada, the Master suspected that at the moment Mr Ramage had no plan.

He bellowed orders that sent men running towards the sheets

and braces controlling the great sails. A quick instruction to the quartermaster set the wheel spinning and soon the *Calypso* was steering north-east on the starboard tack, sailing along her original track.

Mr Ramage was thinking hard but he had no plan: that much was clear to Southwick, who watched him pacing up and down. Then he stopped and stared at the horizon, and rubbed the older of the two scars over his right eyebrow. That confirmed it as far as Southwick was concerned: he rubbed that scar only when he was angry or puzzled, and there was nothing to make him angry.

Southwick watched him as he began walking the quarterdeck again. He was beginning to look like his father: the same easy stride, the wide shoulders, the hands clasped behind his back. His face was maturing too; those brown eyes were more deep-set now and there were tiny wrinkles at the outboard ends of his eyebrows. He was a younger version of his father but with his own sense of humour. He had a disconcerting habit of saying something peculiar with a straight face. If you were not careful you found yourself agreeing before you hauled in what he had said. He had not joked much since the trial of the mutineers, however. It had changed him, but Southwick was hard put to know if it was permanent. He was just the same with the men, he watched all sail-handling with the same sharp eye, he was the same with the officers. Yet Southwick knew he had changed, even if he could not define the difference.

He was beginning to have a suspicion that Mr Ramage was in fact angry. Not with anything on board the *Calypso*—he was not a man to suffer in silence; if something had made him angry in the ship he would have been quick to say so. He had said very little about the trial, but he had mentioned Captain Wallis's behaviour and how free he had been with the cat. And that could be the reason for the change: Mr Ramage trying to keep control of a deep anger—a resentment, almost—against Wallis.

Mr Ramage had very firm ideas about flogging: he reckoned it ruined a good man and only made a bad man worse. In fact he went further: he was convinced that, except for incorrigible seamen (the kind of men who, on land, would spend a lifetime in and out of jail), if a captain had to resort to the cat-o'-nine-tails the captain was probably at fault.

He was not in a bad mood exactly: he had passed the word that the men could fish from the taffrail and four of them were perched there now, cussing and joking as they hooked and lost fish, all within a few feet of where Mr Ramage marched up and down as though trying to wear a furrow in the deck planking.

Whatever Mr Ramage finally decided to do at Santa Cruz—and there was plenty of time, because for the present he was keeping the *Calypso* a hundred miles to windward of it—the ship's company was ready. Gunnery drill and sail-handling showed that Captain Edwards had sent over good men from the *Invincible*. Southwick had expected him to take the opportunity to get rid of his worst men, but he had been fair.

So the *Calypso* was ready for anything; as ready as training and preparation could make her. Down in his cabin was a large-scale chart of Santa Cruz which he had drawn up from various sources. Ironically the best information came from one of the mutineers, who would have been hanged by now: that man had drawn a chart from memory—and it was better than anything available in English Harbour. It showed Southwick that, although he had been guilty of murdering his Captain, the man had not been disloyal to his country as he faced the noose. He must have guessed that the information he had about Santa Cruz was vital, but he had not attempted to bargain with it by trying to get his death sentence reduced to transportation, for instance. According to Mr Ramage, the man had been only too glad to help, as though to make amends . . .

"Deck there! Sail-ho, on the larboard quarter!"

Ramage and Southwick reached the rail at the same time and put telescopes to their eyes. They could see nothing: the distant ship was below the curvature of the earth but just visible to the lookout perched high up in the mainmast.

Ramage turned to the quartermaster: "Pass the word for my coxswain."

A hail forward brought Jackson running aft to the quarter-deck, where Ramage handed him a telescope taken from the binnacle drawer. "Get aloft and see what you make of her."

Three minutes later, after Jackson had spent a long time balancing himself against the reverse-pendulum movement of the masts as the *Calypso* rolled, he hailed: "Deck there. She looks like a schooner. She's steering up to the nor'-east on the same course as us. Could be a Jonathan, sir."

Ramage turned to Southwick: "Bear away and run down to her."

A ninety-mile line of scattered and tiny islands, reefs and cays ran parallel to the Main and up to sixty miles north of it. A prudent master leaving La Guaira, Barcelona and Cumaná would steer north-west to pass safely to the westward; but if he left Santa Cruz he would instead sail out to the north-east, making sure that the west-going current did not sweep him down to the Testigos, the islands marking the eastern end of the line. He would, Ramage knew, steer for Grenada until, sixty miles or so out from the Main, he could risk bearing away for his destination, but even then he would keep a sharp lookout. Many of the shoals west of Testigos barely showed above water; some of the cays were only a few feet high.

Ramage took off his hat and mopped his face and neck: the heat seemed solid; the breeze filled the sails but seemed to ignore the men on deck. Above him the great yards creaked as they were braced round; the men at the wheel hauled on the spokes as Southwick gave them a course which should intercept the ship they still could not see from the deck.

Southwick put a speaking-trumpet to his lips and hailed Jackson: "Masthead there! How is the sail bearing from us now?"

"Two points on our larboard bow, sir."

The Master nodded to himself. The schooner with her fore-and-aft rig would be fast on the wind.

The hailing had brought Aitken on deck, blinking in the harsh sunlight, and as soon as Southwick had told him of the sighting the First Lieutenant said to Ramage: "Could she have come from Santa Cruz, sir?"

"She could, and be clawing up to clear the Testigos."

"She might have some more Jocastas on board."

The idea obviously had not occurred to Ramage, and his eyes narrowed. "I'm more concerned with finding out what's happening in Santa Cruz than providing fodder for courts martial."

"Quite, sir." Aitken understood his Captain well enough not to be offended by the remark: he too imagined vividly the thunder of the *Invincible*'s guns and the hanging figures emerging from the smoke.

Ramage had the telescope to his eye. "I can just make out her mastheads. Have a boat ready for lowering, Mr Aitken. You'll be boarding her. Take six Marines. Mr Southwick, we'll beat to quarters in fifteen minutes' time."

Half an hour later the *Calypso* was hove-to a hundred yards to windward of the schooner, which had hoisted the American flag, and Ramage watched through his telescope as Aitken and her master talked on deck. After a few minutes the two men went below. The Marines were standing where Aitken had obviously placed them, so the American must be cooperating.

On board the *Calypso* the guns were run out, the water which had been splashed across the deck was drying quickly on the hot wood of the planking, and the grains of sand sprinkled over it to give the men a good foothold became myriads of tiny mirrors reflecting the sunlight.

The sea had the dark blue, almost mauve, of the tropical ocean, the sky, with the sun high, was a harsher blue, hinting at infinite distance which would be revealed when darkness once again brought back the stars. And all the time the sun beat down on the ship, making the deck planking uncomfortably hot and heating metal until it was unpleasant to touch. But there was enough breeze now to keep the men cool, once they had finished the heavy work of loading and running out the guns.

Ramage walked the width of the quarterdeck swearing to himself that he would not look across at the schooner again until he had made five traverses. Impatience was a tiring and pointless fault, but one he found it very hard to eradicate. One of the few advantages of being made post was that you could indulge yourself more frequently . . . But now Aitken was dealing with the Jonathan, pumping him dry of information about Santa Cruz, with luck.

The *William and Henrietta* of Boston. Shipowners along the east coast of America were no more imaginative than their counterparts across the other side of the Atlantic. Who was William, and was Henrietta his wife? Or had someone named the ship after his father and mother? He did not give a jot, but speculating about such nonsense passed a few more minutes and by then he had made six traverses of the deck, so he could look again.

He put the glass to his eye. Aitken was on deck again, and folding something and putting it in the canvas pouch he had used to protect the list of known Jocastas from spray. The Marines had not moved and now Aitken was signalling over the side to the boat.

No mutineers! It was as much the wish not to find mutineers

as the hope of discovering the latest information about Santa Cruz that was making him impatient for Aitken's return. He did not want to be a member of another court martial trying one of Wallis's victims. Victims was an odd way to think of murderers and mutineers but it was more of a judgement—a diagnosis, Bowen would call it—than an expression of sympathy.

Now the *Calypso*'s boat was clear of the schooner. The *William and Henrietta* was a graceful vessel, a sweeping sheer lifting to a high bow. She was painted a dark blue with a broad white strake, an unusual colour for an American merchantman: they were usually black or green. Then the headsails, which had been backed, were sheeted home and for a minute or two the *William and Henrietta*'s bow paid off before she fathered way.

Another neutral ship stopped and boarded; another routine dozen-word entry in the log, one of hundreds made every year by ships of the Royal Navy. While Ramage's thoughts roamed, Aitken arrived to stand before him, grinning cheerfully. Startled, Ramage glanced round to see that the boat was already hooked on and ready to be hoisted on board.

Aitken unloaded the pouch. "No mutineers on board, sir, but the master was friendly enough: he left Santa Cruz early yesterday morning and he's bound for St Augustine, in Florida. Cargo of hides—phew, and do they stink!"

Ramage waited with growing impatience. The captain had to be cool, unruffled, patient, the fountain of wisdom . . . which meant that the Captain could not at this moment tell Aitken to stop rambling and report on Santa Cruz.

"Hides, eh?" he said casually. "Of course, they have a lot of cattle along this coast. Poor quality hides, if I remember correctly: some kind of fly that attacks the skin and causes sores."

"Maybe so, sir," Aitken said, "but the master tells me they fetch a good price in America."

"Indeed? What other news from our American friend?"

"Nothing, sir. He says he always finds a west-going current of between one and two knots from here all the way up to the lee of Grenada, which is what we'd reckoned anyway."

"Quite."

"And the *Jocasta*, sir: she's still there and has her yards crossed and sails bent on, but apparently there's barely a hundred seamen on board her now. She was full of troops when he arrived, but they were suddenly taken off and marched inland with some of the town garrison. He reckoned more than five hundred of them altogether. There was a lot of talk of trouble up in the hills at a place called"—he paused and took a piece of paper from his pocket—"called Caripe. I don't know if that's the way to pronounce it. Anyway, there are hundreds of Indians living up in the mountains who are always making trouble for the Spaniards, and they've just massacred the garrison at this place, Caripe. The only troops available to send after 'em were those on board the *Jocasta* and some of the garrison."

Aitken's voice was flat. Did he understand the significance of the news he was relating? Ramage, not realizing that Aitken was copying him, was far from sure, but he was thankful for those unknown Indians who, revolting for reasons he could only guess at, had as if by magic removed three hundred soldiers from the *Jocasta*. That was as good as doubling the number of men he had in the *Calypso* . . . Then he remembered the forts. They were the threat; compared with them the prospect of three hundred more or less on board the *Jocasta* was of little account. Smile, Ramage told himself; Eames was beaten long before he reached Santa Cruz, beaten by a look at the chart.

"A fortunate coincidence," Ramage commented. "A pity we can't help our Indian allies."

Aitken nodded as he peered into his canvas pouch. "And then

there's this, sir." He took out a large sheet of paper which had been folded twice. "The master copied it for me from the one he uses. He vouches for the soundings because he's taken them himself."

Ramage turned his back to the wind. The paper was a good chart of Santa Cruz and the entrance with the forts marked in, and on the windward side of the large rectangular lagoon at the inner end of the channel was drawn the *Jocasta,* showing that she was secured fore and aft to buoys.

He handed it back to Aitken. "You'd better give that to Southwick. It's a great deal better than anything we have."

Ramage resumed his pacing. Even a perfunctory look at the new chart did not alter the major characteristics of Santa Cruz: it was still a square lagoon half a mile inland at the end of a channel which began as a narrow slot through the cliffs, although the hills on either side quickly sloped down so that Santa Cruz itself and the land round the lagoon was flat.

The *Jocasta* was at the eastern end of the lagoon; the town at the western. And high above the middle of the southern side was the Castillo de Santa Fé, taking its name from the high mountain, Pico de Santa Fé, which stood inland like a giant beacon, a landmark visible for twenty miles, though one which Eames's chart neglected to mention.

An American master and a group of Indians: Captain Ramage of the *Calypso* was finding some improbable allies. He turned to find Aitken waiting to speak to him.

"I forgot to mention, sir," he began apologetically, "that the American said there is a Spanish *guarda costa* patrolling the coast. He saw her steering westwards as he left Santa Cruz. They caught a Dutch ship smuggling a few weeks ago, so they're on the watch."

Ramage nodded and resumed his pacing. By now the boat

had been hoisted on board and was being stowed, men waiting with the canvas cover that kept off the sun in the eternal fight to stop the heat drying out the planking. The *Calypso*'s guns were being unloaded and run in; a head pump was already gurgling as men swabbed down the decks to wash away the sand. The *William and Henrietta* was a couple of miles away and sailing fast. There was a lot to be said for a schooner rig, Ramage thought; you soaked up to windward like water through paper.

Wagstaffe, who was officer of the deck, came up to report that the boat was secured, the guns run in, and the ship ready to get under way again.

"Carry on," Ramage said, and went down to his cabin, sending a seaman to tell Aitken and Southwick to report to him with the charts. He slumped down on the settee, pitching his hat on to the desk. He was a hundred miles from Santa Cruz, and had not a single positive idea in his head. He had hoped that after leaving English Harbour a plan would come to mind; that once he was clear of the trial and all the petty irritations inflicted on a ship in harbour, he would suddenly find he had an answer to the problem of cutting out the *Jocasta*. Instead he had become more certain that it was impossible. The only possible chance was to send in the boats at night; rely on boarding parties creeping along the channel past the forts and seizing the *Jocasta* and sailing her out. This meant assuming that the Spanish sentries would be asleep.

It also meant he had to wait for a southerly wind—the only wind that would let the *Jocasta* sail out. But with Santa Cruz surrounded by mountains and hills, one could never be sure from out to sea what the wind direction would be inside the channel: eddies round a hill and gusts rolling down the side of a mountain could change the wind direction in a given spot by ninety degrees. An east wind at the entrance could mean a south wind inside the lagoon. A north wind at the entrance could mean an east wind in the channel. And the *Jocasta* would have only the survivors of the boarding parties to man her and sail her out under the fire of three forts which, with all the noise going on, would be wide awake and ready to sink the frigate before she was halfway down the channel. The boats could not tow her out, he thought bitterly, since none would survive for long enough . . .

Eames had come and looked at the problem and gone back to tell the Admiral it could not be done. It was not a question of courage; it was a problem of wind directions and the courses that a ship could steer; of the amount of punishment a ship could take from dozens of guns firing down at ranges of a few score yards. Now thanks to the American chart, there was less risk of grounding on a shoal but that was his only advantage over Eames . . .

If he decided on towing out the *Jocasta* he had to allow for the fact that the boats (rowed by the survivors, and those not needed on board the frigate) could not possibly tow her at more than two knots, probably less. The channel was half a mile long so it would take a quarter of an hour to get to the entrance, and the forts there could keep up a fire for another fifteen minutes at least after she had reached the open sea, even if it was a dark night. The *Calypso* could not wait close in to take over the tow: she would be taking a big risk if she tried to help from half a mile out to sea.

It couldn't be done; no amount of talking could change that. Eames would be in the clear although he had not even tried; Captain Ramage would be the man who attempted but failed to carry out the Admiralty's orders. Admiral Davis might even explain away Eames's visit by saying it was a reconnaissance . . .

The sentry at the door called: "Mr Aitken, sir, and Mr Southwick."

The two men came into the cabin, Southwick carrying a roll of charts. Ramage stood up and went to the desk, throwing his hat across to the settee. "Let's have the American chart here."

"It's a good chart," Southwick said gloomily and shaking his head, "and all it tells us is—" he broke off and shrugged his shoulders. "I can't see how we can do anything without losing both ships."

Aitken was watching Ramage and clearly expected his Captain to smile and contradict Southwick. Instead Ramage looked down at the chart and said: "I can't either. How about you?" he asked the Scot.

"I—er, well, sir, we'll probably lose one ship."

"Ah, there you are, all you Scots are the same," Southwick said with a sniff. "Too damned mean to lose two!"

"We mustn't be too generous with the King's property," Ramage chided, and once again Aitken remembered the meeting in Captain Ramage's cabin on board the *Juno* before the battle off Martinique, when the Captain was facing the prospect of fighting a French squadron with only two frigates. He still had not got used to Captain Ramage's manner, and Southwick's was just as bad. Here they were, faced with impossible orders, and both of them joking. He supposed there was some sense in it. If the Captain and his officers walked round the ship with long faces before a battle, the men would think it hopeless and would not display the kind of reckless bravado that Captain Ramage seemed to inspire with that truly diabolical grin he wore at the prospect of gunfire. Better die joking than grumbling! But with just the three of them in the cabin and a sentry on the door, was it necessary to keep up the play-acting?

At that moment Aitken realized that it was not play-acting:

he saw Ramage looking down at the chart and guessed that he had long ago weighed up all the prospects. If the Captain could still laugh and joke after that, then he had every right to expect his First Lieutenant to be cheerful as well. Southwick must have been born with a grin on that chubby red face of his, and with an irreverent attitude towards just about anything that other men took seriously—including going into battle and getting killed.

Southwick jabbed at the chart, running his finger along until it reached the eastern end of the lagoon, near where the *Jocasta* was moored. "Perhaps we could land men farther up the coast and let 'em attack overland."

"If they didn't break their necks falling over precipices on the way. These are mountains, you know, not hills—they'd be in fine shape after they'd swum out to the *Jocasta*. They could paddle round her and hurl abuse—their powder would be wet, so abuse would be their only weapon."

"But, sir," Southwick protested, "there are bound to be boats—fishermen tie 'em up to piers and that sort of thing."

"At night they'd probably be out fishing, but anyway they're small boats. Would you gamble on finding enough little fishing boats—with oars left in them—for two hundred men? Forty boats at least?"

Well, no, sir," said Southwick. "Some, though. But you're right about oars: they're all thieves and they certainly wouldn't trust each other enough to leave oars on board."

"You don't think our men could get on board from our own boats, sir?" Aitken asked.

"I'm sure they might, but if they had to tow her out—two knots? More than half a mile to the entrance? Three forts with 50, 36 and 28 guns—a total of a 114 with the range barely above two hundred yards?"

"They might sail her out," Aitken said hopefully.

"Indeed they might. Those would be my orders if there was any guarantee that she's properly rigged and that we could tell from seaward when there's a fair wind in the channel. We know she was originally stripped and her yards sent down. Now we know her yards are crossed and sails bent on. But what of sheets and braces? If I was the Spanish captain, worried about having his ship cut out—don't forget Captain Eames was there less than a month ago—I'd leave reeving sheets and braces until just before I was ready to sail.

"So without being reasonably certain of a fair wind and without being certain she can be sailed, I'm not risking two hundred Calypsos. It wouldn't even be risking, it would be sending them to death or captivity."

"But at least you'd have tried, sir," Aitken protested.

"Yes, but . . ." Now Ramage was smiling. "The 'but' is simple yet important. A dead hero who succeeds is one thing; a dead hero who fails is another. And a dead hero who unnecessarily sent two hundred men to their graves is a knave."

"Quite, sir," Aitken said quietly, suddenly recalling the almost incredible loyalty that Captain Ramage seemed to inspire in men who had served with him, ranging from Southwick to that flock of seamen led by Jackson. "But we don't have much time, sir. The minute anyone on the coast spots us, they'll pass the word to Santa Cruz."

"Yes, indeed," Ramage agreed, "and a neutral ship coming into Santa Cruz might sight us: why, we might even be seen by a *guarda costa*."

"Then, sir . . ."

"This is where the conversation began," Ramage said, still smiling. "Southwick had just said it was hopeless, and I'd agreed."

"But, sir—" but then Aitken found he had nothing more to say. Southwick slapped him on the back and gave a hearty laugh.

"Cheer up—we've all stayed alive up to now and we've a deal of prize-money due soon!"

Ramage turned to Southwick. "How does this American chart compare with the others?"

"More soundings, and I suspect the *Jocasta*'s position is more accurately marked. Aitken said the Jonathan skipper showed where he usually anchored if there was no room at the quay— where he's drawn in an anchor. That's only a hundred yards from the *Jocasta*'s stern, and she's secured to buoys and doesn't swing."

"The distances compare well? I mean the scale of this chart is likely to be correct?"

"Yes, sir. See here, now, the channel's a hundred yards wide at the entrance, almost exactly half a mile long, and tapers down a bit to about eighty yards where it meets the lagoon. As you can see, the lagoon is just about rectangular, as though it was an artificial harbour. A mile long from east to west, half a mile wide."

Southwick took the dividers from a rack on Ramage's desk and used them to point at the fort on the inland side of the lagoon. "I reckon this is the one that could cause the most trouble: Santa Fé. It stands three hundred feet up and can cover the channel from one end to the other. One mile from the fort to the entrance.

"Now, these two at the entrance, they've been sited badly. I don't reckon they can fire down the channel towards the lagoon: I'm sure they can only fire to seaward and just cover the channel between 'em."

Ramage looked closely at the drawing. "What makes you think that?"

"Well, you see how that Jonathan fellow sketched in the run of the hills here. Look, this is Castillo San Antonio, on the eastern side of the entrance. Well, that's how it is on Summers's drawing. I reckon the slope of the hill hides the channel from the fort. None of us spotted it then so it was too late to ask. Both charts agree about the hills on the west side, too, so this other fort, El Pilar, was probably built the same way, with the slope hiding the channel."

Aitken said suddenly: "It would make sense, sir: they site Santa Fé to sweep the channel and stop any ships sailing down it, and build San Antonio and El Pilar to cover the seaward approach. I'm no soldier, sir, but I can't see them siting fortresses to stop ships *leaving* the port!"

"How much of the channel do you reckon they might cover, Southwick?" Ramage asked.

"Maybe half of it: a quarter of a mile."

Ramage shrugged his shoulders. "Towing at two knots, you wouldn't get a rowing boat past them."

"No, sir," Southwick said lamely. "I was just pointing it out."

"How high would you guess the walls of the fort?"

"Forty or fifty feet, sir."

"I think you'll find that guns mounted that high in either fort would clear the hills . . ."

"Yes, sir," Southwick admitted, flushing. "I was going on the plan drawn here. Of course, that'd be ground level. Sorry, sir."

"No, you may be right anyway. I'm only going by the fact Summers didn't mention it when I talked to him. He had sharp eyes, that man; considering he drew his chart from memory, he didn't miss much."

He sat down at the desk and motioned the two men to sit down. "Southwick, have a couple of copies made of this chart. It will be a good job for young Orsini. Clean, accurate copies."

"Yes, sir. You have anything in particular in mind?"

Again Ramage smiled. "Some brilliant idea snatched from a

passing cloud? No, our only hope is something unexpected, so we may as well be prepared. We might have Aitken row in one night disguised as a fisherman—he can bring us back a nice mackerel or two and report on the town."

"I wouldn't trust him in Santa Cruz with all those beautiful Spanish ladies, sir. Wouldn't trust myself, come to that," the old Master said, giving a lewd wink.

"What are your night orders, sir?" Aitken said hurriedly. "Anything special?"

"No, we'll reverse our course at sunset and hope we'll be lucky tomorrow. Now, how are these Invincibles settling in?"

"Very well, sir. Another week and you won't be able to distinguish them from the others."

"And Kenton?"

"He's young, sir—and I don't mean that he's only just past twenty. He's supposed to have had good marks when he took his examination for lieutenant, but—well, I wish the Admiral had sent us someone else."

"Don't be too hard on him," Southwick said mildly. "He's got plenty of spirit! You were a fourth lieutenant once!"

"Aye," Aitken admitted. "But this Kenton—he hasn't half the head of young Orsini. I can hardly believe that boy has been at sea only a few months."

"Sunset," Ramage said, "we reverse course at sunset—and hope for some luck by the time we've had our breakfast."

CHAPTER TEN

AT THE FIRST sight of dawn—the black eastern night sky softening to grey, dimming the stars low on the horizon—the diminutive Marine drummer boy began beating a ruffle as bosun's mates went through the ship, following the shrilling of their calls with bellows of: "General quarters—all hands to general quarters!"

There was no wild rush: sleepy-eyed men stumbled up ladders and went to their guns, to the head pumps and to the magazine. Every ship of the Royal Navy at sea in wartime met the dawn ready for action, guns loaded and run out, in case daylight showed an enemy close by.

The *Calypso's* six lookouts were still on deck, one on each bow and quarter and two amidships; lookouts did not go aloft until the first daylight would let them see at least two hundred yards round the ship.

Aitken was officer of the deck and Ramage joined him as Rennick mustered his Marines aft. The wind was little more than a stiff breeze and as the *Calypso* reached to the south-west her bow occasionally sliced the top off a wave and sent a shower of spray across the fo'c's'le.

The dim candle in the binnacle, lighting the compass card, was growing yellower as dawn spread higher in the sky; soon Ramage could distinguish the wavetops dancing grey and menacing as they swept under the ship, hurried westwards by the Trade wind. He shivered and pulled at his cloak: this was the most miserable part of the day—the grey light washed out colours and the sea always seemed more menacing, and the almost inevitable line of low cloud to windward was stark and black, as though heralding bad weather.

He knew the colours would soon come, the sea lose its threat and the line of cloud would probably disappear once the sun had some warmth in it; but it was the time of day when he had little strength to fight off the doubts and fears which, this morning of all mornings, seemed to wriggle into his soul like silent snakes; the serpents that ate away a man's confidence but which were driven back whence they came once the sun lifted over the horizon. One of the advantages of living on land was you could sleep through the hours of grey doubts.

He looked astern at the *Calypso's* wake, a smooth swathe through the waves. At that moment Aitken shouted: "Lookouts to the masthead!"

The two men standing amidships on each side ran to the shrouds: one started up the ratlines of the foremast, the second went hand over hand up the main. The other four men went to their stations for action. By the time the two lookouts were aloft and had taken a good look all round the horizon, visibility would be two hundred yards. Aitken had timed it well—but he had several years' experience, Ramage thought to himself and, the way the war was going, had several more years ahead of him.

How he hated the smell of damp wool. His cloak had a fair share of salt on it from the spray and it soaked up the damp of the night. It was chilly and he was hungry: he would be glad when the ship stood down from general quarters and the galley fire could be lit. He stared round the horizon, expanding quickly now, and suddenly there was a hail from high overhead: "Deck there! Sail ho!"

"Where away?" Aitken shouted.

"Dead ahead, sir, two miles or less, an' crossing our bow to the westward!"

It would be another neutral; Ramage was sure of that. Another Jonathan bound for one of the Spanish ports along this stretch of the Main with a cargo of salt cod and "notions." She'd have made a landfall at Punta Peñas—probably passing the *Calypso* to windward in the darkness—and was now running westward for her destination. And, arriving there, she would report seeing an English frigate in the area, thus raising the alarm . . .

"Deck there!" This was the lookout at the foremast. "She's a small brig."

"Aye, aye," Aitken acknowledged.

Brig? Still, Ramage thought, she could be an American, though most of them were schooners. She was unlikely to be Spanish this far to the east: Santa Cruz was still about seventy-five miles farther along the coast. It was the nearest Main port to the Atlantic for any ships trying to break the blockade, having slipped out of Cadiz in a gale of wind on a dark night and dodged the patrolling frigates, but such ships were rare.

"I can see her, sir," Aitken said, and told the quartermaster to bear away a point to starboard. "Fine on our starboard bow."

Ramage was more interested in having a cup of hot tea, a pleasure which had now been put off for at least an hour by the appearance of this brig. "Very well," he said, and began walking up and down along the starboard side. There was no way of stopping the wretched American raising the alarm: he would have seen the *Calypso* by now. Damn all neutrals!

All round the ship the men were standing at the guns; along the centre line the ship's boys squatted on the cylindrical wooden cartridge cases they had carried up from the magazine. The sand sprinkled on the dampened deck grated underfoot, but the light was at last bringing out the colours. He went over to the binnacle drawer and took up his telescope. He pulled out the extension tube to the mark filed in the metal to show the correct focus for him and, balancing against the aftermost gun, looked at the brig. She was small, she was pierced for eight guns—and she was Spanish: that was clear from the cut of her sails.

"Mr Aitken," he called and, as soon as the First Lieutenant was standing beside him, said quietly: "Take a good look at her— she's a typical Spanish *guarda costa*. She's looking for smugglers."

The Scot put the telescope to his eye. "I can see now that her sails have that high roach the Spanish like, sir. But couldn't she be American?"

"No—she's Mediterranean-built. Just look at that sheer and stern . . . Ah! She's spotted us—see the men grouping by the guns? Run up our colours—and make the challenge, just in case she's a prize put into service from Jamaica."

Two minutes later three flags streamed out from the *Calypso*'s mainmast: three numbers which were the challenge and changed daily. Any British ship of war would have the diagram which also showed the correct numbers which were the reply.

The *Calypso* was approaching fast and, as though she was bringing the daylight with her, Ramage could see more details. Black hull with a bright red strake; four guns a side, and they were now run out. Men scrambling aloft—going to let fall her topsails, no doubt, though little good they would do her with a frigate approaching. No answer to the challenge . . . if she was a former Spaniard now commissioned into the Royal Navy, the flags for both challenge and reply would have been bent on to the halyards, ready for just such a situation as this.

The familiar sound of a contemptuous sniff told Ramage that Southwick was now standing beside him. "These Dons—they never learn, do they? Can't trim their sails, not even with an enemy frigate bearing down on 'em."

"Come now," Ramage said mildly, "you forget we're a French-built ship! They can see that, and are probably going to quarters as a matter of routine and waiting to cadge a case of French wine."

"They'll soon distinguish our colours," the Master commented, "even though they have the light in their eyes."

Ramage shut the telescope with an impatient snap. He must have been half asleep, because the idea he had just snatched at had been floating round his head, waiting to be hauled on board, from the moment he first recognized the ship as a *guarda costa*. It was not an idea that started him singing like a lark, but almost any idea was welcome at this time of the morning, and if it seemed practical at dawn the chances were better than even that it would be worthy of praise by noon.

Southwick followed as he walked to the quarterdeck rail, and he gestured to Aitken and Rennick to join him. Quickly he gave them their orders and then sent for Wagstaffe, who was standing by a division of guns on the main deck. Finally he walked aft, where Jackson was waiting for him with his sword and a message from his steward that if the Captain wanted breakfast, cold cuts of meat could be served in a moment. The prospect of slices of cold mutton—a sheep had been killed and roasted yesterday—effectively stopped Ramage's hunger pains.

Half an hour later, with the sun a great reddish-gold ball resting on the low band of cloud across the eastern horizon, the *Calypso* was sailing a hundred yards to windward of the Spanish brig and on the same course, rolling slightly. The brig had finally hoisted Spanish colours and Ramage was hard put to avoid laughing as he looked through his telescope. There was a little comedy being played out on the brig's quarterdeck.

Her Captain had watched the *Calypso* approach; then, as they came abreast each other, Ramage had given the order to clew up the courses so that the *Calypso*'s speed under topsails alone matched the Spaniard's. That had been five minutes ago. For five minutes the Spanish Captain had alternately stared at Ramage on the *Calypso*'s quarterdeck and turned to make comments to his officers—judging from his gestures he was both puzzled and agitated.

Ramage looked at his watch and commented to Southwick: "We'll give him another five minutes."

"Aye—he should be done to a turn by then. Do you think he's thrown over his papers?"

"I haven't seen any sign, and I've been watching closely. I think he's forgotten them."

"It'd make sense, sir: first he thought we were French, then it went clean out of his mind when he saw British colours."

"That's why we're going through this pantomime. The more nervous he becomes the easier it is. Fear is not knowing: he doesn't know what's going to happen next. He expected us to range close alongside and fire a few broadsides into him—and instead we are sailing along like his shadow. No guns, no hails, no signals . . ."

"I'd be feeling jumpy if I was him," Southwick admitted, removing his hat and running his fingers through his mop of white hair. "They've been generous with the paint, for once. And not many patches in the sails—though whoever cut them must have used army tents for a pattern."

Ramage, the telescope to his eye once again, began laughing: "He's shaking a fist at us!"

Again Southwick sniffed. "Trying to frighten us, no doubt. Er, what had you in mind after—"

"Let's take her first," Ramage said, looking once again at his watch. The fact was that the first single idea had brought others in its train; now he was mulling over various alternatives, each of which seemed excellent at the moment of birth and absurd the next.

Southwick stared through his telescope and then turned to Ramage: "You know, sir, I'm beginning to feel sorry for that fellow over there."

"I've been sorry for him since I started this," Ramage said. "Still, if you're in a brig with a 36-gun frigate a cable to windward it's better to be stared at than fired at."

He could hear his men at the guns on the main-deck laughing and joking: they could see the antics of the Spanish Captain, and several of them knew from experience what it was like to have the positions reversed.

"Mr Southwick," Ramage said with mock formality, "I'll trouble you to pass the word that number one gun on the larboard side should fire a shot across the enemy's bows."

"It will be my pleasure, sir," Southwick said with a bow, and replaced his hat with a flourish.

Ramage turned aft and watched the Marines getting ready. The sergeant with six men was standing by at one of the quarter boats with Aitken who, with a cutlass slung over his shoulder and a pistol clipped to his belt, waited with ill-concealed impatience. Wagstaffe was inspecting the men who would be accompanying him in the other quarter boat.

Ramage gave a violent start as the gun fired, and then heard Southwick's bellow of laughter.

"You should have seen him, sir—jumped a foot off the deck!"

"So did I, blast it," Ramage growled.

"There!" Southwick bellowed triumphantly, his shout almost drowning the thud of a gun firing from the *guarda costa*'s larboard side—a gun fired in the opposite direction from the *Calypso*. A moment later the Spanish flag came down at the run, the brig's Captain having gone through the ritual which protected him against an accusation of surrendering without firing a shot. Then seamen climbed up into the yards and began furling the topsails.

It took an hour to ferry the *guarda costa*'s crew across to the *Calypso*, and Aitken brought her Captain and officers back in the first boat. The Captain, a plump little man with an amiable face and an excited manner, obviously wanted to talk to the *Calypso*'s Captain, but Ramage was far more interested in what papers, if any, Aitken had managed to find.

The Spanish Captain and his two lieutenants were taken below to Southwick's cabin by two stolid Marines, and Ramage, after assuring himself that the *Calypso* was lying comfortably hove-to, gestured to Aitken to follow him down the companion-way.

He sat down at his desk and eyed the canvas pouch in Aitken's hand. "Had he thrown the books overboard?"

"No, sir—here." The First Lieutenant took a second canvas pouch from the one he was carrying. "This is weighted and has a signal book in it. But I found all these—" he fished out a handful of letters "—in his drawer. I can't read Spanish, but they might be important. I think they are, from the fuss he made when I found them. She's called the *Santa Barbara*."

Ramage flicked through the signal book. It was well-thumbed and likely to be up-to-date. "Where did you find this?"

"In the binnacle box drawer, sir. When I took it out he—the Spanish Captain—waved at our challenge and pointed at the book and shook his head."

"He saw the challenge before he could make out our colours, probably," Ramage said as he began looking through the letters. The first contained orders for the *Santa Barbara* to patrol for two weeks between Punta Peñas and the eastern end of Isla de Margarita, returning to Santa Cruz by nightfall on 24 June— tomorrow, Ramage noted. Any ships suspected of smuggling were to be boarded and sent into Santa Cruz. Care must be taken to avoid any enemy ships of war but, with the exception of one English frigate, none had been sighted off the coast for many weeks. The orders were signed by the Governor of the Province of Caracas.

The remaining letters concerned stores, the supply of seamen and complaints that various reports had not been sent in to the Port Captain and Mayor of Santa Cruz. The brig carried stores and water for three weeks, a small enough margin when sending a ship out on a two-week patrol. Ramage put the letters down and realized that Aitken was obviously keen to know what he had found.

"Just his orders—the rest are routine."

"But you read them all so quickly, sir. I didn't know you spoke Spanish."

"It comes in useful sometimes. Now we'll have that Captain up here with his officers, and see what we can find out. Perhaps you'd fetch them. We don't need Marines—you've a pistol, and I don't think there's any fight left in them."

"I don't think they were issued with any to start with, sir," Aitken said dryly as he made for the door.

Ramage put the letters and signal book in a drawer and pitched the canvas pouches into a locker: it would do no harm to let the Dons think that no one was very interested in papers.

Aitken came back, leading the fat little Captain and two young men, obviously his lieutenants but, from the foppish way they wore their clothes, probably owing their appointments more to the influence of their families than to their knowledge of seamanship.

"This, er, this gentleman is the Captain of the brig, sir," Aitken said, "I didn't catch his name."

"You speak English?" Ramage asked pleasantly.

The Spaniard pointed to the elder of the two lieutenants, who stepped forward and bowed. "I speak English," he said truculently.

"Then introduce your Captain and tell him I am Captain Ramage."

The fat Spaniard's name was Lopez. Ramage, speaking slow

and precise English, introduced Aitken and then waved for the three Spaniards to sit on the settee.

"I have some questions to ask your Captain," he told the lieutenant, watched by a puzzled Aitken. "You will translate. First, what are his orders, and who gave them?"

The lieutenant translated, and Lopez, his eyes on Ramage, said with relief: "Ah—he hasn't read the letters. Tell him I was patrolling the coast—on the orders of the Governor of the province. Looking for smugglers."

Ramage nodded as this was translated into careful English. "And from which port did you sail?"

"Do not tell him," the Captain said quickly, after the translation. "Tell him Cumaná."

Again Ramage thanked the lieutenant. It was absurd how often people assumed that, because they had not heard you speak their language, you did not understand it.

"I want to know what ships are in Santa Cruz."

The Captain sniffed. "Tell him I do not know. I have not been there for months."

Ramage looked puzzled when the lieutenant translated. "I am trying to find the English frigate," he said helplessly. "Tell your Captain that."

Lopez was watching him closely as the lieutenant translated. "I guessed that! Tell him she has sailed for Havana. Sailed a month ago."

Ramage waited for the translation and then carefully arranged his features to show disappointment and disbelief. "But . . . but," he stammered, "she was in Santa Cruz six weeks ago!"

The lieutenant translated and Lopez, looking smug, said: "Tell him to look for her in Havana. She escaped all the English corsairs!"

Ramage could not blame Lopez for his attempted deception,

but was thankful he had met the *William and Henrietta* yesterday, otherwise Lopez might have succeeded. But the way the Spaniard was patting his knees, confident he had misled the Englishman was irritating. It was time to jolt him.

"I hope your Captain is telling the truth. I shall be looking into all the ports between here and La Guaira, and if I find he is telling lies it will be easy to punish him: he will be on board . . ."

The lieutenant translated, trying to conceal his nervousness—he was obviously wondering if he and the other lieutenant were included in the threat—and Lopez shrugged his shoulders: "He'll never see her: he'll never get into—" he just caught himself in time to avoid naming the port "—the place, so we've nothing to fear."

Ramage listened to the lieutenant's hurriedly invented answer: "Captain Lopez says your frigate is not on the coast; you should look for her in Havana."

Now Ramage shrugged his shoulders. "Oh well, we've missed her, then. Still, I'm sure we'll find some prizes in Santa Cruz."

"Santa Cruz?" the lieutenant exclaimed. "Surely you will not try to enter there?"

"Why not? I have charts—and this is a powerful frigate, you know."

"But the forts—they will blow you out of the water!"

"You, too," Ramage pointed out just as Lopez demanded to know what was being said.

The lieutenant said hurriedly that the English Captain was going to enter all the ports, starting with Santa Cruz, and he had warned him that the forts would blow the ship out of the water.

"And us, too," Lopez exclaimed, beginning to turn pale. "Ask him if we can be exchanged—there are many English prisoners at La Guaira. An exchange could be arranged. We must go first to La Guaira and send a message to the Captain-General. A flag of truce—the *Santa Barbara* could go in under a flag of truce while this ship waits out of range of the guns."

Ramage listened patiently to the translation, his expression becoming more and more vague. "Tell Captain Lopez my orders are clear: I cannot waste time making exchanges."

"But—we will all be killed!" the lieutenant exclaimed, his face white.

"There is that risk, of course. But you would have been killed if we had fired into you this morning."

"But you didn't! You would never attack such a small ship! It would be dishonourable and cowardly!"

"A few years ago," Ramage said reminiscently, "I commanded a cutter about the size of the *Santa Barbara*, perhaps a few tons smaller. She was sunk by a Spanish ship of the line."

Lopez, his face running with perspiration, ordered the lieutenant to translate, but the young man was shaking now. He made an effort to translate coherently to Lopez: "He hates the Spanish! He was in a small ship that was sunk by one of our ships of the line. This is his revenge—to have us all killed as he tries to get into Santa Cruz. Orders, he says; he cannot arrange an exchange because it is not mentioned in his orders. *Caramba!* That tells you what sort of man he is."

"Compose yourself," Lopez said sharply, wiping the perspiration from his face with a large, lace-edged handkerchief. "If we die then so does he!"

"But he doesn't *care* about death!" the lieutenant protested. "They're heretics, these English; they place no value on life; they glory in killing people."

"I wish I could kill *him*," Lopez said bitterly. "Anyway, it was your uncle that gave us the orders and made me take you as a lieutenant. A poor captain like myself can only obey the Captain-

General. You asked him to let you sail in the *Santa Barbara*. You wanted to impress your friends with your bravery. You have only yourself to blame. Me—I am just an ignorant naval officer. I live or I get killed. I knew that years ago, when first I went into the Navy."

Ramage snapped his fingers. "What is Captain Lopez saying?"

The lieutenant looked down at the deck. "He is shocked at your cruelty. You have no right to risk our lives with your foolish ideas!"

"Young man," Ramage said heavily, "you know well enough what the buccaneers used to do along this coast a hundred and fifty years ago with people like you. Yes, they'd light a fire and hang you over it on a spit, or make you walk off the end of a jib-boom . . ."

"You would never—"

Ramage deliberately looked disinterested and callous. "Today, prisoners can fall over the side—accidentally, of course—and—"

"You would never dare! You would be punished. My uncle is the Captain-General of the province: he would protest to Madrid and—"

"How would he ever know?" Ramage asked casually.

Lopez, alarmed at his lieutenant's high-pitched protest, demanded to know what was being said.

"He threatens to roast us on a spit over a fire, like the corsairs did. I warned him. I told him my uncle would have him punished."

"You did *what?*"

"I told him my uncle was the Captain-General of the province and he would be punished."

"You fool," Lopez said contemptuously. "Until now you were an insignificant lieutenant. Now, with your own tongue, you have made yourself a valuable hostage!"

Ramage told Aitken to take the prisoners away, and the lieutenant jumped up to continue his protests, but when he looked up at the English Captain he found that the vague, almost bored expression was gone; instead a pair of deep-set brown eyes seemed to bore into him, and he realized with a suddenness that left his knees weak and his lips trembling that he should never have asked his uncle for the commission appointing him to the *Santa Barbara*.

Ramage watched with his telescope as Wagstaffe shouted orders through his speaking-trumpet on the quarterdeck of the *Santa Barbara*. Swiftly men of the prize crew swarmed aloft and let fall the topsails, which were then hoisted and sheeted home. The brig gathered way and then turned north, away from the distant coast, and when she was a mile off Ramage nodded to Baker, now the second senior lieutenant: "Follow her and keep this distance astern."

He waited until Baker had given the necessary orders and then went down to his cabin, where Aitken and Southwick were going through the roll of charts found on board the *Santa Barbara*. Some had been removed, and sent across to Wagstaffe, but Southwick hoped to find harbour plans.

"Nothing of interest to us, sir," he grumbled. "No chart at all of Santa Cruz. The rest—Cumaná, Barcelona and the like—don't tell us anything we didn't know already. The Spanish don't seem very strong on charts."

"Very well. We discovered more from the *William and Henrietta* than from this damned *guarda costa*—except that we now have on board the nephew of the Captain-General of the province as a prisoner."

"The Captain-General's nephew, sir?" Southwick exclaimed. "The whole province?"

"Yes. He began threatening me. Said his uncle would punish me if I took him on shore and roasted him on a spit or made him walk off the end of the jib-boom!"

"I heard you remind him the buccaneers used to do that," Aitken said. "He was terrified."

"The *Jocasta*, sir," Southwick said anxiously. "Did you find out anything about her?"

"No—except that she's in Santa Cruz. The Captain was very anxious to assure me she had already sailed for Cuba, and the lieutenant warned me we'd be blown to pieces if we tried to get into Santa Cruz. That's why he's so scared."

"What now, then?" Southwick asked. "I see you've decided to head out to sea again."

Ramage nodded casually. He could afford to be casual now he knew what to do. The Governor's nephew had not given him the new idea, but it had come as he watched the beads of perspiration forming on the young man's upper lip, almost as if the sheer terror it revealed had been the source of inspiration.

"Yes, we stay out of sight for today; then we sail up to Santa Cruz tomorrow and have a good look."

"Had you any particular time in mind, sir?" Southwick asked sarcastically.

"Yes, towards dusk. It'll be cooler then. I don't want to put you to any effort during the heat of the day."

Southwick gave a grin which revealed his relief. The Captain was functioning again; he had a plan at last. Southwick did not care what it was; the mere fact that it existed was enough. Well, he had to admit that he was a little curious, but obviously it had something to do with the *Santa Barbara*. Or maybe using the Captain-General's nephew as a hostage? Or both; the *Santa Barbara* to go in with a flag of truce to negotiate an exchange of the *Jocasta* for the nephew. That did not sound too likely: no

Captain-General would dare agree to such an exchange.

Southwick heard himself asking diffidently: "You have a plan, sir?"

"No," Ramage said, "just an idea. The *Santa Barbara* was on a two-week cruise against smugglers. She's due back in Santa Cruz by tomorrow night."

He went to his desk and took the Spanish signal book from a drawer. He opened it at a page and showed it to Southwick. "Here are their signal flags, all carefully coloured by some loving hand. They use the same sort of numerary system, one to nine, and nought. And three substitute flags—these here. Give the sailmaker three men. I want him to make a complete set of flags and have them ready by tonight. We'll have to go up within hailing distance of Wagstaffe and get the dimensions. I want them to be the same size as those in the *Santa Barbara*."

"Any special orders for me, sir?" Aitken asked hopefully, still ruffled that Wagstaffe had been put in command of the *Santa Barbara*.

Ramage thought for a moment. "Make sure we have the second copy of our own signal book ready, and check through the *Santa Barbara*'s charts. Make up a portfolio—borrow duplicates from Southwick, or make copies. And the spare set of our own signal flags—have them ready too."

At first Aitken was delighted to have some task obviously associated with whatever idea the Captain had in mind; then he realized that "we" could also mean the *Calypso*. But why a second set of charts? Either the Captain was teasing them or whatever he had in his mind was exactly what he had said, just an idea.

"And cutlasses and pikes," Ramage added. "Get the grindstones up on deck and sharpen everything. But keep an eye on the men—we want some metal left."

"Aye, aye, sir." Aitken waited in case there were more orders, but Ramage had nothing more to say.

CHAPTER ELEVEN

JACKSON LED his men round the deck, pointing here and there, and Stafford and Rossi spattered small pieces of slush—the thick greyish fat that the cook skimmed from the top of the water after boiling salt meat—and smeared it into the wood with their feet. The American then sprinkled sand. They had already covered half the decks.

"What a game this is," Stafford grumbled. "It'll take weeks to get these decks clean again. An' the brasswork—just look at it. Amazin' wot a few hours' soaking with salt water can do." He stopped for a moment and pointed to the bosun and his mates. "Look! Cuttin' off lengths of old rope and fraying the ends into cow's tails!"

He shrugged his shoulders and resumed his scuffing of the specks of slush, but all three men stopped a few minutes later at the sight of the cook, a bucket in his hand, following Southwick.

"A few drops here," the Master said, and the cook dipped his hand into the bucket and then spattered blood over the deck by the break of the gangway on the starboard side.

"'Ere! Whose blood is that?" exclaimed a startled Stafford.

"They just kill one of the officers' sheeps," said Rossi cheerfully.

As the cook followed Southwick, pouring a mugful here, spattering with his hand there, one of the bosun's mates walked past with a length of rope and tucked it round a belaying pin at the mainmast, careful that the frayed end hung down. He walked back a few paces, inspected it and then went back and slid the frayed rope across the deck with his foot to dirty it. Jackson gestured aft as the cook passed him: "Look, it's drying fast. Soon loses that nice rich red!"

"Looks like a slaughterhouse!" the cook said nervously. "There'll be a lot of scrubbing to do when all this is over!"

By now the purser had come on deck, followed by seamen carrying bundles of shirts and trousers. "Ah, come on cookie," Southwick said. "We've got to do this next job very carefully!"

The seamen began spreading the clothes on the deck and the cook, holding his bucket carefully against the rolling of the ship, began sprinkling them with blood.

"Wipe your hand on some of them," Southwick instructed. "Not too much, make it look realistic. Now, how many shirts are there? Only 25? Come on, Mr Purser, we need another couple o' dozen!"

The purser went below again with his men, muttering under his breath, and as Ramage walked up to inspect the work Southwick said: "The purser's wondering how he'll be able to sell these as new!"

"He won't—you'll list them as destroyed in action!"

"Ah," Southwick said. "I'll tell him that." Action—he guessed that the *Calypso* was supposed to have been in a fight with the *Santa Barbara*. Was Wagstaffe to fake some damage to the brig as well?

Ramage continued his inspection, walking slowly round the deck, hands clasped behind his back. By now the bosun's mates had fitted more tails of frayed rope and Jackson's men had almost completed their task of making the decks look filthy. Aitken came from forward after supervising the seamen sprinkling more salt water on the brasswork.

"I never thought to see this, sir," Aitken said cheerfully. "The Captain, First Lieutenant and Master of one of the King's ships doing their best to make her look like a hulk!"

"Like a neglected slaughterhouse," Ramage commented. "Give the grease a few hours to soak into the wood, and time for that blood to darken . . ."

The First Lieutenant paused for a few moments, hoping Ramage would say more, but he continued walking forward and Aitken called to the seaman with the bucket of salt water: "The brass rods protecting the glass in the Captain's skylight: go up to the quarterdeck and douse them again."

He looked round the ship, proud of the morning's work yet dismayed and appalled by it. In the days since the *Calypso* left Antigua, he had kept the ship's company busy holystoning, scrubbing and polishing, making up for a year's neglect by the French. The metal surface of most of the brasswork was now smooth enough to take an easy polish with the brickdust; the last dirt had been scrubbed and holystoned from the grain of the deck planking and the last grease stain removed. Now—in a couple of hours—it had been transformed so that even the French would be impressed. All the ship lacked, he thought sourly, was the reek of garlic and the stench of unpumped bilges and you'd think she was back in French hands.

Captain Ramage had specified exactly what he wanted: dirty decks, gritty with sand, ropes with cow's tails, unpolished brasswork, bits of food lying around in the scuppers, bloodstained decks . . . Well, he had it now; the *Calypso* looked like a ship which had fought a desperate battle, lacking only damage by round shot.

There had not been a word of explanation: Captain Ramage had said nothing to Southwick—who, as far as Aitken was concerned, seemed to have been born without any curiosity at all.

Not a word to his First Lieutenant, not a comment to Baker or Kenton. Of course he did not expect the captain to confide in third and fourth lieutenants, but a passing comment might have revealed more of what he had in mind.

There was enough heat in the sun now to speed up the work: the water dried almost immediately on the brasswork, leaving a fine crust of sparkling salt crystals; the drops and blobs of blood were turning a rusty brown and he wished he was over in the *Santa Barbara*, still a mile ahead. The peak of Pico de Santa Fé was gradually lifting on the larboard bow, but high clouds inland drifted across to hide the tip from time to time. If he was over in the *Santa Barbara* it would be up to Wagstaffe to reduce the *Calypso* to a shambles . . .

The dirt, the frayed ropes' ends, the dulled brasswork offended him. His mother had been a great one for the scrubbing brush, whether it was cleaning the grey stone floor of the kitchen or the backs of her young sons standing shivering in the high-walled yard as they were doused with buckets of water for their weekly bath. The kitchen table, the bread board, occasionally the carpet—all were scrubbed with a cheerfulness belying the effort needed.

The great rolling hills of Perthshire seemed a million miles away; the village of Dunkeld on a hot summer's day was colder than the chilliest night in these latitudes. The people of Dunkeld would never believe him if he said that for much of the day men never stood still on deck if they could avoid it because the wood was too hot underfoot; that a man off watch who stretched out on the deck for a nap was liable to wake up to find his shirt striped with pitch from the caulking. They would nod politely when he told them this accounted for the seamen's phrase "taking a caulk," meaning having a nap. They would be equally polite when he said that the sun heated metal so that it became uncomfortably hot to touch. They would nod politely, but they would not believe a word of it. Likewise it would be just as hard describing snow or frost to people born in the Tropics.

Ramage walked back to the quarterdeck and stood at the rail looking forward over the ship. It all looked unreal. Although he had given the orders which had transformed the *Calypso*, he seemed remote from it. The dirty bloodstained deck, the frayed ropes—she lacked shot holes and splintered woodwork, otherwise anyone would think she had been in battle and then left to drift for a week or two.

What was he really trying to do? The problem was that he was far from sure, but was risking everything on it. What was "it"? His own questions made him impatient, because they only underlined that he was grasping at straws. The straw, for example, that led to the order to make the *Calypso* look like a hulk. Now Southwick and Aitken waited confidently for the next orders, for the next stage in the plan to be revealed to them.

The only difficulty was that there was no next stage. I've used my ration, he thought ruefully, and it isn't enough. I have a dirty, bloodstained ship and an appointment at dusk off Santa Cruz, and that's all. A little picture was trying to intrude into his mind with the tenacity of a woodpecker; a picture which, if studied carefully, might yield a plan. "Might"—a longer word than "if," but no more certain . . .

In an hour or two, after the men had finished their dinner, Wagstaffe expected to come on board the *Calypso* to receive his orders. Captain Ramage could hardly greet him with: "I'm most apologetic for bringing you over to no purpose, Wagstaffe, but I have no orders for you because I have no ideas."

The picture seemed a little clearer now, as though the lines and colours had grown stronger at the thought of apologizing to Wagstaffe. Yet the problem was not the clarity, it was the absurdity. The picture represented a plan whose success was enormously dependent on luck and even more on the Spanish.

He would need to keep his plans flexible, and if he was to achieve surprise he had to be careful not to be surprised himself.

The first surprise was that he seemed to have turned a picture into a plan, and even as he stood there, too stupid to move over a few feet out of the sun and into the shade, he was adopting the plan and dividing it up between the two ships . . .

How the situation would appeal to Gianna's sense of humour. Young Paolo had entered into the spirit of it too, as though adding his quota to the confusion while acting as an agent for his aunt—a word Ramage had always associated with old ladies and white hair, bony fingers, sharp knuckles and watery eyes! Gianna was an aunt with raven hair, an oval-shaped face, high cheekbones, eyes that laughed—or, when she was angry, stabbed. Aunt Gianna was slim with an imperious body and jutting breasts that made the ship and the sea fade as he thought about them.

He pushed these thoughts to the back of his mind. Lopez and the Spanish prisoners could be a problem. The lieutenant had been bubbling with indignation and protests because the three of them were not allowed on deck for some exercise, but Ramage could imagine the expression on Lopez's face if he saw the ship now. All the prisoners, officers and seamen alike, had to remain in ignorance of what was going on, and they would have to be told that they might get their throats cut if they made any noise—an idle threat they would readily believe.

He went down to his cabin and spent half an hour poring over the Santa Cruz chart. The port was about thirty miles away now and the west-going current seemed to be less than a knot. The wind had been steady from the east for the past two days, strong enough to overcome any land or sea breeze and likely to hold all the way to the coast. The entrance channel to Santa Cruz ran almost south-east and north-west, and any ship trying to enter it now would probably have to be towed in by boats. Pico de Santa Fé would be deflecting the wind down on to the lagoon and port so that it funnelled through the channel and out between the headlands on each side of the entrance, Punta Reina and Morro Colorado.

He rolled up the chart and put it back in the rack. And that, he told himself sheepishly, is how battles are won or lost: the crazy picture trying to lodge in his imagination had now changed into Captain Ramage's plan. Not a bad plan, come to think of it, but not a good one either. A good one left nothing—or very little, anyway—to chance.

Wagstaffe would be ordered on board to get his instructions after dinner, and at the same time he would explain everything to the rest of the officers. Then he would muster the ship's company aft and tell them. Not that anyone would need much explanation. Once you knew the basic idea, the rest was obvious.

After a dinner of mutton, he thought gloomily. It was a pity they had had to kill another sheep so soon, but they had needed the bucket of blood. Apart from cutting the Captain-General's nephew's throat, the sheep was the only source of supply. Antigua sheep must lead hard lives; the meat from the last one was the toughest he had tasted for a long time.

He took out the Spanish signal book to compare it with the one used by the Royal Navy. The Spaniards must find it hard to communicate at sea; there were no more than fifty signals listed in this one, compared with nearly four hundred in the *Calypso*'s book. Number 7 was a useful one: "Keep in close order." He made a note of it, cursing while he retrieved a pencil which rolled off the desk as the ship gave an unexpectedly heavy roll. Number 33: "Lead the Fleet"; then 41: "Anchor"; and 48: "Keep in the Admiral's wake." Finally he noted number 50: "The signal not understood although the flag can be distinguished."

He put the signal book back in the drawer. By now the Spanish lookouts in the Castillo San Antonio and in El Pilar, the fort on the west side of the entrance to Santa Cruz, would be watching for the *Santa Barbara*. They would have been told she was due back from her two-week patrol and they would not get excited when they saw her. Like lookouts and politicians the world over, they would see what they expected to see.

Ramage's steward knocked on the door and came into the cabin to see if the Captain was ready for dinner, the main meal of the day. "That lamb's roasted up a treat, sir."

"Lamb?" Ramage exclaimed sourly. "That was a very ancient sheep. Did the officers want to buy some of it?"

"Well, no sir; they said they was off mutton for a while, and I'd best salt the rest of it."

"They're wise—and tactful. That sheep had the muscles of a mountain goat and not a spare ounce of flesh on it."

"The sweet potatoes, sir," the steward said soothingly, "they're nice and fresh. An' a bottle of wine to celebrate?"

Ramage stared at him suspiciously. "Celebrate what?"

"Why, sir, that we're almost in sight of Santa Cruz."

"Did you think we wouldn't find it?"

"Oh, no, sir," the steward said hurriedly, disconcerted by Ramage's surly tone. "All the men are excited, and what with the ship all of a mess I thought perhaps—"

"You know I never drink at sea."

"Yes, sir, but I thought this once—"

"Jepson, stop thinking for a day or two, and if you're a wise man, I'd sharpen the knives so that the meat seems less tough." He glanced up at the clock on the bulkhead. "All right, you can serve now."

While the *Calypso* rounded up and hove-to for Wagstaffe to come on board from the *Santa Barbara*, Ramage sat at his desk writing his Journal. Nine columns had to be filled in, beginning with the date ("Year, month and week day"), and giving wind direction, courses steered, miles covered, the latitude and longitude at noon, and ending with a wide column headed "Remarkable observations and accidents."

The ship's log, more usually called the Master's log, normally gave a more complete picture of the ship's activities, and Ramage copied the details into his Journal. Under "Remarks," Southwick had listed the morning's activities—"Ship's company employed dirtying decks, making bloodstains, taking the shine off brasswork."

In the "Remarkable observations" column of his Journal, Ramage wrote the brief note: "Ship's company employed changing character of ship. *Santa Barbara* in company." The latitude—a few miles short of eleven degrees north—was the furthest south he had ever been; only a few hundred miles short of the Equator.

He put his Journal away, closed Southwick's log, and took out a fresh sheet of paper. He glanced at the small pile in his drawer, saw the last number and wrote "19" at the top of the page. His letter to Gianna—it could not be posted until he returned to Antigua—was getting long, but he tried to write a few sentences each day so that what she received was more of a diary than a letter, and he knew she read extracts to his father and mother. He liked writing it because it helped sort out his thoughts and ideas, and talking to Gianna through his pen eased the loneliness forced on the captain of one of the King's ships; the man who at sea commanded all that he surveyed, but who also lived in almost monastic seclusion.

He had described the court martial, but had forgotten to tell her that Summers had been rescued by the *Kathleen*. The story would sadden her because he had been given command of the cutter just after rescuing her: she had stayed in Bastia while he sailed northward up the Corsican coast to see what could be done about the stranded *Belette*. Later Gianna, the valuable refugee, had sailed for Gibraltar with him in the *Kathleen*. Yet he wanted to tell her about Summers; about the tragic coincidence which had made the seaman's rescuer one of the five judges who had to condemn him to death.

He finished one side of the page and then turned it over to give news of Gianna's favourites, Jackson, Stafford and Rossi. He described how they, and most of the frigate's men, had spent the morning dirtying the decks, but he gave no explanation: that would follow later, when he knew the result, but he could imagine Gianna turning the page impatiently. "Read this to father," he wrote, "and make him wait a few minutes before telling him the rest of the story, which I hope to write tomorrow."

Ramage wiped the pen and put it in the rack. If only he *could* guess the rest of the story! By midnight—if he was still alive—he would know; but by midnight something unexpected might have happened so that Gianna never received the letter. Now the depression and doubting was coming back . . . It always happened: like the cold and misery of the hour before dawn, this chill spread over him before going into battle. Not exactly fear but something dam' close to it. The feeling of not being sure whether he was going to be sick or fall ill with a fever, yet appearing confident or whimsical, firm or flippant, in front of his officers and men.

There was shouting on deck: Aitken was giving orders that would get the ship under way again, so Wagstaffe must have boarded and his boat would be towing astern. A minute or two later the Marine sentry announced him and the Lieutenant, his face sunburned despite his tan—there was no awning over the *Santa Barbara*'s quarterdeck—appeared, clear-eyed and cheerful.

"How do you find the *Santa Barbara*?" Ramage asked.

"She handles well, sir. Just about every rope is badly stretched and turned end for end, but the sails are in good condition. The whole ship's riddled with vermin, though; the lice are fighting the fleas for a chance to get at us."

Ramage nodded and told Wagstaffe to sit in the chair beside the desk to receive his orders.

"First, the papers. This is a copy of the signals in the Spanish signal book and here are drawings of the flags—Orsini has been busy with his watercolours in case the actual flags aren't marked. These are your written orders—don't bother to read them now because I want to talk to you about them—and here," Ramage paused a moment as he selected a roll from the rack over his head, "is a chart which shows all we know about Santa Cruz."

For the next fifteen minutes Ramage outlined what Wagstaffe and the *Santa Barbara* would do. There were three possibilities, and he emphasized that he would probably leave it to the last moment before deciding which to select. "Now, the boats. Your two boats and the Marines are the key to the whole thing. They must work fast but they mustn't make mistakes. Pick a dozen good men for each one. I'll let you have more if you think it leaves you short."

Wagstaffe shook his head. "No, sir, just the extra boat will be enough." He hesitated, and then began: "But, sir . . ."

Ramage raised an eyebrow, guessing what was coming.

"Could—well, sir, Baker is experienced now, and I feel I can be of more help if I—"

Ramage held up his hand. "You have this job for one reason. I need Aitken for something else. You are next senior. In fact if you make one mistake you'll wreck everything. I've told you all the alternatives that I can think of, but I can't be expected to guess everything the Dons can do."

He spoke very deliberately. "It's a great mistake to assume the enemy is a fool: many battles are lost through underestimating the opposition. But sometimes the enemy can be more foolish than you expect, or unprepared, or a dozen other things. For instance, the three hundred soldiers on board the *Jocasta* have just been taken off and sent into the hills against the Indians. That was unexpected from everyone's point of view."

He tapped the top of the desk for emphasis. "The forts may blow us out of the water, the Mayor may come out in a gilded barge to take the Captain-General's nephew to a banquet, you might run the *Santa Barbara* aground, it might suddenly pour with rain so we can't see what we're doing . . . You agree all those things are possible?"

Wagstaffe nodded uneasily, wishing he had kept his mouth shut.

"Very well. In every case *you* will have to do the right thing without waiting for orders from me. And there could be a dozen more things."

The Second Lieutenant was still not convinced, but then Ramage said: "Aitken wants to change jobs with you. He doesn't know what I have in mind for him, but he'd like to command the *Santa Barbara*. Do you really want to exchange?"

Wagstaffe paused for a second and then shook his head vigorously. "No, sir; indeed, I'm flattered you have such trust in me."

Ramage shrugged his shoulders. "You can do it, all right; it's just that I don't want you to underestimate what you might have to do. And remember, no more men on deck than the *Santa Barbara* had in her original Spanish crew—twenty, was it?"

"Twenty-one, sir. Oh yes, I need a fat man."

"Do you, by Jove!"

"The Spanish Captain: he's a very distinctive—ah, shape. There's a spare uniform on board. I thought I might—"

"Take the cook's mate," Ramage said, and laughed at the thought of the plump little man dressed up as the Captain of the *Santa Barbara*. "Take care of him, though; no one slaughters and dresses a sheep better than he does. Any questions? Very well, you'd better get back on board the *Santa Barbara* and steer for Santa Cruz. But wait for a few minutes while I give Rennick his orders."

In his cabin an hour later Ramage looked round at Aitken, Baker, Southwick and Paolo. Either the plan was better than he thought or familiarity was breeding affection. He had explained it three times now—to Wagstaffe, Rennick and now the three staying with him in the *Calypso*—and so far no one had pointed out a flaw. Nor, he realized, had anyone pointed out how much it depended on luck, so their opinions were of little significance. He looked across at the First Lieutenant.

"Aitken—you have everything ready?"

The Scotsman tapped the rolled chart and signal book. "Ready for whatever is served up, sir."

"Baker . . . Southwick?"

Neither the Third Lieutenant nor the Master had any questions, and Ramage glanced across to Paolo, who was present as part of his training. "Orsini, you look as though something is bothering you!"

"Should I have a cutlass or a pistol, sir?"

Ramage smiled at the boy's eager face. "Have both. Now, you understand what you have to do?"

"Oh yes, sir!"

"Very well. Now, gentlemen, I want to emphasize this. In a few hours you'll be actors on a stage, but if you're unconvincing you'll get cannonballs fired at you, not boos and catcalls."

They all laughed, but they knew that the Captain was only

just joking. Ramage guessed that no group of the King's officers had ever received such bizarre orders. He had a sense of unreality in giving them, and could only admire the way they had all simply nodded from time to time as he spoke, as though they were routine instructions for entering harbour and saluting the Commander-in-Chief. No doubting looks, no carefully-worded questions intended to hint that the Captain was wrong. On the contrary: if anything they seemed both amused and pleased with their orders.

"Very well, Mr Aitken; muster the ship's company aft and I'll let them into the secret."

Ten minutes later Ramage stood on top of the big capstan looking down at his men grouped round him on the quarterdeck. He was puzzled and his face was flushed. Just at the moment the men should have been looking serious and listening attentively, they had burst out laughing. Jackson, the cook, Rossi, Stafford, the shrivelled little gunner were amused; they were slapping each other on the back and two or three were pretending to start a hornpipe.

Suddenly he realized the significance of their reaction and he grinned and waited for the laughter to subside, as though he had expected it. Then he held up his hand.

"Tomorrow, I'll remind you, is a new day. Half a dozen of you will have to clean up the decks, and the First Lieutenant will need half a dozen men to polish the brass—"

He broke off again as the men roared with laughter, and one man—was it Stafford?—called out: "Half a dozen men? You're spoiling us, sir." This was the moment to stop; they were in high spirits and just in the mood for the task in hand. He gave a wave, vaulted off the capstan and went down the companion-way to his cabin, catching sight of Pico de Santa Fé as he turned. It was very close now, towering high and forbidding; he could

imagine it being the legendary home of proud and vengeful
Indian gods . . .

CHAPTER TWELVE

THE SUN was low enough to throw the eastern sides of
the tumbling hills and cone-shaped Pico de Santa Fé into
deep shadow. The channel into Santa Cruz was now a dark slot
cut through the cliffs, a forbidding canyon at the far end of which
Ramage could just see the lagoon with the castle of Santa Fé
crouched at the foot of the peak, a square block of stone, its battlements like bared teeth, its guns covering every inch of the
entrance.

The wind was light, the sky clear except for streaks of cloud
on the horizon, and Ramage felt strangely free. He looked down
at his bare feet and was vaguely surprised to see his toes on the
planking of the quarterdeck, the flesh startlingly white compared
with his tanned hands. The white duck trousers were suitably
creased and grubby but a good deal more comfortable than
breeches and stockings. A bloodstained purser's shirt, open at the
neck, felt light and loose after years of wearing a stock and heavy
uniform coat. His hair was bound at the back with a bit of cord
and like everyone else on board he was unshaven and unwashed.
It took very little to change the *Calypso* into a ship apparently
run by mutineers.

Southwick was pacing round the quarterdeck like a bear
dressed up for a carnival: he too was wearing a pair of purser's
trousers and a bloodstained shirt, and his usually unruly white
hair looked more than ever like a twice-used mop. He had a

pistol tucked into the top of his trousers; his great sword slapped against his leg as he walked. The once-smart First Lieutenant now wore a red shirt; his white duck trousers were smeared with blood and dirt. A black cloth served as a scarf tied over his hair and gave him the look of a Highland brigand.

The *Calypso*'s cook was—under orders—swaggering round the ship with a great meat cleaver hanging from his waist; thirty men were perched in various parts of the rigging while a dozen more were skylarking, occasionally scrambling down the mainstay. The frigate yawed from time to time, and Ramage knew that all the Spaniards watching from Castillo San Antonio and its twin of El Pilar must realize she was being badly sailed. What they did not see was Jackson, acting as quartermaster and giving the orders to the men at the wheel which produced the sudden flapping of the topsails. The courses and topgallants were badly furled—it had taken Southwick an hour before he was satisfied with them, straining his patience as he complained that it was harder to furl them badly than neatly.

Ramage walked aft, hitching at the cutlass-belt over his shoulder and kicking at a piece of bread lying on the deck. The ship stank of rum; not fifteen minutes ago Southwick and the purser had sluiced a bucket of it over the quarterdeck and now a barrel was lashed against the skylight with half a dozen mugs beside it. It normally held forty gallons of rum and was obviously placed so that any man could have a mugful when he felt like it—or so it would seem to a casual eye.

The *Santa Barbara* was following a hundred yards astern, sailing in the *Calypso*'s wake, the red, gold and red of the Spanish flag streaming out in the breeze. From her foremast flew two flag signals—"Lead the fleet" and "Keep in close order." The *Calypso*, like an obedient bear obeying a small boy, was leading the way into Santa Cruz, obviously a prize. Instead of the Red

Ensign, she also flew the flag of Spain; a flag of the same size as the one hoisted in the *Santa Barbara*, which had obviously supplied it. And from her foreyardarm the frigate flew two more flags which the Spanish lookouts should by now have interpreted: a plain red flag—the "bloody flag" of buccaneer days and now the symbol of revolution—and below it, obviously vanquished, a Red Ensign.

"Brother Jackson," Ramage called, "I'll trouble you to bear up for a moment and shiver those luffs!"

"Aye, aye, brother Ramage," Jackson said cheerfully.

"Brother Ramage," Southwick called self-consciously, "according to my revolutionary quadrant we're exactly a mile off the entrance."

Ramage nodded. They were approaching the coast at an angle, and there was now no doubt that the wind in the channel was blowing out through the entrance. In another ten minutes they would be in position. He looked aft anxiously, but Wagstaffe was waiting deliberately in the *Santa Barbara:* he could measure distances as well as Southwick. One mile: they were within range of the guns of both forts, but neither had opened fire.

"Brother Jackson," Ramage growled, "there's no need to flog the sails into shreds. If you luff too much again I'll bring you before the committee."

All the men on the quarterdeck laughed cheerfully and gave their Captain credit for being a waggish fellow, but in fact Ramage could detect a stiffness among them. The habit of discipline, the respect for officers and obedience to orders was hard to drop in a couple of hours, but they were now supposed to be mutineers. There were no officers on board; according to the story that each of them would tell if questioned, all the officers had been murdered two days ago and their new officers were the leaders of the mutiny—brother Ramage (the former bosun), brother

Aitken (a Marine sergeant) and brother Southwick (who, Ramage decided, had been the cook's mate, a choice which brought Southwick close to mutiny). The automatic use of the word "brother" might serve to convince a doubting Spaniard; it might gain a few minutes when seconds mattered. Or it might be a complete waste of time. In any case, Ramage had decided, it amused the men; it took their minds off the menace of the forts.

"Brother Ramage!" a seaman hailed from aloft. "The *Santa Barbara*'s hoisting a signal!"

Ramage put the telescope to his eye. Number 29.

"Brother Aitken, I'll trouble you to heave-to the ship, but not too skilfully please."

Having spent all his sea-going life in ships that were always handled correctly, Aitken had to concentrate on his orders so that as the *Calypso*'s bow swung across the eye of the wind the fore-topsail was not braced up enough to ensure that the pressure on the forward side trying to push the frigate's bow one way was balanced by the pressure on the after sails trying to thrust the bow the other. Instead of lying stopped in the water like a waiting seagull, the bow continued to swing.

"Brother Aitken!" Ramage said, surprised how easily he could substitute "brother" for the more usual "mister." "If we wear right round now and try again I think we'd demonstrate to our new Spanish friends on shore that we are lubbers!"

"Aye, aye, sir—brother, rather."

The *Calypso*'s bow paid right off, spinning the ship round like a top. Sails flapped and slatted like enormous curtains, then filled with a bang; men hauled on sheets and braces, Jackson gave quick, sharp commands to the men at the wheel. The *Santa Barbara*, taken by surprise, had to bear away to avoid risk of collision and then tack to get up to windward of the frigate.

Soon the *Calypso* was lying hove-to, with the *Santa Barbara* hove-to a hundred yards to windward. Ramage could see the corpulent cook's mate over on the brig, resplendent in the gold-trimmed uniform of a Spanish captain, climbing down into the brig's boat, which had been towing astern and was now hauled alongside. With him was a seaman rigged out in a lieutenant's uniform. Now the boat was cast off and the seamen began rowing down to the *Calypso*.

Army officers would be watching with telescopes from the walls of the forts. Ramage hoped it would all be clear to them by now. Somewhere along the coast the *Santa Barbara*, one of His Most Catholic Majesty's ships, would have found the *Calypso* flying the "bloody flag" of mutiny and with her mutineers anxious to follow in the footsteps of the *Jocasta*. Captain Lopez would have ordered her to make for Santa Cruz after having put people on board to keep an eye on things.

Hoisting the signal "Lead the fleet," the *Santa Barbara* had then followed the *Calypso*. Now, off the entrance to Santa Cruz, Lopez would have found the wind foul for the entrance, so that both the *Calypso* and the *Santa Barbara* would have to be towed in. What could be more natural than having both ships heave-to while he went across to the *Calypso* to give the mutinous Englishmen their final orders?

The *Santa Barbara*'s boat came alongside and the cook's mate climbed on board with his lieutenant to make his way to the quarterdeck while the boat was hauled aft to tow astern. The cook's mate's appearance at the gangway was met with hoots of laughter and catcalls: he was a popular man and, with the cook, one of the wealthiest men on the lower deck. Selling slush to his shipmates was one of his perquisites: it helped soften the board-like bread, or bind it together when it had become so old it began to crumble. The cook's mate had quick wits and a ready tongue, and as he made his way aft he kept up a barrage of imitation Spanish. Finally he reached the quarterdeck with his lieutenant and Ramage called: "Don't salute anyone: come up to me!"

The *Calypso* was close enough to Castillo San Antonio that anyone with a powerful telescope could see down on to the frigate's quarterdeck. When the cook's mate—looking remarkably like Lopez—reached him, Ramage saluted him with a flourish.

"Captain Lopez!"

"Well, brother Ramage that's what Mr Wagstaffe said I was to call you once I got this uniform on—well, as I was saying, sir, Mr Wagstaffe said as 'ow I was to tell you for sure, sir, that there weren't no message, sir."

"Good. Now I want you and your lieutenant to keep striding up and down here on the quarterdeck. Make sure that you can be seen by everyone in these forts up here—they're watching us with telescopes. You see the entrance channel? Good, point along it. You've just given me my orders. Now I understand what you mean. Oh no I don't!" He called to the seaman dressed as the Spanish lieutenant. "Come closer—you are supposed to be translating everything to me."

Ramage turned back to the cook's mate. "Point up at one of the forts. Now the other. When I salute, you start marching up and down. Not like a Marine," he added hastily. "You're in charge of everything, so swagger about!"

It was time to hoist the boats out. The men already had their orders—that was the only way to ensure enough confusion to satisfy the watchers from the forts—and Ramage said: "Brother Aitken, the committee would like you to hoist out the boom boats and choose enough men to row them. You'd better double-bank 'em; it's not a long row but the quicker we . . ."

Ramage turned to the Master as Aitken hurried forward:

"Brother Southwick, I must disturb your revolutionary thoughts long enough to have the quarter boats lowered."

"Aye, brother Ramage. You know, sir, I get a strange feeling when I think this was the way the *Jocasta* really did come in."

Ramage grinned reassuringly. "I had the same feeling yesterday when you and the cook were scattering all that sheep's blood!"

Ramage watched the cook's mate and the seaman: they made a passable counterfeit of the real thing—the cook's mate was waving his arms, gesturing with Latin exuberance. The seaman, not to be outdone, began gesturing back and Ramage was just going to interrupt when he realized that the real Captain Lopez probably had to put up with a lot of interference from his young but influential second-in-command.

Shouts from amidships and the squeal of ropes rendering through blocks told him that a tackle was beginning to lift one of the boats and would soon be swinging it over the side and lowering it.

"Brother Baker," Ramage called. "To the fo'c's'le please, and stand by the hawsers ready for taking the ship in tow."

"Aye, aye—I mean, yes brother Ramage."

Everything was proceeding at a leisurely pace; the current was slowly sweeping the *Calypso* and the *Santa Barbara* to the westward, but Ramage had allowed for an hour's delay. Normally, heaving-to and hoisting out the boats would take less than fifteen minutes. However, the longer the *Calypso* was lying in front of the two forts the better; the Spaniards were getting used to the idea and there was time for messengers on horseback to be sent off to report to the Mayor. Everyone, Ramage thought to himself, was being reassured; it was another *Jocasta* all over again; another frigate to be added to His Most Catholic Majesty's fleet for the expenditure of a small reward to the leading mutineers.

Finally Aitken came back to the quarterdeck. "All ready for towing, sir—I'm sorry, sir, I mean brother Ramage. The boats are alongside, the hawsers are ready to run."

Ramage looked over towards the entrance. He could sail the *Calypso* another five hundred yards, and save the men rowing, but could the leader of a group of mutineers? Summers could, from his own account, but it was not worth the risk of arousing the suspicion of the Spaniards.

"It's time for our Captain Lopez and his lieutenant to return to the *Santa Barbara*. As soon as they're clear, we'll furl the topsails. First the main, then the fore. That'll pay off the bow to starboard, and by the time the boats have the slack out of the hawsers we'll be heading in the right direction."

He called over to the cook's mate, giving instructions. The man strutted over, stopped in front of Ramage and then swung round and pointed dramatically to the maintopsail. A moment later his hand moved out again towards the foretopsail.

"How's that, sir?"

"Fine. Now—you are the translator," he told the seaman in the lieutenant's uniform. "Translate!"

"Do I need any of the armwaving, sir?"

"No, just talk. All right, that's enough! Now, Captain, you will go back to the *Santa Barbara*—after I've saluted you."

With that Ramage saluted and went to the break of the quarterdeck as the two men walked to the gangway. It was all going well—even to the thin layer of cloud forming to leeward of Pico de Santa Fé, which would cause a spectacular sunset. But in fifteen minutes, he realized, the *Calypso* would be in the entrance to Santa Cruz, midway between the forts, the muzzles of their guns a bare seventy-five yards away on either side.

Aloft, the men furled the maintopsail quickly, but they were deliberately careless with the gaskets. Some of the strips of canvas were tied tighter than others; three were not tied at all. The *Calypso's* bow began to pay off, and then the foretopsail was furled, and again some gaskets were left untied. All the fewer to untie when he gave the order to let fall the sails, Ramage noted, and was pleased that the men had remembered their orders.

Now the *Calypso's* bow was turning towards the harbour entrance, pulled by the boats which were out of sight from the quarterdeck, hidden by the bow. And the closer the frigate approached, the narrower the channel seemed to become.

"Brother Aitken," Ramage said, "take your mutinous thoughts to the fo'c's'le and pass them aft at the top of your voice if we seem to be straying out of the fairway. I can't see properly from here."

"Aye, aye."

At that moment Southwick sidled up to him and sniffed: "Don't like this one bit, sir—brother, rather."

"How so?"

"I don't know. The feeling that those damned Dons are watching every move we make. It's uncanny. Here we are, towing in, large as life, and they're just staring at us . . ."

"You'd sooner they were shooting, eh?"

Southwick laughed, a laugh which began deep in his large belly. "Not at this range! But I never guessed, and that's a fact; I had it all wrong!"

"Never guessed what?"

"How you were going to get us into the place, sir—brother! I thought all the blood on the deck was to show how the *Santa Barbara* captured us. Didn't seem very likely to me; I nearly said so. Aitken was worried, too."

Ramage swung round and stared at the Master. "You never guessed? Why, it was so obvious I didn't bother to explain!"

"Not to us, it wasn't, not until you said we'd mutinied and

we were to call each other 'brother.' I suppose we'd got it into our heads that you'd take the *Santa Barbara* in, and leave the *Calypso* anchored outside. Fill the brig up with men and send her in under the Spanish flag to cut out the *Jocasta.*"

"Too risky," Ramage said, and stared up at Castillo San Antonio, now towering over the *Calypso*'s larboard side. He counted the muzzles. "Fourteen guns facing this way, and fourteen to seaward. And that other one over there, El Pilar, has twenty to seaward and sixteen covering the channel."

"Why too risky with the *Santa Barbara* alone, sir—brother?" Southwick persisted.

"The Dons in the forts would get suspicious. Just think about it. If mutineers *had* handed the *Calypso* over to Lopez his first concern would be to get her into Santa Cruz. He wouldn't trust them an inch and he wouldn't leave her anchored outside with her ship's company still on board while he went in with the *Santa Barbara*. Why leave her there? No, he'd want to see her go in first."

Southwick sniffed again, showing his doubts. "He might want to rush in first to make sure he gets all the credit."

"No one else can take that away from him. Anyway, if the *Santa Barbara* went in first, the Mayor, Port Captain, Bishop—they'd all swarm on board. Where would you hide your boarding party? How would you persuade the real Lopez to make the right answers?"

"Didn't think of that," Southwick admitted cheerfully. "We tied ourselves up with the idea of making use of the *Santa Barbara*. Here! Look at that!"

Flags had been hoisted from on top of San Antonio. Ramage grabbed a telescope and saw that they made up a three-number signal. Three? There were only one- and two-flag signals in the Spanish book. It was obviously addressed to the *Santa Barbara,* and whoever had ordered it to be hoisted knew that Lopez would understand it. What the devil could it mean? Suddenly the fourteen muzzles came into sharp focus. Through the telescope he could see the heads of the Spanish artillerymen. There was an officer peering down at them, using a small glass. What if they opened fire? The *Calypso* must not fire back. Cause confusion—yes, if San Antonio opened fire, Ramage decided, then the *Calypso* would hoist signal flags wherever a signal halyard was rove. Two-flag signals which would send the Spaniards running to the book; two-flag signals which would buy time because every minute that passed saw the *Calypso* getting further along the channel, further from the muzzles of those guns.

Fear was chilling him; the breeze dried the cold perspiration that was soaking his shirt. Three flags, three pieces of coloured bunting flapping at the top of San Antonio's flagstaff, could wreck everything. He glanced at the channel. If there was any chance of the *Calypso* being badly damaged, he'd sink her so that she blocked the middle of the channel.

He swung the telescope round to look at the *Santa Barbara* and remembered telling Wagstaffe that the whole operation could depend on him. It could, and at this moment it did. He saw two flags being hoisted on board the brig: number 50. Yes, Wagstaffe had been quick to react; number 50 meant: "Signal not understood though flags distinguished."

What the devil *were* the Dons asking Lopez? Something was needed to divert their attention! Ramage picked up the speaking-trumpet, noting that the *Calypso* was now in the middle of the channel and precisely between the two forts.

"All you men—quickly, get up in the rigging and stand by to cheer. You on the fo'c's'le, get muskets and pistols and stand by to fire into the air when I give the word!"

In a minute the shrouds of all three masts were thick with men.

"Now—wave like madmen. Stand by to cheer. Hip, hip . . ."

"Hurrah!" two hundred voices shouted and the roar echoed down the channel, the sound bouncing from the hills.

"Hip, hip . . ."

"Hurrah!"

"Hip, hip . . ."

"Hurrah!"

By now startled birds were wheeling and more faces appeared along the walls of the forts.

"Stand by with those muskets and pistols. Ready? Fire!"

A ragged volley echoed along the hills. More faces appeared at the walls.

"Now, just cheer like madmen! You're mutineers getting your freedom!"

The men shouted, screamed and waved, and for a moment Ramage wondered if the *Jocasta*'s men had behaved like that when they arrived off La Guaira. Someone waved back from the walls of San Antonio and was followed by another man. Soon twenty or thirty Spaniards were waving, and more joined in from the walls of El Pilar.

"That should convince 'em," Southwick grunted. "It's nearly convinced me!"

The wind in the channel was not as strong as Ramage had expected; the four boats were towing the *Calypso* at a good speed, two knots or more, because the forts had now drawn aft until they were on each quarter.

"We've got through the gate," Southwick commented. "I hope we don't find it closed when we want to get out! How do you reckon we're doing for time, sir—brother, rather. Sorry, sir, I can't get used to it."

Ramage looked at his watch. "We're doing well enough. It'll be dark in about forty-five minutes."

"Supposing the Captain of the *Jocasta*—or whatever they call her now—supposing he hasn't received the word that we're coming in?"

Ramage walked to the ship's side and peered out through a gun port, then returned to the rail. "He'll have his orders by now, but even if he hasn't the musket shots will rouse him enough to find out what's going on."

The steep hills on either side of the channel were now beginning to slope down; a hundred yards ahead the land was flat. Then Ramage saw the hills to larboard stop abruptly and the eastern half of the lagoon came in sight—with the *Jocasta* lying there, her bow to the north, seeming placid and content, like a cow in a meadow.

Southwick, telescope to his eye, began describing what he saw, as though reading from a list: "All her sails bent on—courses, topsails and t'gallants. Sheets and braces are rove—that's a relief. Headsails are bent on and the sheets leading to larboard; she's ready to get under way on the starboard tack. Gun ports closed. Hey, what the devil is going on?"

Ramage was looking by now, watching a score or more men swarming along the *Jocasta*'s larboard side. They were dragging large white cylinders . . . putting fenders in place; the big sausage-shaped cylinders made of old rope and used to protect the side of the ship when she went alongside in the dockyard, or secured next to another ship.

"That answers a question," Southwick commented cheerfully. "They're expecting us!"

Ramage went down the quarterdeck ladder and walked forward to join Aitken on the fo'c's'le. It was a curious sensation—the ship gliding along in a silence broken only by the creaking of the boats' oars and the rustling of the water at the stem. The light was going quickly now, and with the last of the colour fading from the hills the water turned silvery-grey. Although the land was flat on each side and a track ran parallel with the water, presumably leading up to each fort, there was a lot of undergrowth: bushes and stunted trees stretched into the distance, finally climbing up the side of the hills to reach the foundations of the forts.

For a moment, as he glanced aft and saw the two forts, squat and walls black in the shadows, Ramage felt sick as he thought of the orders he had given Rennick. When he had drawn up the plan he had tried to assume the worst, that the countryside would be rocky and covered with bushes. It was no worse than he had anticipated, but there seemed little chance that even one of the Marines would survive the night's work. Forty Marines, yet the Admiral would consider their lives a small price to pay for the *Jocasta*.

"We'll go alongside the *Jocasta* just as we planned," he told Aitken. "They're expecting us. I want us towed round so that our bow is to seaward, too. You give the orders to the boats; I want to come alongside as though an admiral was watching."

"But, sir—but, brother Ramage: would they expect a gang of mutineers to do it perfectly?"

"The Spanish Captain of the *Jocasta* is very proud of his new ship. He's ready to sail. All the paintwork is new. We want him coming on board us with a welcoming smile, not screaming with rage because we've just ripped out channels and rigging or scored his paint!"

Aitken grinned sheepishly. "I don't have your knack o' imagining myself in the enemy's boots, sir!"

Ramage walked aft, giving orders as he went. Baker came hurrying up to supervise men preparing lines along the starboard side, ready for securing to the *Jocasta*; other seamen were placing loaded muskets out of sight under the carriages of the guns. All now had pistols stuck in their trousertops and cutlass belts over their shoulders, though the cutlasses were still scattered round the deck, apparently in random piles.

As soon as he reached the quarterdeck Ramage told Southwick: "Have the yards braced sharp up so we don't hook up in the *Jocasta*; then make sure the topmen don't move five yards from the ratlines."

"Brother Ramage," Jackson called from abaft the wheel. "I've a pair of pistols here ready for you, sir."

"I'll get them in a minute or two."

Hellfire, it was getting dark quickly now. He looked aft along the channel and was thankful to see that the *Santa Barbara* was just coming into the entrance, her two boats out ahead like water beetles, the brig little more than a black blob. There was no disturbance along the walls of San Antonio, no flashes of guns or muskets, so whatever that three-flag signal had meant, it obviously did not matter. The commandants of the forts must be relieved—the horse was in the stable and the door was bolted. What were they doing up there now? Toasting each other, no doubt; slapping themselves on the back and jeering at the English Navy and its mutinous men.

He could smell the plants and shrubs growing on shore: the faint hint of spices. They were only a few hundred yards from the mangroves and he thought he smelled charcoal—a charcoal-burner at work, or someone preparing to cook his supper? And the curious high-pitched rattling of frogs, blurred by distance. And above him the creak of the great yards as they were braced round so that the outboard ends should not foul those of the *Jocasta*. Let's hope the *Jocasta*'s Captain remembers, too . . .

Looking forward again he was startled to find that the *Calypso* had finally reached the end of the channel and was now gliding into the lagoon. And over to the west, at the far end of the lagoon, were the dim lights of Santa Cruz itself. It would be hot in the houses; the small windows kept the sun out but the rooms trapped the heat of candles. Little pinpoints of light dancing on the water showed that fishermen were busy near the town, fishing with lanterns, and there were four dark shapes, merchant ships at anchor off the quay. Three were laden, one was high in the water. A peaceful scene, Ramage noted; over there, almost a mile away, people were going about their evening business. Wives would be preparing meals, old men would be supping wine. Some of them might notice a frigate being towed into the lagoon but few would be interested; curiosity counted for very little in the Spanish character.

Now the *Calypso* was beginning the slow turn across the eastern end of the lagoon, a long curve that would end, if Aitken directed the boats properly, with the frigate coming alongside the *Jocasta* perhaps ten minutes before it was dark. With the yards braced sharp up and the lines led ready to be passed to the *Jocasta*, there was nothing more to be done on board, and men stood silent, each alone with his thoughts. Aitken, on the fo'c's'le and now standing on the knightheads with a speaking-trumpet so he could shout down to the boats when necessary, was reminded of the lochs on the west coast of Scotland: long stretches of water, some surrounded by steep hills, others with hills in the distance. But of an evening they had the same tranquillity, the same atmosphere of time passed, of witnessing events that left no mark. When the Captain had described it all in the cabin earlier, Aitken had pictured Santa Cruz rather like a cave; he had expected to feel an overwhelming sense of being trapped—as indeed they were—but instead he was reminded of a peaceful evening's walk beside a loch.

Jackson, walking from one side of the ship to the other to keep an eye on the edges of the channel, now mercifully disappearing astern as the ship came out into the lagoon, was reminded of Italy, not by the water but by the hills. They were smoothly rounded and rose higher and higher as they moved inland. This was, he thought, like southern Tuscany: that big peak could be Monte Amiata. The land on either side of the channel was covered with the same tough scrub of the macchia, like the countryside where they had found the Marchesa. He wondered if it had jogged the Captain's memory. At times like this he always seemed busy, working out angles and distances, ranges and trajectories, or what the enemy might be planning, but afterwards —perhaps long afterwards—he'd make some comment that showed he had missed nothing.

Stafford, squatting on the breech of one of the aftermost of the quarterdeck guns with Rossi, felt uncomfortable. The long channel back to the sea, with the fort on each side, reminded him of a heavy door. He had never been in the Bridewell, but he knew plenty of men who had, and they all commented on the jail doors slamming behind them as they entered, then the long walk to the cells. The long walk was what they remembered, down a corridor that seemed to go on for miles.

"Be glad to get out o' here," he commented to Rossi.

The Italian turned to look at him. "Oh? Is not so bad, you know; the French build a good ship."

"I don't mean the *Calypso*," he said impatiently. "I mean this place, Santa Cruz."

"Is quiet enough now, Staff," Rossi said complacently. "Just like the Captain said."

"He didn't say it'd be quiet going out, though. I'll take my oath on that!"

"We'll soon know. Remember when we were in Cartagena?"

"Aye, that's what I'm saying. Trapped. Same sort of place— Spanish, mountains, narrow entrance . . ."

"We sailed out of Cartagena all right!"

"But he'll chance 'is arm once too orfen, mark my words."

Rossi spread both arms, palms upwards. "Always you get like this, Staff. For ten minutes you think of ways we can all get killed. Then you forget all about it."

"'Ere!" Stafford exclaimed, jumping from the gun, "that bleedin' *Jocasta's* gettin' close. Come on, Rosey, time we got ready to invite the Dons on board."

Ramage watched the *Jocasta:* she was a hundred yards ahead, fine on the starboard bow, but the men at the oars were getting tired now and the *Calypso* was slowing down, yet he wanted some way on her so that the rudder would have a bite on the water for the final slight turn that would bring the *Calypso* alongside.

Suddenly he swung round: "Jackson, the signal lanterns: have you checked that they're ready?"

"Just done it, sir. Slow matches too; I've got three of them going."

"Very well." And keep control of your voice, he told himself; that all sounded rather agitated. A glance back at the channel: they were too far into the lagoon to see along it now, but he could not distinguish the *Santa Barbara's* masts across the land. What's delaying Wagstaffe? Don't say he's put the brig aground!

Southwick was standing beside him muttering: "Not much breeze, sir. From the south, a soldier's wind for getting out of here down the channel."

"We'll need it," Ramage said briefly. "Jackson! Four spokes to larboard!"

It was hardly a standard helm order but it should be just enough, a quarter of a turn of the wheel. The *Jocasta's* stern was

showing up black, like the end of a barn, with the Spanish name
picked out in white paint (and probably a lot of gilt, too, but it
was too dark to see that). And the masts, spars and rigging made
a complicated but beautiful web of lace against the sky, like a
Spanish mantilla.

Ramage saw that dozens of men were lining the *Jocasta's* bulwarks, waiting for lines to be thrown. Dozens—a hundred or
more and others streaming up from below. Many were running,
but they were spurred on more by curiosity than orders.

"Two more spokes!" he snapped. The *Calypso's* bow was abreast
the *Jocasta's* stern; now level with her mizen. Men were shouting in Spanish from her quarterdeck. Now abreast her mainmast,
and the ship was moving a little too fast.

"Wheel hard a'starboard!"

That would stop her; at low speeds the rudder put hard over
acted as a good brake. And now the *Calypso* was precisely alongside the *Jocasta,* bow to bow, stern to stern, and he tried to keep
the excitement out of his voice.

"Bowline, brothers; pass a bowline! Aft there, get a sternline
over. You there amidships—pass the after spring! Come on, brothers, look alive and get the fore spring across!"

Every Spaniard on board the *Jocasta* seemed to be yelling at
once and at least two men were bellowing through speaking-
trumpets. There must be a hundred voices within fifty feet, all
shouting orders, advice and encouragement on how to get the
Calypso safely alongside, and all ignoring the fact that she was
already there.

No sign of the *Santa Barbara*, although she was so small and
the channel was in such deep shadow that her masts might not
show up. The shouting on board the *Jocasta* seemed to be reaching a crescendo amidships, as though the Captain was demanding
to be allowed through.

"Brother Southwick," Ramage said, "I think we'd better join brother Aitken at the gangway, and form a welcoming committee. Brother Stafford, bring up some lanterns!"

CHAPTER THIRTEEN

THREE SPANISH sailors carrying cutlasses leapt on to the Calypso's bulwarks, scrambled down to the deck and then stood round in a half-circle, looking rather sheepish as Ramage led a round of cheering. A moment later three officers followed them, led by a tall and gaunt man in the uniform of a Captain.

As soon as he was standing on the Calypso's deck the captain squared his hat, gave his sword-belt a twitch and looked around him. It was a slow, calculating stare, and although the last of the light had almost gone, Ramage sensed that the Spaniard had not missed much, the dirty, gritty decks, the untidy ropes, the dark stains on the planks . . . At the moment he was obviously trying to determine which of the dozens of men standing round was the leader of the mutineers.

"Que pasa?" he demanded.

Ramage stepped forward and gave a clumsy salute which the Spaniard did not bother to acknowledge. "You speak English, sir?"

"A little."

"Well, sir, me and my mates you see, we took the ship and—"

Ramage stopped as Stafford and Rossi came up from below with lanterns, one in each hand.

"Where j'yer want 'em, brother?" Stafford asked the Spaniard, the complete mutineer addressing everyone as his equal.

The Spanish Captain gestured towards the quarterdeck. "Aye, aye, sir!" Ramage said quickly, leading the way aft to the ladder. "Bring them up here, brothers."

Rossi put one lantern on the binnacle and another on top of the capstan; Stafford put a third on the binnacle and continued to hold the fourth.

"Now, sir," Ramage said in an ingratiating voice, "may I present the committee—"

"Committee?"

"Yes, sir. When we took the ship the men elected a committee. Three of us to run the ship. Make decisions, and things like that."

"I understand. You are the leader?"

"No, sir, there are three of us. Me—Nicholas Ramage, sir. And this here is brother Southwick, and here is brother Aitken."

"This 'brother,' I do not understand it. You have different names; how can you be brothers?"

"It's a sort of . . . well, sir," Ramage said, careful to keep the ingratiating note in his voice, "a greeting, like 'mister,' only it—"

"I do not care for this 'brothers,'" the Captain interrupted. "I have taken command of this ship. What is her name?"

"The *Calypso*, sir; she's French-built and—"

"I want the ship's documents. Signal book, log . . ."

Ramage held up his hands. "I'm sorry, sir, we couldn't save the papers—"

"What happened to them?"

"The officers, sir. You see, before we could take control, the officers—the First Lieutenant it was—threw the bag over the side."

"What bag?"

"The bag—a bag with a lead weight in it. The one they kept all the papers in. Sunk it, he did, before—"

"Your men," the Spaniard interrupted. "How many?"

"Two hundred and four left, sir."

"Show me round the ship."

With that he gestured to Rossi and Stafford to pick up lanterns and began to walk round the quarterdeck. He inspected the binnacle, the capstan, the wheel and then the guns. He paused from time to time and Ramage saw how the sharp eyes noted the pieces of food in the scuppers, the grease spots on the deck, and then the barrel of rum and the mugs beside it. The Spaniard stopped by a bloodstain and told Rossi to hold the lantern lower, but he made no comment.

Ramage cursed the lanterns: the light had destroyed his night vision, yet he had to know where the *Santa Barbara* was. The Spaniard had been on board about ten minutes—and already part of the plan was breaking down: apart from the three Spanish seamen and the two lieutenants, the Captain had not brought more men on board. Ramage had expected that all the Spanish seamen from the *Jocasta* would stream on board the *Calypso*, where everyone was ready to seize them. The groups of British seamen apparently lounging around on the main deck were in fact all near piles of cutlasses; most of them had pistols and loaded muskets ready. But the Spanish seamen were still on board the *Jocasta;* it had not yet occurred to the Spanish Captain that he must take control of the *Calypso* and the *Jocasta's* men were—judging by those now idly spitting over the side and walking away from the bulwark—rapidly losing interest in the proceedings.

Ramage sensed that at this moment he risked losing control of the situation. Because his plan for seizing the Spanish seamen had collapsed, the advantage could easily swing to the Spanish

Captain without the man realizing it. Surprise, he thought to himself; I must get this fellow off balance. He walked over to him and said insolently: "Sir, the men have not had their dinner yet."

"They must wait."

"But, sir, the committee agreed that all meals should be piped on time and—"

"The committee! *Caramba,* I command now! Tell your committee that! I want all the men paraded here, now. Give the order!"

If one part of a plan goes adrift, Ramage thought bitterly, another soon follows. The men must stay where they are; that was vital. The problem was that the Spaniard was too confident: Ramage had underestimated him. He should have sent his men swarming on board to take control the moment the *Calypso* came alongside, but instead he was walking round making a leisurely inspection by lantern light. And all the time the *Santa Barbara* was getting into position in the darkness and waiting; Wagstaffe was watching for the signal.

Aitken was close and the Spanish Captain was striding away towards the quarterdeck ladder, the gold lace on his uniform glinting in the light of Rossi's lantern. The three Spanish seamen remained on guard at the gangway.

"Can you see the brig?" Ramage hissed at Aitken.

"I just caught sight of her five minutes ago coming clear of the channel, but I haven't seen her since. These damned lanterns . . ."

Aitken was tense—Ramage could detect that from his clipped voice. The young Scot knew that the success of the whole venture was at this very moment in the balance: one wrong word to the Spanish Captain and it would fail; instead of losing the *Jocasta,* the Spanish would gain the *Calypso.*

"Captain!" Ramage called.

Ramage braced himself. Insolent self-assurance, that was what he had to convey in the dim light thrown by the lanterns, and he had only a dozen paces in which to achieve it. Just enough to provoke the man, to cause sufficient anger to cloud his judgement and make him act pettishly.

Now he was standing in front of him on the quarterdeck, staring him straight in the eye: "Me and my mates want dinner."

Ramage deliberately slurred the words and the Spaniard, provoked by the tone although he could not fully understand what was said, snapped his finger to attract one of the lieutenants as he said: "Speak slowly. What did you say?"

"Me—and—my—mates—want—our—dinner. Now."

The lieutenant hurried up the ladder and stood waiting. "Send the men to quarters," the Captain said in Spanish, careful to keep his voice casual. "Load and run out all the guns on the larboard side. We might have trouble with these men."

"Brother Ramage," Aitken said urgently in the darkness. "Brother Ramage—brother Wagstaffe says he's ready for dinner."

Like the tumblers of a lock clicking as the key turned, Ramage assessed the significance of the Captain's brief order to the Spanish lieutenant: the Captain was not confident, and he was stupid; he had boarded the *Calypso* with only two lieutenants and three seamen—because he had not considered there was any danger—and left the *Jocasta* completely unprepared: until the lieutenant shouted the Captain's order the frigate was defenceless, the men gossiping on deck like idlers in a town *plaza*, not a gun loaded nor a pistol ready.

"Brother Jackson and you, Staff and Rosey," Ramage said conversationally, making the lieutenant pause for a moment, "stop our brothers here from shouting."

Two lanterns were put down on the deck and suddenly there was a blur of movement. The lieutenant gave a great gasp, struggling for air, and the Captain suddenly collapsed like a rag doll dropped by a child. A moment later the lieutenant fell beside him, seeming curiously bulky. Then Ramage saw that Jackson had knocked out the Captain with the butt of a pistol while Rossi had seized the lieutenant from behind, an arm round his neck and throttling him. Both men had fallen to the deck and Stafford had knelt down, seized the lieutenant's head and banged it on the deck. In the silence that followed the other lieutenant down at the gangway began calling plaintively: *"Que pasa?"*

There was no shout from the *Jocasta*, nor did the three Spanish seamen, out of sight at the gangway, raise any alarm.

"Both of 'em unconscious, sir," Jackson reported. "Here, Staff, quick, get some rope and cloths to gag them. Or did you want 'em slung over the side, sir?"

"No, tie them up. Make sure you're not seen from the *Jocasta*. Where the devil's a speaking-trumpet? Oh, thank you, Aitken. We seem to be getting short of time, so let's be quick now." He put the speaking-trumpet to his lips and turned forward to bellow: "Do you hear, there! Calypsos! There's a change of plan! Now then—board the *Jocasta!*"

Immediately the whole starboard side of the frigate seemed to give a convulsive twitch in the darkness as more than a hundred seamen leapt on top of the bulwark, cutlasses waving and all shouting "Calypso!" and swarmed on board the *Jocasta*.

As Ramage made for the bulwark Jackson grabbed his arm. "Your pistols, sir!"

Ramage took them and paused to jam the barrels into his belt, picturing for a moment what would happen if one of them fired accidentally. Then he was scrambling up on to the bulwark and leaping across the gap of black water between the two ships—a gap at the bottom of which a man was already splashing and screaming in Spanish.

"Calypso!" Ramage began shouting as he landed on the *Jocasta*'s

quarterdeck, followed a moment later by Jackson and several other men. But the quarterdeck was deserted; all the shouting was amidships, the bellows of *"Calypso"* punctuated by the sharp clash of cutlass against cutlass.

Ramage plunged forward down the ladder to the main deck and found two Spaniards on the steps climbing backwards as they tried to fight off seamen attacking them from below. A slash of the cutlass sent the nearest man collapsing on top of the one below and as he scrambled over the bodies Ramage remembered to keep on shouting "Calypso," the prearranged call so that the men could distinguish friend from foe.

By now Ramage's eyes were becoming accustomed to the darkness. He was conscious of a dim, yellow glow from the *Calypso*'s quarterdeck where lanterns still guttered in the light breeze, and he could see the *Jocasta*'s main deck packed with men fighting in isolated groups, a dozen Calypsos against a dozen Spaniards.

And there were many more Spaniards than he expected: with the three hundred soldiers away in the hills he had assumed only a hundred or so Spanish seamen would remain on board the frigate; little more than a "care and maintenance" party. He paused a moment to have a good look round, conscious that Jackson and some men immediately closed up like a bodyguard.

How many Spaniards? More than a hundred, but the Calypsos had the advantage of surprise. Yet the Spanish were quickly recovering themselves; they had found cutlasses and grabbed boarding-pikes from the racks round the masts, and they were fighting with the desperation of men who knew their lives depended on it.

Ramage found himself breathing fast, fighting back the excitement that crowded out logical thought. Group against group, man against man: this was useless; he needed his men concentrated, not spread out all over the ship. He took a deep breath.

"To me! To me!" he bellowed. "Calypsos, to me!"

In the darkness he sensed rather than saw the mass of men give a spasm of movement as the Calypsos disengaged themselves from their opponents; then a black wall seemed to move round him. "Calypsos! To me! Let's drive them forward and trap 'em. Southwick—get back to the quarterdeck with a dozen men. Now then, the rest of you, follow me!"

With that he ran towards the Spaniards who, finding the enemy had left them, were hurriedly grouping themselves. He kicked a coil of rope and staggered a few paces as he recovered his balance, but in that instant a dozen screaming Calypsos had passed him and began hacking and slashing at the Spaniards.

Now only instinct kept a man alive: a cutlass glinted and Ramage managed to deflect the blade sideways and then stab at the frenzied Spaniard wielding it. As the man collapsed Ramage turned to fight off two more Spaniards armed with pikes. There was so little room that they could not wield them properly; they seemed to Ramage like women trying to sweep with brooms. He jabbed at the nearest man and as soon as the point of his cutlass drove home he wrenched it away and swung the blade sideways at the shadowy figure of the other man, who saw it coming but could not parry with his pike nor duck out of the way.

Ramage was conscious that the Spanish were being driven back; the yelling Calypsos were slowly moving forward, step by step in a deadly saraband where the music was shouts and the crash of steel against steel. As Ramage half turned, looking for his next opponent, a cutlass blade suddenly flashed horizontally out of the darkness and he could not parry in time. It sliced into his stomach and he thought the wound must be fatal. A sharp pain made him gasp but he could still move and he slashed down at the dark figure who staggered off-balance. The man went down and Ramage, registering that he was still alive, fought on: hack, parry, step over a body, jab, parry yet again. No pistols were firing; there was just the clashing of cutlass against cutlass, blade against ash pikestave, the screams of men mortally wounded, the convulsive movements underfoot of wounded bodies.

Suddenly he found he was close to the breech of a gun and the Spanish were vanishing: the man he was just going to attack leapt on to the barrel, flung away his cutlass and vaulted over the side into the sea with a curious, despairing wail. A dozen more figures on either side followed him, and Ramage realized that the only men now left on the main deck were a wildly dancing group still shouting "Calypso!"

He shouted: "Stand fast, Calypsos!" but his voice came out as a scream which rasped his throat. "Stand fast!" he repeated but it was still too shrill. He took a deep breath but he was panting too hard to be able to hold it for a moment. He knew he was on the edge of losing consciousness and the pain in his stomach made him pause. His hand came away dry, but the pain seemed to be worsening.

The immediate fighting was over but the ship had not been secured: not all the Spaniards had leapt over the side—the majority of them feared water more than a cutlass blade. There had been more than a hundred on board—perhaps even double that number. Some were probably hiding down on the lower deck.

Now Aitken was reporting the fo'c's'le clear of Spaniards; Southwick was waiting for orders, wiping the blade of his sword on his sleeve. Time was racing past and he tried to guess whether the alarm would have been raised in the town across the water. There had been no shots—an indication of how unprepared the Spanish had been. The ring of steel against steel would not carry far, but a fisherman out there in the darkness sitting in his boat, tending net or line, would have heard and even now might be rowing to raise the alarm.

A mile to row in the darkness, ten minutes to persuade anyone in authority in Santa Cruz to listen to him, and another ten minutes to rouse out armed men and get them into boats, then a mile to row to the anchorage . . . there was no direct danger from the town. But a galloping horseman could warn the forts . . . Yet there was nothing to be gained from rushing; he had to risk an alert fisherman, or a suspicious sentry on the walls of Santa Fé. Wagstaffe could be relied on to wait in position, and all would be quiet in the town; at least, that was what Ramage hoped. The fox had managed to get into the hen run and was now swallowing the fattest bird, but he still had to finish the meal and then get out again. He had to keep calm and work methodically. First, clear the lower decks of Spaniards, and for that lanterns were needed. Then muskets to guard them—there was no time to send prisoners on shore.

He sent a dozen seamen across to the *Calypso* to fetch lanterns; a couple of dozen went over for muskets but were warned that they were to do nothing until all the Spaniards had been captured. As guards they were to fire only as a last resort, because the sound of musket shots would carry across the water and raise the alarm . . .

By the time the lanterns arrived Ramage had divided his men into three groups, one under Aitken to get to the lower deck down the fore hatch, another which he would lead himself down the after hatch, and a smaller group under Southwick to cover the main hatch to prevent the Spaniards scrambling up the ladder to the main deck.

A look over the starboard side revealed a couple of dozen Spaniards swimming close to the ship and shouting for help. Ramage ordered some seamen to throw them ropes and take them to the fo'c's'le under guard as soon as they were hauled on board. They had leapt overboard to avoid being spitted by British cutlasses; now the same British seamen were saving them from drowning.

The parties of men were now waiting ready at the three

hatches, each with half a dozen lanterns whose light threw strange and conflicting shadows. Those weird angles were the shadow of the cranked pump handle, and that broad band came from the mainmast. Aloft the light caught the underside of the yards and the furled sails, with the shrouds and ratlines looking like nets reaching up to the stars.

Ramage stared down the after hatch. The lower deck was a dark, silent pit. The lanterns lit the ladder but beyond that he pictured frightened men in the darkness clutching their cutlasses—there had been no time for them to grab muskets or pistols—and staring up at the pools of light in the hatchways. How much fight was there left in the Spaniards? Knowing they were trapped, would they be desperate or resigned? Was there a leader down there to rally them? Or, he thought for a moment, a leader who could speak for them all and negotiate?

He was far from sure how many of his own men had been killed or badly wounded: there were many bodies lying round the deck. Just then the light of a lantern reflected on his cutlass blade and showed the stain on the metal, and he knew he wanted no more killing if he could avoid it.

He called to Southwick, who came trotting aft: "Take over here for a moment. Don't go down the hatch."

As he walked to the main hatch Ramage called to Aitken, telling him to stand fast. Like the after hatch, the main hatch was a regular black pit; twelve-pounder shot gleamed round the coamings, sitting in semi-circular depressions cut in the wood, like large black oranges on display.

Anyone standing at the edge of the hatchway and shouting at the Spaniards below was lit up by the lanterns, a perfect target, towering over them like a figurehead. Well, he had already decided the Spaniards would not have had time to pick up muskets or pistols; in a minute or two he would know if he had been wrong. The possibility of a shot coming upwards out of the hatch reminded him of the dull pain gripping his stomach, but there was still no blood.

Yet *would* the Spaniards be crouching round the main hatch? Would they bunch themselves amidships where they could be trapped by parties coming down the fore and after hatches? No, he realized; they would be right forward, waiting for their enemy to come down the fore hatch.

He walked the few more paces that brought him to the small fore hatch where Aitken waited with his men, obviously uncertain what Ramage intended to do. But Ramage knew that while he was prepared to lead men in a wild dash down the ladder, he had little appetite for perching on the coaming like the target in a shooting contest. It had to be done though, and he found himself standing at the edge and taking a deep breath.

"Below there!" he called in Spanish. "Your ship is captured. Throw away your weapons and come up on deck unarmed."

"Let our Captain speak to us," someone answered.

"Your Captain is dead," Ramage said harshly, for the moment less concerned with the truth than persuading the Spaniards to make up their minds quickly. "And so are your officers. You must surrender!"

"No! Help will soon arrive! The soldiers are back in Santa Cruz—they will come on board in the morning."

"By then you will all be dead," Ramage said, speaking slowly and evenly. "You have only two choices: to live by surrendering, or to die when we come down there after you."

He paused for several moments, letting the Spaniards absorb his words. "If you want to live, you must come up on deck without your arms. If you want to die—well, the moment I give the order, two hundred men will come down there and slaughter you. You saw what happened up here."

A dozen voices began talking; more joined in and several men began shouting to make themselves heard. Ramage listened carefully. There seemed to be no quarrelling; although he could not distinguish the words he was sure they were all agreeing with some decision. Suddenly there was a silence broken by the same Spanish voice.

"You will kill us if we surrender?"

"Of course not. You will be prisoners."

"How can we be sure you will not kill us?"

"You cannot be sure," Ramage said, "but we have just been saving the lives of some of your shipmates by pulling them out of the water. Do you want to talk to them?"

There was a clatter of cutlass blades. Were they fighting or tossing away their weapons?

"We surrender," the voice said, "and I will lead the men up."

Ramage turned to Aitken and said quietly: "They've surrendered and are coming up in a moment. Have the men with muskets stand by." With that he walked aft to tell Southwick, and then went up to the quarterdeck to collect his thoughts. Three shadowy figures followed him, and as he paused by the binnacle Ramage, startled for a moment, recognized them as Jackson, Rossi and Stafford, who had obviously appointed themselves his bodyguards. It was a sensible precaution; half a dozen desperate Spaniards could be lurking anywhere in the ship, and by now they would have recognized which of the disreputable-looking men was the leader.

Gradually his night vision returned. The lanterns on the main deck were throwing a lot of light, but by facing aft he found he could first pick out the great black peak of Santa Fé, then the hills on either side of the entrance channel. Then he saw a grey patch, moving very slowly if it was moving at all. Gradually the patch became an outline, and he recognized the *Santa Barbara* lying hove-to.

Wagstaffe was in position, the *Jocasta* had been captured, and the first half of the plan had succeeded. But it was the easier half; many a schoolboy had found to his cost that it was easier to climb up a tree than down.

CHAPTER FOURTEEN

FIFTEEN MINUTES later Ramage settled himself comfortably at the desk in the captain's cabin of the *Jocasta* and grinned at Aitken and Southwick, who were sitting on the settee sipping cups of coffee.

"This is poor stuff, sir," Southwick said, squinting in the lantern light. "These foreigners don't have the right quality beans to start with."

"Aye, there's no body to it," Aitken commented. "Still, we shouldn't be complaining, I suppose."

"It'll make a tale to tell your grandchildren," Ramage said. "We shan't be able to tell the Admiral because he would not believe it."

"I wouldn't blame him," Southwick said after draining his cup and putting it down on the deck beside him. "'What did you all do after sailing into Santa Cruz with the *Calypso* and seizing the *Jocasta?*' Well, sir, Captain Ramage found the *Jocasta's* galley fire was still alight, so he ordered hot soup for the men and coffee for the officers."

"'And pray, Mr Southwick,'" the Master added, giving a good imitation of Admiral Davis's voice, "'how did Mr Ramage justify wasting so much time, with two of the King's ships lying in a heavily defended enemy harbour?' 'Well, sir, Mr Ramage said it was much too dark for gentlemen to be blundering around the lagoon in frigates, so he scrapped his plans and sat down sipping his coffee.' How does it sound, sir?"

"Well enough," Ramage admitted. "All we lack is the Marchesa serving us thin slices of cake!"

"Aye, she'd enjoy all this."

"However," Ramage said, "I trust you'll tell the rest of the story!"

"Oh yes, sir," Southwick said airily, "but sticking too closely to the facts does wreck a good tale, you know. 'Well,' I shall tell the Admiral (if he asks me), 'we'd seized the *Jocasta* without raising the alarm on shore, so Mr Ramage changed his mind: instead of sailing out with a fanfare of trumpets and bonfires lit along the sides of the channel to show us the way, we'd wait half an hour for the moon so that we could sneak out like guilty lovers.'"

As Aitken sipped his coffee he watched Ramage. He was unshaven, his seaman's shirt bloodstained, his trousers torn and grubby, but there was no mistaking that he was the Captain. Put him in a line with a couple of hundred seamen, and you would know he was in command. Quite why it was, Aitken was far from sure. Eyes deep-set, cheekbones high, nose narrow and slightly hooked, mouth firm but quick to twist into a smile. You would pick him out on appearances, even though the stubble on his face and the tangled hair were great levellers and at least temporarily counteracted the hint of aristocratic lineage. Aitken liked the word "lineage" and was proud of his own, even though it contained no titles. Thomas Jackson, seaman, had as much lineage as Nicholas Ramage, heir to the Earldom of Blazey. The reason for the curious relationship between Captain and coxswain was probably that both men knew and acknowledged this without ever giving it any thought.

The Captain sat in his chair, not exactly sprawling, but not sitting bolt upright either. Sitting comfortably—confidently was the word. Some captains needed well-pressed uniforms, formality, remoteness, the backing of the Articles of War, to create an atmosphere of authority round them, but most of them, however carefully they cultivated it, could not achieve what Mr Ramage did without realizing it, sitting back grubby and cheerful, a grin on his face as he teased Southwick.

Aitken heard a faint call, answered from the gangway. "The boat's come back, sir. I'll make sure that Kenton found Wagstaffe and delivered your orders."

Southwick looked at his watch as the First Lieutenant left the cabin. "Another fifteen minutes, sir. I do wish you'd let me land with Rennick and the Marines. There's no telling—"

"Not again," Ramage interrupted. "Rennick is competent and agile. He knows what to do. There'll be enough work for you on the way out. Anyway, you're no mountain goat, and you need to be one for the job I've given him."

"Yes, sir, but—"

"But you don't feel comfortable because the escape of two frigates probably depends on one lieutenant of Marines!"

"Aye, sir," Southwick said stubbornly. "That's the long and short of it."

Ramage looked up as Aitken came back to report that Kenton had found the *Santa Barbara* and handed Wagstaffe his orders. He had waited until they had been read and reported that there was no message from Wagstaffe, who had understood everything perfectly.

Aitken then waited a moment and said: "I wish you'd let me take half the prisoners in the *Calypso,* sir; I'm afraid they'll rise on you. You have fewer than a hundred men to work the ship and guard them."

Again the First Lieutenant saw the teasing smile. "Don't disturb those poor Spaniards, my dear Aitken: they're crowded together under the watchful eye of four boat guns loaded with grape. If one prisoner so much as sneezes he risks having them all wiped out. Now, is everything ready on board the *Calypso?* Baker and Kenton have their orders?"

"Yes, sir."

"And you remember your own orders?"

Aitken looked puzzled. "Well, sir, just to follow you out but to pass you and get clear of the entrance if you go aground."

"Good. I just wanted to make sure you understood that you don't take any ships in tow."

Aitken grinned cheerfully. "I understand, sir."

At that moment the sentry reported that Mr Bowen was waiting to see the Captain, and the Surgeon came into the cabin, bloodstained and weary and holding a folded sheet of paper. Ramage saw him and stiffened, knowing that the Surgeon came to report the casualties.

Bowen held out the paper but Ramage said as he took it: "Tell me how bad it is."

"We were lucky," Bowen said. "It could have been much worse. Five Calypsos dead and nineteen wounded."

That, Ramage thought to himself, is the price of the *Jocasta* so far. Admiral Davis would regard it as cheap—almost unbelievably cheap. But Admiral Davis would read Bowen's list in a different way: to him the names of the dead would mean nothing. He would not recall faces and accents, habits and problems. Obviously the captain of a ship knew each man in his crew; obviously admirals were concerned only with totals—but it did not make it any easier to bear the fact that you have just been responsible for the death of five of your men, with others possibly maimed for life. And there was the enemy, too.

"How did the Spaniards get on?" he asked.

Bowen shook his head. "You'll hardly believe it, sir. Twenty-three dead and forty-one wounded. I don't know how many will see the dawn. And if you'll excuse me, sir, I'll get below again. The only thing is there are no gunshot or splinter wounds."

Ramage nodded as the Surgeon turned away. Sixty-four Spanish dead and wounded—nearly a third of her complement. Ramage had discovered from the Spanish Captain that there had been 181 men on board. Another third were missing—they had jumped overboard—and a third, seventy or so men, were prisoners, along with the twenty from the *Santa Barbara*.

Tomorrow there would be funerals. Five British and twenty-three Spaniards would "go over the standing part of the main sheet." Twenty-eight times the bodies of men, sewn up in hammocks and with a round shot at their feet, would be put on a wide plank hinged on the bulwark in way of the mainsheet where the standing part was secured to the ship's side; twenty-eight times Ramage would have to read the appropriate passage from the funeral service, and the plank would be hinged up to allow the body to slide off into the sea. Twenty-eight times—providing the *Jocasta* managed to get past the forts without being fired on.

Twenty-eight men dead because a seaman called Summers talked his shipmates into mutiny—although one should include the Captain and officers who were murdered, and the various mutineers later executed. Twenty-eight men dead, the ghost of Summers might argue, because Captain Nicholas Ramage saw fit to attempt a cutting out which another captain had already said was impossible. Yet, blaming himself, Summers, Admiral Davis or Eames didn't bring anyone back to life; he knew he should be thankful to Bowen, because without even looking he knew that several of the wounded were alive only because of the Surgeon's skill.

Southwick pulled out his watch. "Five minutes to moonrise,

sir, then we'll have to wait another ten minutes or so before it gets up clear of the hills."

"Very well, you and Aitken had better make sure that we are all ready."

When the two men had gone Ramage took the four books which had been sitting on top of the desk, slid them into a drawer and turned the key. The Spanish order book, letter book, captain's journal and the signal book for the *Jocasta—La Perla*, rather. The first two would make interesting reading; it was a pity there was no time to go through them now.

The muscles of his stomach gave a spasm of protest as he began to get up. That he was lucky to be alive was plain from the damaged pistol now in the second drawer of the desk and the cut in the front flap of his trousers. The horizontal slash from that Spaniard's cutlass had hit him in the stomach, but the blow had been taken by one of the pistols tucked in his belt. The blade had hit the side of the butt and been deflected, sliding down an inch or two before coming hard up against the steel and pan cover, which had absorbed most of the impact. Sea Service pistols were clumsy and heavy, but he would never again complain about them; the sturdy construction and sheer bulk had saved his life. Nevertheless it would be a few days before he would be able to sit or walk comfortably; he felt as if he had been kicked by a horse. Apart from the pain, he did not want to think about it. His imagination ran riot when he thought of dying from a stomach wound.

On deck there was a faint lightening in the eastern sky. The moon was almost in its last quarter, just the right strength: it would be light enough to show the edges of the channel, but Ramage was hoping it would not help the Spanish gunners in the forts too much.

Half the *Calypso*'s ship's company were now on board the *Jocasta*: they already knew their jobs on board the prize—whether they were topmen or afterguard, which gun they served, if they were to be armed with cutlass or pike, pistol or tomahawk. Fortunately that had not been a tiresome job: Aitken and Southwick had simply taken the watch, quarter and station bill for the *Calypso*, which showed where each of the seamen and Marines on board went for the various evolutions. The Marines and twenty men now in the *Santa Barbara* were removed from the list and the remainder, about 180 men, were divided into two parties: half the topmen—the nimblest and best seamen—would stay in the *Calypso*, half would go to the *Jocasta*. Aitken was now commanding the *Calypso* with Baker, the Third Lieutenant, and Kenton, the Fourth, to help him. Ramage would command the *Jocasta*, with Southwick. He would have young Orsini with him, and the Surgeon. The reason for Bowen was obvious: it was better that the wounded did not have to be transferred to the *Calypso*.

Ramage looked inland, past the Pico de Santa Fé, which was now becoming more clearly outlined as the moon lifted over the hills and added its quota to the light from the stars. Over there, he reflected, up in the mountains beyond the Santa Fé, were a group of Indians who, by revolting against the Spanish, had played their part in the recapture of the *Jocasta*. The soldiers serving in the ship and sent off against the Indians were now back in Santa Cruz, their task completed. Had they returned a day earlier the story of the *Jocasta*'s recapture would have been different.

The moon was rising with its usual startling speed: the small thin crescent was now clear of the land and a silvery path of reflection was reaching across the water towards him. It was quiet and peaceful here, the two frigates lying secured to the same mooring buoys; a quiet broken only by the occasional irritable squawk of birds—night herons, complaining and chatting in their own little world.

He found himself speaking quietly as he said to Southwick:

"Have the men stand by to cast off the *Calypso's* lines." He picked up the speaking-trumpet and called over to Aitken: "*Calypso*, get under way when you are ready."

Aitken had obviously been waiting, and a series of orders crackled across the *Calypso's* decks: topmen were sent aloft ready to let fall the topsails; the afterguard waited to sheet home the sails and brace up the yards; more men took in the lines securing the ship to the *Jocasta*.

For the moment the *Calypso* had to drift clear; bracing up the yards too soon and letting fall the sails would simply lock the two ships together. Ramage jumped on top of the foremost gun on the larboard side of the quarterdeck and looked forward. The gap between the two ships was widening and the *Calypso* was also moving away crabwise to larboard: although she had no sails set at the moment the wind was moving the ship.

"You're well clear," he called to Aitken. Now the *Jocasta* could also get under way and lead the way to the channel. Wagstaffe, waiting with the *Santa Barbara*, would have seen the blurred outline of the two frigates gradually divide into two distinct ships, and that would have been enough to start him on his way. And all the while the town of Santa Cruz slept, with perhaps the Mayor wondering why Captain Lopez had not come over to brag, but secure in the knowledge that the Spanish Captain of the *Jocasta* would have dealt with everything. With any luck the officers and men of the forts too would have celebrated the bloodless capture of a new ship, so that the sentries would be careless.

He looked up at the Castillo de Santa Fé. Was she a threat? The *Santa Barbara* had stayed out in the middle of the lagoon, hove-to, for a couple of hours, occasionally letting her sails draw as she sailed back up to windward, and there had been no interest shown at the fort. He hoped that the brig's unusual behaviour would have been interpreted by the soldiers up there in Santa

Fé as something to do with guarding the two frigates. Or, more likely, the soldiers had taken no notice; they knew the *Santa Barbara* was a Spanish ship . . .

But what would they do when they saw the *Calypso* get under way? He was gambling that they were likely to do nothing—because the *Jocasta* followed. That would make it all right; they had not been told the ships would be moving, but obviously someone had forgotten to pass the word.

As the topmen raced up the ratlines to the yards Ramage shouted two orders rarely heard in a frigate because it was unusual for such a ship to be using mooring buoys while in commission.

"Let go forward!"

A splash and then a shout from the fo'c's'le told Ramage that the buoy had been dropped to starboard.

"Let go aft!"

A call from Southwick told him the buoy and buoy pendants were clear of the rudder. Now the wind was beginning to drift the *Jocasta* ahead, to the north, with the entrance channel over to the north-west. Ramage pointed the speaking-trumpet aloft to give the next sequence of orders to the topmen which would bring the topsails tumbling down like great curtains.

"Trice up—lay out!"

In the darkness the men scrambled out along the yards, their hands feeling for the gaskets, the canvas strips securing the furled sails, while the studding-sail booms were triced up out of the way.

The next order was to the afterguard down on deck: "Man the topsail sheets!" Again the speaking-trumpet was pointed up at the yards: "Let fall!" The topsails flopped down and at the same instant Ramage snapped: "Sheet home!" The wind slowly pressed out the creases in the canvas; then the sheets put a curve into the sails.

Ramage gave the final orders to the topmen. The studding-sail booms were lowered back into position; then came: "Down from aloft!"

But the topsails were still far from being ready to draw. "Man the topsail halyards," he shouted, and as soon as the seamen were ready: "Haul taut!"

A shout had the men ready at the braces, but first came: "Hoist the topsails!"

The yards were hoisted several feet up the masts and then Ramage gave the orders which turned the *Jocasta*'s wheel to head her two points to larboard, braced the yards round and trimmed the sails on the new course.

Ramage could hear the water bubbling along the frigate's side as she picked up speed. The lagoon was almost mirror smooth, and the moon, higher now and showing the wind shadows, out-lined the channel running north. The *Santa Barbara* was already sailing along the channel heading for the sea; the *Calypso* was over on the *Jocasta*'s larboard quarter, and Aitken was preparing to follow into the channel.

Southwick stood beside Ramage ahead of the binnacle. "Thought we'd hear from the castle up there," he said, gestur-ing over his shoulder at Castillo de Santa Fé, now astern of them.

"We might at any moment," Ramage said, irritated by a super-stitious fear that the guns would start firing now Southwick had mentioned them.

"Doubt it. I'll bet they're chattering about it though."

"I'm glad I'm not the commandant. Just imagine it: the two frigates he's supposed to be protecting suddenly get under way."

"Aye—does he open fire or doesn't he?" Southwick said.

"And he's fairly certain that it's all a mistake. Someone—the Mayor or the Port Captain—notified him that they would be get-ting under way, but the letter went astray."

"That's true, sir: no Spaniard trusts his own folk with paper-work; he knows the things that can go wrong."

Ramage turned to Jackson and gave him a new course. The *Jocasta* turned slightly to larboard and then Ramage saw all the way up the channel. The hills cast too many shadows to be sure at this distance that he could see the forts on either side, but he could distinguish the *Santa Barbara* as a small black patch at the far end.

Then the *Jocasta* was in the channel with a following wind that was steady. The land was low on each side but within a few hundred yards it began to rise like petrified waves, higher and higher until it ended in the sheer drop of the cliffs forming the entrance.

The *Santa Barbara* was back in the middle of the channel: she was too far off for him to be sure but it looked as though her topsails were being let fall again. It was likely: Wagstaffe would have clewed them up to take some of the way off the ship while the Marines climbed into the boats.

"That Rennick," Southwick growled. "I hope he doesn't lose his head."

"The only way would be for a round shot to take it off," Ramage said. "He's calm enough."

"Aye, sir, but—"

"We'll soon see," Ramage said shortly. "Just inspect the men at quarters."

The guns had been loaded and run out, and although their twelve-pound shot would make little impression on the forts they might keep the Jocastas happy if they came under fire. He knew from experience there was nothing more demoralizing than being shot at without being able to fire back.

He saw that the *Calypso* was now in the channel too; Aitken was following less than one hundred yards astern of the *Jocasta*.

In line with the *Calypso's* masts was the Castillo de Santa Fé, brooding over the lagoon. It was not as high as Ramage had originally thought, and the range to a ship at the entrance would be a mile. Just right for trained gunners firing in daylight, but perhaps too much at night for excited men who were rarely drilled.

Ramage picked up the night-glass and looked forward. One of the irritations of using a night-glass was that it gave an inverted picture, and he could see the *Santa Barbara* sailing along upside down with the sea in place of the sky. However there was no doubt that she was under way; another fifty yards or so and she would be abreast the two forts, while another fifty yards would bring her to the open sea. And there were her boats, hauled up on the narrow strip of beach on each side of the channel. But there were no flashes along the battlements of Castillo San Antonio or El Pilar; neither the firefly-flicker of pistols and muskets nor the red lightning of cannon.

CHAPTER FIFTEEN

RENNICK had selected his two parties with care. Although he was an officer short—a 36-gun frigate should have a Marine second lieutenant as well as a first lieutenant—at least the Admiral had given him the full complement of NCOs and men. Lacking a second lieutenant, he had put his sergeant in command of the second party, but he was a steady man who had the sharper of the two corporals to back him up.

Every one of the Marines had looked carefully at the hills and the forts as the *Santa Barbara* had sailed in: half of them had watched to larboard studying San Antonio, half to starboard had watched El Pilar. Rennick knew there was no chance of the men remembering all that they had seen; it was more important that they saw the kind of task that faced them, particularly up the twisting paths, which were little more than goat tracks.

Rennick grinned to himself as he recalled the looks on the faces of the sergeant and corporals as he passed on the orders given him by Captain Ramage. They would all wear dark clothes— if necessary they were to dye or dirty duck trousers. Every man's face and hands were to be blackened—they had been lucky to find a supply of corks in the boatswain's store on board the *Santa Barbara*. The men were to be armed with pistols and cutlasses or pikes; they were not to carry muskets. And a few minutes before they went in to attack they were to tie narrow strips of white cloth round their foreheads to distinguish friend from foe. The blackened faces and dark clothes were to disguise them as they approached the castle; once inside it would not matter.

Now the seamen stopped rowing and the keel of the boat scraped on some coral before running up on the sand with a hiss. The grapnel dropped a few yards out held the boat's stern so that she did not broach, and Rennick gave his first low-pitched order: "All Marines out and rendezvous at the back of the beach."

He listened intently, but there was no crack of wood or metal hitting wood: the men were being careful with their cutlasses and pikes. That kind of noise carried a long way on a night like this. A moment later he was vaulting out of the boat, squelching through the water and then up the sharp slope of the beach.

There was the corporal acting as the marker: within a few moments the men were lined up in two ranks. "Everyone has a head-band? Pistols at half-cock?"

All Rennick could really distinguish in the dim light were eyes and the white of teeth: the men's blackened faces, arms and hands, and their dark clothes, blended with the rocks and bushes behind them.

"First rank, follow me." With that Rennick led the way along the steep path that snaked upwards from the beach. As the *Santa Barbara* passed in daylight, he had inspected the path with a telescope. It was steep, it twisted and turned, but it went up towards the Castillo San Antonio, going round a crest near the top and apparently leading to a rear entrance.

As Rennick felt the muscles tighten in the back of his legs he found himself once again worrying about the top of the path. He and Wagstaffe had agreed that the path was used very frequently and the castle was probably supplied from the beach: it would be much easier for a boat to land provisions there so that men could carry them up the path than trying to get supplies across a mile or two of steep hills. That being the case, then the path would naturally go to a back entrance. But if the castle was supplied over the hills then the path was worn by sheep and goats and might not reach the castle . . .

There would be sentries marching along the battlements, watching to seaward; that much was obvious. No matter how slack the Dons were someone up there would be keeping a lookout, however sleepy-eyed and spasmodic. But what about that back entrance? Was it the only entrance? Was there a sentry at the door? Was the door bolted at night?

He glanced back and saw that although the men were following close behind him they were hard to see: they blended in perfectly. If they had been in uniform their pipeclayed crossbelts would have marked out every man. He looked across at El Pilar, where the sergeant's party should be well up the path. No shooting, so they had not been detected—yet.

Why would the Spaniards in San Antonio bolt the door? Why a sentry? It all depended on how they regarded San Antonio. Was it a fortress guarding Punta Reina, the headland on which it stood—in which case there would be sentries covering every direction—or was it part of the defence of the harbour entrance, its eyes and guns aimed to seaward, with no one bothering about back doors?

He paused a moment to look back along the path, which was getting steep now. He seemed to be trailing a bulky black caterpillar whose undulations were men climbing upwards, each trying to keep the ordered yard from the man in front. A hiss as a man breathed in sharply, the shrill whine of mosquitoes, the murmur of waves sucking and slapping at the beach below. And the *Santa Barbara* well clear of the entrance. And then suddenly Rennick saw that the beach where they had landed was indeed out of sight from San Antonio, as they had hoped, hidden by projecting ledges of rock and folds in the hills. He had forgotten to look up towards the castle once they landed on the beach, but he realized now that the Spanish sentries would have seen only the *Santa Barbara* sailing along the channel and out into the open sea. They might have watched her clew up her topsails, but it was unlikely that they had noticed her cast off the two boats that she had towed the length of the channel. In daylight the sentries on San Antonio would certainly have seen the sergeant's boat rowing across the channel to El Pilar; but they would not pick her out in the darkness: he could not see her on the distant beach, even though he knew where to look, because there were so many shadows made by rocks and landslides.

Rennick was beginning to feel weary. From his bird's-eye view he estimated he was more than two-thirds of the way up to San Antonio. The *Jocasta* should be leaving the lagoon and entering the channel by now. It was hopeless trying to look at his watch while still climbing, and he passed the word for a halt. The men could have a brief rest; he could check the time and hope the sergeant across the channel was doing the same. To the minute, Captain Ramage had said of the final attack; the difference of a minute between the assaults on San Antonio and El Pilar could lose all the surprise and cost lives.

He managed to make out the hands of the watch in the faint moonlight. Eleven minutes to go. Better wait at the top than here, he thought, and started off again, followed by his men. The path was smooth, slippery with sheep and goat droppings, and soon began to level out, still with the hill to the left. Then, with startling suddenness, Rennick found the castle towering above him: the path came out from beside a sheer outcrop of rock some five yards from the western side. He ducked back and then squatted down, peering upwards across the gap at the grey walls.

It was unlikely that they would be seen. A sentry leaning over this west corner and staring downward might spot them, but the chances were about the same as being hit by a bolt of lightning. He whispered an order to the Marine behind him and waited until he saw him pass it to the next man.

He moved slowly across the gap until he was against the wall of the castle, then pulled the strip of white cloth from his pocket and tied it round his head. More Marines, all moving slowly, joined him and followed as he led the way round the castle, a sheer face of shaped stone. From here he had a fine view of El Pilar across the channel: the moon was higher now and the shadows shorter. Then he was at the corner and peering round it along the south side of San Antonio. The doorway, blast it, was halfway along the wall with no cover, and hundreds of mosquitoes seemed to be living in the cracks of the stonework, all of them with a whine that made a shrill chorus.

He watched carefully but there was no sign of movement. If there was a sentry, he would be inside the door. Mr Ramage had stressed that the attack had to begin at a certain time, but, Rennick found himself puzzling, did the attack begin here, or inside the castle?

He pulled out his watch. Four minutes to go. Here or inside

the castle? He asked himself the question again and decided to risk there being a sentry down there; the one who could raise the alarm by seeing the flashes of guns at El Pilar was up on the battlements. He signalled the men to follow and crept along the wall. The darkness played tricks with distance, making the castle seem bigger than it was, and he was surprised how quickly he reached the door. It was enormous, studded with circular bolt-heads which were intended to blunt the axes of an enemy trying to cut their way in—and it was shut. He gripped the big handle, lifted it and pulled. The door moved a few inches with a spine-chilling creak and Rennick waited to see what the noise provoked. Nothing moved on the other side and he pulled it again so that the door was open just wide enough for them to slip through one at a time.

He cocked his pistol, quietly drew his cutlass, then led the way through the opening. There was a big courtyard, most of it hidden in shadow. The castle was a hollow square with a building against the north wall which was probably used as a barracks for the garrison. A smaller building a few yards beyond was most likely the officers' quarters, while another nearby would be the kitchen. To one side, stone steps led up to the top of the wall, where the guns sat, waiting.

By now all the Marines were through the door. Rennick found the corporal and gave him his orders, then took his own section of men and whispered their instructions. He looked at his watch. Two minutes to go. He hissed a warning to the men, repeated it when a minute had gone, and then counted the remaining seconds, finishing with a "Go," when he led the rush across the square.

The corporal's section went straight to the two barrack buildings while Rennick raced to the steps. As he reached the bottom one he saw the dim outline of a man standing at the top. He knew it was hopeless to try a pistol shot in the bad light, and anyway the noise would raise the alarm quicker than a shout. The man had vanished and was shouting as Rennick rushed up the steps, all tiredness vanishing in the spasm of fear as he pictured alert men waiting to shoot him as he reached the top.

Down below there was a thudding interspersed with the sound of cutlass blades, then shouts in Spanish. Rennick reached the top of the steps and paused a moment, trying to distinguish where the sentries were. There was a flash of a musket from the western end of the wall and a shot twanged away in ricochet. The rest of the Marines streamed up the steps, but Rennick had already realized that there was only one sentry who must have bolted back from the steps to seize his musket. Now he would be gripping the empty weapon and feeling lonely and defenceless.

"Secure him!" Rennick said loudly, and looked across at El Pilar. There was no noise, no flashes. With luck the sergeant had caught the Spanish asleep there too.

He ran down the steps followed by several of his men and found that the corporal was already beginning to line up a row of sleepy but frightened prisoners. Three Marines dragged a figure from the smaller building, a man wearing a long nightshirt and clearly the commandant. He too was forced into the line, which comprised about twenty men. Yet there had been only one man on sentry duty. It had been just on the hour when the man appeared at the top of the steps, so he was probably coming down to arouse his relief.

As Rennick thought of the commandant, the man in the long nightshirt, he realized that the castle was in his hands.

"Corporal," he called, "the lanterns!"

"They're here ready, sir."

"Light them, then put them up on the west wall!"

Three lanterns each set three feet apart on the west wall

would tell the *Jocasta*—and the sergeant over at El Pilar—that San Antonio had been captured. Half the task was completed, and he looked round carefully before setting off to complete the other half.

He saw it in a few moments, and realized that he must have passed within a few feet of it in the rush to the steps. It was in the centre of the courtyard, and in the moonlight it looked as if it could be a well. He reached it to find a horizontal trapdoor which reminded him of a hatch in a ship. There was a padlock on it and he called for an axeman, one of the men who would, if necessary, have battered down the castle door.

A dozen well-placed strokes cut out the section of plank on which the hasp was bolted. Willing hands grabbed the door and swung it back, and Rennick saw that steps cut in rock went down into what was little more than a cave. He handed a Marine his pistol and cutlass and went down the steps. It was the magazine; stored in the cave were enough barrels of powder and cartridges to withstand a year's siege. He felt one barrel after another, and finally gave up counting before he came across bales of felt wads. Many hundredweights of powder; probably several tons. More than enough to do the job.

He called for the corporal and, after being assured that the three lanterns were in position on the west wall, helped unwind a length of slow match which the man had coiled round his waist.

Then Rennick carefully worked at the bung of one of the barrels, loosening it and finally pulling it out. He could feel the powder inside, and taking one end of the slow match he pushed it down until several inches of it were buried. Then he stepped back to the entrance of the magazine, carefully unwinding the match so that a sudden strain did not pull it away from the barrel. It had been cut to a special length, and would take half an hour to burn.

He sent the corporal up the steps first and then followed himself, patting his clothes to make sure that no loose grains of powder clung to the material.

"Now, are the prisoners ready?"

"They're under guard by the door, sir, all ready to march."

Rennick thought of the half-hour fuse. "Very well, you can start off for the beach with them. Wait by the boat for me. Leave two men on guard here. Now—" he looked round for two particular Marines "—Lumley, Rogers! Ah, there you are; come on, let's attend to those guns!"

As the corporal gave the orders which would start the prisoners down the path, Rennick ran up the steps to the guns, followed by the two Marines, each with a hammer tucked in his belt. Twenty-eight guns to spike, Rennick thought crossly, but at that moment he looked across the channel and saw the *Jocasta* emerge into the open sea. Mr Ramage would have seen the lanterns and known San Antonio was secured. What about El Pilar? He could just make out three horizontal lights on El Pilar's walls showing that the sergeant had done his job.

As soon as Rennick reached the first gun, one of the Marines produced a small piece of steel rod, slightly tapered at one end. At an impatient gesture from Rennick he pushed the tapered end of the spike into the touchhole and gave it a gentle tap with the hammer to seat it. Then he increased the weight of the blows and the spike was slowly driven down into the touchhole, the top burring over slightly so that by the time it reached the rim of the touchhole itself it was fatter and needed one final heavy blow to drive it flush.

As they moved on to the next gun Rennick saw the *Calypso* gliding out of the entrance, following the *Jocasta* and the *Santa Barbara*. The entire Spanish naval strength of Santa Cruz, he thought idly, was now outside the harbour, prisoners of the Royal Navy, and the town slept peacefully.

The second Marine was now busy hammering home spikes, starting with the guns overlooking the channel. Rennick checked each man's work and finally watched the last spike being driven home. The Spanish would find it difficult to bore out these rivets so that the guns could be used again, but spiking was not an absolutely sure way of wrecking a gun, even if done carefully. Mr Ramage had refused him permission to put a double-charge of powder and three round shot in each gun, a degree of overloading that usually blew the barrel apart like ripping the skin from a ripe banana.

Rennick led the way down the steps to the courtyard, which was now deserted except for the two sentries guarding the magazine. He was carrying one of the lanterns, which he put down well clear of the entrance.

"Lumley," he said, "give me a hand here, and you others go and wait by the gate, though you won't be far enough away if I make a mistake!"

The slow match came up the steps from the magazine like a thin snake. Rennick reached down and unwound the rest of it, leading it to windward of the entrance in as direct a line as possible—a sharp kink sometimes made it go out, and it was all too easy to run it through a puddle without noticing it.

"Fetch the lantern, Lumley, but don't drop it!"

As soon as the Marine came back Rennick told him to put the lantern on the ground. Then he knelt down and swung open the door. The piece of candle flickered slightly in a gentle breeze, and Rennick took out his watch, looked at the time, and picked up the slow match. He held the end against the candle flame and after a few moments the match began to splutter. Rennick put it flat on the ground and watched the tiny, slightly bluish flame as it moved along almost imperceptibly. It was burning steadily; in half an hour the flame should have reached that barrel of powder and gone down into the bunghole . . .

"Come on!" Rennick said, and swung the castle door shut as he went out. He gave a nervous giggle as he realized the futility of what he had done, then hurried after his men,

They caught up with the Marine party and prisoners halfway down the path, the Spaniards so stunned by what had happened that they were not even talking among themselves. Rennick hoped they would not have recovered by the time they reached the beach: the boat taking them out to the *Calypso* would be overloaded.

C H A P T E R   S I X T E E N

WHEN RAMAGE saw the row of lanterns appear on Castillo San Antonio he gave a sigh of relief which brought a laugh from Southwick. "So you were worrying about Rennick, sir!"

"I was worrying about the job, not the man," Ramage said impatiently. He glanced astern. "We're still in range of Santa Fé . . ."

Southwick sniffed yet again. "I still can't see the commandant ordering his gunners to open fire on the *Jocasta*, or whatever her Spanish name was. On the *Calypso*, perhaps."

"They can't tell which is which by now—ah, there are the lights on El Pilar. Both in our hands. I hope those Marines step lively on their way back to the boats."

Southwick stared up at each fort as the *Jocasta* passed through a line joining them. "I hope they don't make any mistake with the slow match," he said. "I wonder how much powder they have in the magazines."

"Plenty," Ramage said. "Poor quality but plenty of it."

"Let's hope there's enough to do the job. That San Antonio must have walls ten feet thick."

The two men watched as the *Jocasta* came clear of the two headlands. Ramage brought her round to starboard a couple of points, well up to windward, so that when she was hove-to the current would slowly take her back towards the entrance. The *Santa Barbara* was still close in with the entrance but the *Calypso* was now showing up clear of the headlands.

Ramage looked at his watch. "They should be spiking the guns now."

"Waste of time, to my way of thinking," Southwick grumbled. "Double charge and three round shot: there's no chance of repairs, then."

"Too risky," Ramage said, remembering that Rennick had made the same argument. "Sixty-four guns altogether. Someone's bound to get excited and fire one gun too soon. And why rouse out the town and Santa Fé before we have to?"

Southwick shrugged his shoulders. The fact was that he agreed, but he was annoyed that his role in the night's activities had been slight. True, he had boarded the *Jocasta*, but he had expected to be given the job of taking Castillo San Antonio, and he was enjoying his grumbles.

"Take the conn, Mr Southwick," Ramage said. "Heave-to the ship now, and make sure the *Calypso* heaves-to reasonably close. I want to go through some of those Spanish papers in my cabin."

The Spanish Captain of the *Jocasta*, he discovered as he began reading through the papers, was Diego Velasquez, and the way the letters were kept in neat bundles tied with different coloured tapes showed that he was a careful and precise man. Red tape denoted letters and orders from the Captain-General of the province of Caracas (the bulk was due more to the thick wax seals than the amount of paper), while blue tape secured correspondence with the Mayor and *junta* of Santa Cruz.

A quick glance showed Ramage that the Mayor of Santa Cruz, although given a lot of power and acting more like a governor, was very careful when drawing up orders to make it clear that he was acting for the *junta*. If wrong orders were given, the Mayor was obviously determined that his council would at least share the blame. Every order was issued on behalf of the *junta*, and to make doubly sure the Mayor listed the members present at each meeting. They ranged from the judge to the city treasurer; ten of the city's leading citizens.

The Mayor's letters dealt mostly with routine matters—reporting that casks of provisions had arrived and were ready for Velasquez, asking about the progress being made in refitting the ship, complaining of the strain on the city's finances caused by the need to feed all the troops sent on board . . . Then the almost hysterical warning to Velasquez of the insurrection among the Indians in the mountains, followed by a peremptory order (in the name of the *junta*) to send the troops on shore for them to march inland and put down the insurrection.

The Mayor was clearly happiest when forwarding instructions to Velasquez which came from the capital of the province, Caracas, a few miles inland from the port of La Guaira. "His Excellency the Captain-General has honoured me with his latest orders, which the *junta* of Santa Cruz forwards to you and which I direct you to obey with all speed . . ." was his regular formula.

Ramage had begun by reading the Mayor's letters on the assumption that they would give the latest orders to Velasquez, but by the time he had read a dozen it was clear that they dealt mostly with provisioning and manning. Anything of any importance from the Captain-General had been sent direct to Velasquez. He tied up the Mayor's letters again and with a sigh turned to those from the Captain-General. Letters from the Admiralty in London were usually brief to the point of being taciturn; only formal documents like commissions used archaic and flowery language. But the Spanish were different: a letter from the Mayor telling Velasquez that ten casks of rice and five of chick-peas were being sent to Santa Cruz from La Guaira meant three lines of elaborate introduction and another three to end the letter.

The first he read from the Captain-General was even worse: His Excellency referred not only to his *junta*—which dealt with the whole province "on behalf of his sacred Catholic Majesty"— but to the head of every department involved in the particular order. Hardly believing what he read, Ramage saw that the letter was telling Velasquez that an application for timber to replace some deck planking was not approved. Velasquez's request, the Captain-General wrote, had been submitted to the *junta*, which had referred it to the *Intendente*, the man who controlled the province's treasury. The *Intendente* passed it to the Commander of the Privateering Branch (apparently, Ramage noted, the *Jocasta* had been commissioned under the Spanish flag as a privateer, not taken into the Navy). The worthy commander had refused to pay for the wood, saying that "because of recent decisions" it was not now an item that could be charged against the Privateering Branch's funds, which were for operating privateers, and anyway had been exhausted.

The request, the Captain-General told Velasquez with all the relish of a bureaucrat saying no, had therefore been referred back once again to the *Intendente*, who had refused to provide the money because the *junta* had decided a year ago that the ship was not a regular ship of war but a privateer, and as such was not the concern of the Royal Treasury, whose funds ("which are for the moment exhausted") the *Intendente* administered.

Ramage, fascinated at the way a few planks of wood could cause so much trouble, re-read the letter and several others dealing with refitting the ship. Finally he realized that the Captain-General, who was the administrative ruler of the province, was at loggerheads with the *Intendente,* who was the head of the Treasury, and that the cause of their quarrel was the control of the *Jocasta.*

As a ship of the Spanish Navy she would come under the general control of the Ministry of Marine in Madrid and, if based at La Guaira, the local control of the Captain-General, with the Royal Treasury in Caracas—the *Intendente,* in other words—paying the bills. As privateer, she would still be under the general control of the Captain-General, but the commander of the Privateering Branch would decide how she operated, and would pay her expenses out of the Privateering Branch funds.

All that seemed straightforward but, Ramage discovered, the ship had recently been ordered by Madrid to sail to Havana and then on to Spain, which meant that the Privateering Branch would lose her, and obviously the commander did not want to pay for anything more, claiming that the Royal Treasury should foot the bill. But the *Intendente* would not agree—she was not a ship of the Spanish Navy (though, Ramage could see, it was clear that once she arrived in Spain she would be added to the Fleet), because she had been commissioned as a privateer.

It was hard luck for the Privateering Branch: the letters made it clear that the Branch had paid for all the refitting so far but as soon as she was ready to go to sea she was ordered to Havana, bound for Spain. It said a lot about Spanish officials that it had taken them more than a year to commission the ship, and that the chattering of clerks—people like the *Intendente* might be higher up the scale, but they still had clerks' mentalities—meant that although the *Jocasta* had been in Spanish hands for two years all they had done was move her from La Guaira to Santa Cruz. Those Spanish clerks were the best allies that Britain had, Ramage reflected. The *Calypso* frigate had winkled her out of Santa Cruz, but the clerks had quite effectively seen to it that she stayed there until the *Calypso* arrived. Did his Most Catholic Majesty realize that, albeit unwittingly, his clerks were guilty of treason?

He had just picked up the next batch of the Captain-General's letters, hoping to find the latest orders to Velasquez, when he heard someone hurrying down the companion-way, and a moment later the sentry called: "Mr Orsini, sir!"

Paolo knocked on the door and came in, his eyes glinting with excitement in the dim lantern light. "Mr Southwick's compliments, sir: he says it wants about five minutes before the castles blow up!"

Ramage was tired; he was anxious to know Velasquez's orders. The castles would blow up if Rennick and his sergeant had done their work properly—and providing the slow matches burned true. But there was nothing that Nicholas Ramage, Captain, could do to help or hinder the process. For that matter, it was of no consequence as far as his orders were concerned whether the castles blew up or not. Admiral Davis would lose no sleep if both fuses went out: he would have the *Jocasta* back again, which was all that mattered. The castles were the bonus, and anyway Ramage wanted to continue reading the letters. But the cabin was hot and stuffy and Paolo was holding the door open, waiting to follow him on deck. How like Gianna the boy was; the same heart-shaped face, the same eyes.

Ramage put the papers in the top drawer, locked it, and stood up to find Paolo holding out a cutlass, but he motioned it away.

"The ship's company aren't about to mutiny, are they, Paolo?"

"No, sir," the boy said, "but we have more than a hundred Spanish prisoners on board!"

Ramage took the cutlass and slipped the belt over his shoulder. In the excitement of sailing out of Santa Cruz he had forgotten the prisoners; seizing the ship seemed like something that had happened last week.

On deck the stars and waning moon were enough to light up the ship. Southwick, incongruous in his mutineer's garb, waved to the south: "I didn't think you'd want to miss the excitement, sir. Any minute now, taking half an hour from the time we saw the lights."

"It should be quite a sight," Ramage said, making an effort to sound cheerful so as not to spoil an otherwise exciting occasion: nearly every man on board except the lookouts was up in the rigging or on the hammock nettings—Southwick had obviously given permission—eagerly staring at the top of the cliffs.

The ship was lying hove-to, with the *Calypso* five hundred yards away to the east.

"Where's the *Santa Barbara?*" Ramage asked.

Southwick pointed to the west. "She's well clear of the entrance, sir. I saw her with the night-glass. Towing her boats, so she must have recovered the Marines and Spanish prisoners. She's making up for us, like you told Wagstaffe."

"Prisoners!" Ramage said crossly. "We'll soon have more Spaniards out here than there are in Santa Cruz."

"Don't forget the soldiers, sir."

Ramage gave a short laugh. "No, if we'd arrived twelve hours later we'd be the prisoners."

"I didn't mean that, sir," Southwick protested, but Ramage felt too drained to do anything more than watch the cliffs. It was hard to believe that less than three hours earlier the *Calypso* had first approached Santa Cruz to begin a dangerous game of bluff. Certainly it had worked and he had hooked the *Jocasta* like a fisherman landing a lethargic perch, so he should be cheerful and content. Instead he felt as taut as a flying jib sheet hard on the wind. He had expected to lose half of these men who were now waiting in the shrouds and on the hammock nettings like excited starlings perched in a grove of trees. So, he told himself, he should be cheerful because only a handful had been killed.

The fact was that he was far from being a natural gambler; he had little patience with those pallid fellows crouching over the gaming tables at Buck's, terrified that the turn of a card or the tumble of a die would ruin them, yet always hoping desperately to win. Obviously all they lived for was the fear of losing and exaltation of winning, but it was sad to think that grown men hazarded their futures on the face of a card or the spots of a die. A house that had been a family seat for a couple of centuries often changed hands because a die stopped rolling to show a three instead of a four.

Yet . . . yet . . . he had just done much the same thing, except that no gambler at Buck's or one of those other elegant establishments would play against such odds: no one wagered a guinea to win a guinea, unless he was drunk or desperate, yet he had just risked a frigate, and more than two hundred lives, to win a frigate.

Castillo San Antonio suddenly exploded. A great lightning-flash radiating outwards lit the surrounding hills, the entrance channel and the *Calypso* as though it was day and then equally suddenly plunged everything into a darkness that seemed solid. A moment later a deep rumbling coming through the water made the *Jocasta* tremble, while a noise like a great clap of thunder skated across the sea, followed by echoes bouncing off the mountains and gradually fading into the distance. Then came the startled mewing of seabirds wheeling in alarm and the sudden chatter of excited men.

Ramage blinked rapidly, dazzled and still hardly able to believe what he had just seen. "The night-glass !" he snapped at Southwick.

The hard, rectangular outline of the castle on top of the cliff was hidden in an enormous wreath of smoke and dust, the top of which swirled snakelike in the moonlight. Gradually it thinned out, blown clear by the wind, and finally Ramage could make out the remains of the castle.

"What can you see, sir?" Southwick asked excitedly.

Ramage realized that every man within earshot was straining to hear his reply, and he spoke loudly: "The centre has gone, right down to the foundations. The western corner is still standing . . . yes, the smoke's clearing more: the whole eastern side has collapsed."

"I wonder how much powder there was in the magazine?" Southwick asked incredulously.

"Enough! Ah, there we are, the smoke has cleared completely. Yes, three-quarters of the castle—all except the western end—has gone. A lot of the stonework has slid down the hill in an avalanche."

"Rennick needn't have bothered to spike the guns," Southwick muttered, obviously determined to have the last word on the subject.

Ramage swung the night-glass to find the *Santa Barbara* and saw that she was still beating up to join the *Jocasta*. For a moment he had feared she might have been close enough to be damaged by lumps of stone hurled up by the explosion.

A red eye winked at the far end of the channel.

"Santa Fé!" he exclaimed. "They've woken up and started firing down the channel."

"Aye, they probably think the English are coming," South-wick said contemptuously. "Look!" he added as more red flashes followed, "that first gun woke up the rest of them!"

At that moment El Pilar blew up. Again a blinding flash lit up the hills—showing San Antonio a wrecked shell, the western wall throwing the rest into heavy shadow—followed by a shock through the water and a dull blam-blam, as though the side had fallen away from a mountain.

Ramage handed Southwick the night-glass . "We'll go down to meet the *Santa Barbara*. The sooner our prisoners are trans-ferred to her the better. I'm going below to finish reading the Spanish orders."

"Ah, we might find a few prizes to take back with us," South-wick said cheerfully.

"The *Jocasta*'s enough," Ramage said crossly.

"Yes, sir, but don't forget that Isla de Margarita is the pearl island, and they find emeralds farther along the coast."

"We'll collect enough oysters to make a crown of pearls for you," Ramage said sarcastically, "then hurry back to English Harbour for the coronation." With that he went below, hearing Southwick beginning the string of orders which would take the *Jocasta* down to the *Santa Barbara*.

Captain Velasquez had the irritating habit of putting the earliest letters at the top and the latest at the bottom, but Ramage was curious about the way the Captain-General had handled the *Jocasta* affair. Here, written at great length, was the first letter to Velasquez describing how English mutineers had brought the ship to La Guaira—"under the command of an officer named Summers"—and handed her over to "the municipality." Clearly the Captain-General was determined not to take any personal responsibility even at that early stage. The *junta* had ordered the ship to be taken round to Santa Cruz because the port was well defended and there, the *junta* directed, Velasquez would take command.

That letter alone would have hanged Summers, Ramage thought, and the very next one again referred to the seaman, saying he would act as master for the voyage, and when he handed over the frigate to Velasquez he was to be allowed to return to La Guaira, unless Velasquez had any use for him in refitting the ship "in view of his particular skills."

Then came a series of orders dealing with fitting out the ship. The English were always so short-handed that they sailed the ship with fewer than two hundred men, the *junta* noted, but it regarded three hundred as the absolute minimum. The master shipwright had assured the *junta* that the frigate could carry more guns without endangering her stability, so Velasquez was to consider fitting six more, but the *junta* did not specify the size of the guns, nor whether they were to be mounted on the quarterdeck and fo'c's'le or on the main deck.

In later letters there were complaints—obviously referring to reports by Velasquez—about the amount of work and cost of commissioning the ship. Then, the most flowery letter so far, the *junta's* unanimous decision on the ship's new name, *La Perla*. This, the Captain-General ordered (for once he took the credit for it), was to be painted or carved on the ship's transom after all traces of the original English name had been removed, the letters painted in red on a gold background, "to match the glorious flag of Spain." The Pearl, Ramage thought, was hardly a suitable name for a ship of war.

Further letters reported that Spanish merchant seamen had been pressed and were being sent to Santa Cruz to man the ship. Another told Velasquez that soldiers were being used to make up the number, volunteers from two regiments recently arrived from

Panama. These men would make excellent seamen, the Captain-General assured Velasquez.

There were more letters about provisions—mostly saying that various things were not available—and, at last an urgent warning to Velasquez that an English "corsair" had been sighted and was probably bound for Santa Cruz to attempt to recapture the frigate. From the date of the letter Ramage saw that it referred to Captain Eames's arrival on the Main.

Several letters had mentioned dates by which Velasquez should have the ship ready, and then came the first to mention Havana. This was an order telling Velasquez that because of instructions just received from the Ministry of Marine in Madrid —"from the hand of the Secretary of State for the Navy, His Excellency Don Juan de Langara"—*La Perla* was to proceed to Spain by way of Havana, and Velasquez was to prepare for the voyage accordingly "and report at once if the ship has any needs."

A letter dated twelve days later and referring to one from Velasquez seemed to show that *La Perla's* Captain had suddenly found a dozen excellent reasons why the frigate could not sail for Spain, but the Captain-General, obviously mindful of the order from Madrid, dismissed them all: the ship would sail as soon as one or two ships bound for Havana were assembled so that *La Perla* could escort them and "protect them from English corsairs."

Ramage saw from successive letters that as the days passed the idea of a convoy to Havana grew in the minds of the *junta:* obviously the businessmen in the province of Caracas were thankful for this rare opportunity to send goods from La Guaira to Cuba and Spain under the protection of a frigate. Then came more specific information for Velasquez: ships from Vera Cruz, Cartagena and La Guaira would assemble in Havana, ready to sail as a convoy for Spain, escorted by a 74-gun ship and four frigates, of which *La Perla* would be one.

Ramage sighed as he struggled with the handwriting. The letters were full of abbreviations, and the clerks obviously cared little if blots of ink obscured words providing the big wax seals were perfect. He was tired of phrases like "very magnificent, sir" used by almost anyone when writing to a superior; he was bored with the decisions of the *"Real Audiencia y Chancilleria."*

The convoy for Spain was due to sail from Havana "any time after the first day of August" in one letter; another put the date back at least two weeks. Velasquez was to sail from Santa Cruz to arrive at La Guaira by the beginning of July—except that the next letter from the Captain-General delayed it two weeks. Then came a definite order: *La Perla* was to be ready to sail from La Guaira on 26 June, escorting one ship.

One ship? Ramage read the paragraph again. From the previous references he had understood there would be at least four or five ships. The next paragraph told Velasquez that the *junta* was awaiting orders from His Excellency the Viceroy of the Indies, in Panama, concerning this particular ship, but the Captain-General trusted that in any case *La Perla* was ready to sail.

Why on earth would the Viceroy—the man who ruled the whole of the Spanish Main and Central America in the name of His Most Catholic Majesty—be concerning himself with one ship? Was she going to carry important passengers? Was he travelling in her himself?

Ramage had been conscious of a lot of bustle on deck, and the sentry's call warned him that Southwick was coming to see him.

"We're all ready to begin sending the prisoners over, sir," the Master reported. "Wagstaffe had the sense to send Marines over with his two boats to help guard them. I'm using two of our boats as well. Two trips for each boat."

"Very well. Tell Wagstaffe to come over and bring his sea bag with him. And Captain Velasquez will go over to the *Santa Barbara* in the last boat. I want to see him first."

"Aye, aye, sir. I'll be glad to see the back of 'em and get the lower deck scrubbed out and aired. You wouldn't credit the mess they've made."

Ramage went back to the letters. His eyes ached, his head buzzed with weariness. Only two more letters remained of the bundle from the Captain-General, and he cursed the time he had wasted. It was, he admitted, sheer curiosity: it mattered not a damn when the Captain-General of Caracas or the Mayor of Santa Cruz ordered Velasquez to sail for La Guaira and Havana: the ship was back in the Royal Navy and half a ton of Spanish correspondence and a ton of His Most Catholic Majesty's sealing wax could not affect that.

Wearily he wriggled in his chair: the candle in the lantern was burning low and he turned the letter to catch more light. The *junta* had received a communication from His Excellency the Viceroy, and as a result it had been decided to entrust "a particular cargo" to the ship which *La Perla* would escort. His Excellency the Viceroy had further ordered that another "particular cargo" from the province of Columbia should also be despatched to Spain in the same ship. This valuable cargo had already been sent round from Cartagena in smaller vessels and was now safely on board the ship at La Guaira, and the ship would be ready to sail when *La Perla* arrived on 23 June.

The 23rd of June: that was the day before yesterday, Ramage realized, but *La Perla* had been delayed by the wait for her troops to come back from the mountains. They had returned to Santa Cruz yesterday; they were due to board today. The Captain-General would know all that, and would expect *La Perla* to sail for La Guaira by noon.

Suddenly he awoke with a start, realizing that he had been

half asleep while reading. Slowly he repeated to himself what the letter was telling him: a merchant ship loaded with "a particular cargo" important enough to involve the Viceroy and described by the Captain-General as "valuable" was at anchor at La Guaira waiting for *La Perla* to arrive to escort her to Havana.

He reached up to the rack of charts overhead, selected the one showing the coast from Santa Cruz to west of La Guaira, and unrolled it on the desk, hurriedly weighting it down with an inkwell at one end and his hat at the other.

His hand was trembling slightly as he reached for the dividers and measured off the distance between Santa Cruz and La Guaira. Just over two hundred miles in a direct line, but the road ran like a snake over mountain ridges and across valleys, skirting round a great gulf . . . A messenger on horseback would have to cover a good three hundred miles, and much of the way must be simply mule tracks climbing over the great saddle of mountains to Caracas, some peaks of which were 9000 feet high. The chart showed few villages and only two small towns on the way, so changing horses would be difficult. No messenger from Santa Cruz with the warning that *La Perla* had been captured could reach La Guaira or Caracas by land in less than thirty hours— probably more like forty-eight. *La Perla* herself—the *Jocasta*, he corrected himself—might make it in twenty-four.

CHAPTER SEVENTEEN

RAMAGE rolled up the chart and told the three men standing round the desk to sit down. All of them were physically weary, worn out by the mental strain of the past few hours and the lack of sleep, but the news that Ramage had just given them had brought a gleam to their eyes.

"I wonder what 'particular cargo' means," Southwick said. "It could be anything."

"The Captain-General refers to it later as 'valuable,'" Ramage commented. "And I can't believe the Viceroy of the Indies would concern himself personally with something unimportant."

"Ah, you know what these Spaniards are like, sir. It's probably some gift to a minister; a bribe to get something. Or a present for the King."

Aitken looked up: "It's valuable enough for the Viceroy to want a frigate to escort it."

"Bulky, though," Southwick said. "The letter says 'coasting vessels' were bringing it round from Cartagena. Not one vessel, but several."

"He might have wanted to spread the risk," Aitken pointed out. "A small amount in several vessels."

Ramage laughed dryly. "The three of you are dreaming of gold bars and pieces of eight!"

"Why not, sir?" Wagstaffe asked. "The Dons mine enough gold and silver!"

"Not along the Main. That comes from Peru and they send it up to Panama. And from Mexico, of course, and that is sent out through Vera Cruz."

Wagstaffe looked puzzled. "The Spanish Main, sir—I thought this was where Sir Harry Morgan and the buccaneers were always raiding. Along this coast and beyond Cartagena."

"They raided it, true enough, but as far as I know they usually made their money by ransoming a town's leading citizens. The only time Morgan found a lot of gold was when he marched across the Isthmus to Panama."

"If the Viceroy is so worried about this cargo, sir," Aitken said cautiously, "why didn't he send it direct to Havana from Cartagena? Sending it round to La Guaira means an extra six or seven hundred miles . . ."

"That puzzled me," Ramage admitted, "but the obvious explanation is probably correct: they just don't have the ships. Probably there was one merchant ship in La Guaira and none in Cartagena. There were coasting vessels in Cartagena capable of the voyage round to La Guaira, but none that could be relied upon—or spared—to get to Havana. It was easier to have the one particular cargo from La Guaira loaded on board in La Guaira itself, with the other one from Cartagena being sent round.

"The *Jocasta's* arrival a couple of years ago must have seemed like a miracle: she's the only frigate on the whole coast. Apart from her, the *Santa Barbara* is probably the only ship o' war they have along the Main."

"I can believe that," Southwick said. "We certainly never hear of anything being sighted, or captured."

"That was why their Lordships were anxious to get the *Jocasta* back," Ramage pointed out. "They didn't want the Dons to have her."

"But the Dons never used her," Southwick protested.

"Blame that on the quill-pushers in Caracas. The Captain-General has been arguing with the man who holds the purse-strings, and they have no money anyway. But make no mistake, they want her desperately."

"What was she going to do, sir?" Wagstaffe asked. "I mean, before she was ordered to Spain."

"They were going to send her to sea as a privateer—I think the Captain-General hoped she'd pay for herself with prize-money. They couldn't afford to pay enough seamen; that's why they were using soldiers: they are paid by Madrid."

"So just as she's ready to sail as a privateer, they get orders to send her to Spain," Southwick commented. "They must be hard up for ships over there; I'd have thought she'd have done more good out here."

Ramage nodded; he had given that a lot of thought while reading the letters. "I think Madrid has always regarded the Indies simply as a gold mine. As soon as there's enough bullion ready, they send a small fleet to escort it to Cadiz. In between times the Indies have to look after themselves."

"Pity we don't have gold mines," Aitken said. "When you want to build another dozen ships of the line you just send to the Indies for some more gold."

"Hasn't done 'em much good in the past," Southwick said contemptuously. "They've been digging out gold for nearly 250 years, and neither their fleet nor their army is worth a tinker's cuss."

There was a knock on the door and Ramage's clerk came in holding several sheets of paper: "The orders, sir, for your signature."

Ramage took them and sat at the desk. He glanced through the top page, signed it and gave it to Wagstaffe.

"There you are. Now you are in command of *Calypso,* and you send fifty men back to the *Jocasta.* You're sure you can handle her with the rest?"

"Quite sure, sir. Sixty men are more than enough."

"Very well. The rendezvous is given: wait three days and if we don't meet you before then, make your way to English Harbour and give the report to Admiral Davis."

Ramage signed the report addressed to the Admiral, and gave it to the clerk to take away and seal.

"I'm sorry to bring you back from the *Calypso,*" Ramage told Aitken.

The young Scot grinned cheerfully. "I'm glad to be back in the *Jocasta*, sir. It's not often we get a chance of cutting out ships. I'm getting a taste for it!"

Ramage turned back to Wagstaffe. "You are satisfied with Baker and Kenton? It looks as though it's going to be watch-and-watch-about for you for a week or two."

"We'll be all right, sir, although I think they were looking forward to taking the *Santa Barbara* back to English Harbour."

"I'm sorry to disappoint them, but if you take a prize on the way back they can toss up for the honour of commanding her."

The clerk brought back the report for Admiral Davis, and Ramage, after inspecting the seal, gave it to Wagstaffe. He listened to the movement on deck for a few moments. "I think the last of the prisoners are ready to be taken over to the *Santa Barbara*. Southwick, you'd better send Velasquez to see me."

With that the three men left. Ramage rubbed his face with a towel and was thankful it was not a humid night. He tugged his stock straight, ran a comb through his hair, and put the rolled-up chart back in the rack. He glanced round the cabin—it looked exactly as Velasquez had left it when the *Calypso* came alongside.

A stamping of feet down the companion-way warned him that Velasquez was being brought down with an escort of at least two Marines.

"Spanish officer, h'under h'escort, sir," the sentry announced.

"Send him in, but the escort can stay outside."

Velasquez came into the cabin warily, as though expecting a wild animal to leap at him out of the shadows.

"Good morning," Ramage said in Spanish.

Velasquez had not seen him sitting at the desk and he took a step back.

"Come in," Ramage said. "Sit on the settee."

"You speak Spanish!" Velasquez exclaimed. "Why—you are

the leader of the mutineers! But that uniform! Why do you wear it?"

"It fits me rather well, doesn't it?" Ramage remarked conversationally.

"Yes, but—"

"It should, of course; it was made for me by one of the best tailors in London."

"But you are a mutineer!"

"No," Ramage said quietly, "you just thought I was."

"The rest of the men," Velasquez said lamely. "I just saw some of them in Army uniform . . ."

"Marine uniform," Ramage corrected him.

Velasquez flopped down on the settee. "I do not understand. They sent me a warning from El Pilar that the *Santa Barbara* was bringing in another English frigate with a mutinous crew. I assumed all the details had been arranged by that fool Lopez, and that she was just to berth alongside me."

"Lopez was a prisoner; the *Santa Barbara* was an English prize by then."

"Yes, I realize that now. But you, *señor?*"

"Nicholas Ramage, at your service; a captain in the Royal Navy."

Velasquez was about to rise and bow, but Ramage gestured for him to remain seated: time was getting short, with all the prisoners out of the *Jocasta.*

"Captain Velasquez, all your men will soon be on board the *Santa Barbara,* along with the brig's original crew and Captain Lopez—oh yes, and the nephew of the Captain-General. There are 41 of your men, wounded in the fighting. And here—" he took a piece of folded paper from his pocket "—are the names of the 23 killed. One of the wounded identified them. The garrisons of the two forts are also on board."

"You mean Castillo San Antonio and El Pilar?" Velasquez asked incredulously.

"Yes. You heard two explosions?"

"My God, yes!"

"You'll see what caused them when you sail back."

"Sail back?" Velasquez asked suspiciously.

"Back into Santa Cruz. You will be taken over to the *Santa Barbara* in a few minutes and you will allow the remaining English Marines on board to depart in the boat that takes you over. Then you will sail the *Santa Barbara* back into port."

"You mean I will be free?"

"Yes—you and all the prisoners I have taken, providing you give your word that you will not prevent my Marines leaving. I should warn you that the *Calypso*—she was the frigate that came alongside you in Santa Cruz—is close by, so that between us we can sink the *Santa Barbara* in a matter of moments."

"You have my word," Velasquez said, and Ramage knew he meant it. "You have my word," he repeated bitterly, "although God knows that from now on my own people will place little value on it."

Ramage looked puzzled, and Velasquez held his hands out, palms upwards. "As soon as the Captain-General hears of this, I shall be put under arrest. There was not even a pistol loaded when you boarded us."

"At least you are still alive!" Ramage exclaimed, surprised and vaguely irritated by the sympathy he was beginning to feel for the Spaniard.

"I may live to regret that," Velasquez said bitterly. Then he glanced up at Ramage. "Have you captured any of the English mutineers who originally brought in this ship? Many have sailed in neutral ships."

"Some. In time we'll capture most of them."

"There was one man, one of their leaders. He could handle the ship well. He brought her round from La Guaira—with a Spanish guard, of course. I remember him well. His name—for the moment I cannot remember it."

"Summers?"

"Ah, that was it. You know him?"

"He was captured a few weeks ago and court-martialled."

"And?"

"And he was hanged."

"He deserved it," Velasquez said quietly. "He brought us a frigate, but he was evil. He boasted that he planned the entire mutiny and was responsible for killing all the officers. I think he was the most evil man I ever met. It was wrong for Spain to benefit from the activities of such men. We needed the ship, but mutiny knows no frontiers."

Ramage suddenly felt a kinship with Velasquez; the kinship of men who faced the responsibilities of command. He stood up and held out his hand.

"I have your word about my Marines?"

"You have." Velasquez shook hands. "And thank you for freeing us. I am in your debt. Now you return to report to your Admiral?"

"Yes," Ramage said, thinking of the letters in the drawer.

"What about the other English frigate, the one which came a month ago?"

"Her Captain was making a reconnaissance," Ramage said. "We needed to know if we could cut out *La Perla*."

"And he reported that you could?" Velasquez asked incredulously. "*Caramba!* He must be a brave man! And you, Captain Ramage, you have done the impossible."

CHAPTER EIGHTEEN

BY SUNRISE the *Jocasta* was running westward under studding-sails with a stiff north-east wind. To the south a series of mountain peaks stretched into the distance along the coast of the Main, fading purple like old bruises, while ahead, fine on the starboard bow, was Isla de Margarita, its high mountains making it seem as if the island had been formed by a giant wrenching off a handful of the mainland and tossing it into the sea a dozen miles from the coast. There were two small islands in the channel between, Coche and Cabagua.

Daylight had been a melancholy time on board the frigate because Ramage had to conduct a funeral service for the 23 Spaniards and then for the five men from the *Calypso* who had been killed while boarding the *Jocasta*. Yet the ship's company had soon cheered up after the last body, sewn into a hammock and with a round shot at the feet, had disappeared over the side. Ramage sensed that the men had, like him, expected far heavier casualties, and most of them were too concerned with the wonder of being alive to mourn five lost shipmates for long.

Ramage paused to look ahead at Isla de Margarita and then resumed his pacing of the starboard side of the quarterdeck. By now the *Santa Barbara* would be in Santa Cruz and Velasquez and Lopez—and the Captain-General's nephew—would be telling their story. By now a messenger (two or three of them if the Mayor had any sense) would be galloping along the coast, carrying the warning to the Captain-General in Caracas that *La Perla* had been captured. Looking across the mountains, which swept on westwards like enormous petrified waves, Ramage did not envy the messengers.

The last cast of the log showed that the *Jocasta* was making nine and a half knots. If they could keep up this speed they would arrive off La Guaira soon after dawn tomorrow. In fact it mattered little whether it was dawn or noon, providing they reached there in daylight and before the messengers.

"A particular cargo." The phrase nagged him. The word "particular" had a certain significance when used in the Royal Navy, usually meaning that something was both important and secret. When Admiral Nelson had been given the task of covering the English Channel against the threat of invasion, he had been given command of a squadron "to be employed upon a particular service."

Ramage cursed his deficient Spanish. Normally it was good enough to pass himself off as a Spaniard, but occasionally he was caught out by the deeper significance of a particular word. Southwick might be right; the "particular cargo" from Cartagena could be a present from the Viceroy, something intended to curry favour at Court.

In steering for La Guaira he was now acting without orders. If anything went wrong Admiral Davis would be quite justified in accusing him of actually disobeying orders, since his instructions had been commendably brief: he was to sail to the Main, recapture the *Jocasta* and bring her back to English Harbour. There was not an inch of slack in the wording.

If Ramage brought back a nice fat prize, the Admiral would not throw up his hands in horror and refuse his share, but if Ramage lost the *Jocasta* or the *Calypso* while going after a prize of unknown value, it would be a different story. Captain Ramage would probably spend the rest of his life on the beach on half-pay, being used as an object lesson to other young captains, like a carrion crow strung up on a piece of string beside a gamekeeper's lodge.

Should he forget about that damned merchant ship?

Supposing he managed to cut her out and found that the "particular cargo" was an elaborate suite of furniture made of some exotic tropical wood, or even cages of parrots or rare birds intended to amuse the vapid ladies of the Spanish Court? It could be something like that, because the normal exports to Spain from the Main were items like indigo, tobacco, hides and sometimes cotton.

From Admiral Davis's point of view, he could have had the *Jocasta* back, with the destruction of the two fortresses guarding Santa Cruz as a bonus. His orders would have been obeyed. He could report to the Admiralty that their instructions were carried out. If Ramage brought back a merchant ship full of birds and furniture as a prize it would be doubtful if the Admiral's despatch to London would even mention it.

He picked up the telescope and looked to the north. There was no sign of the *Calypso*. The lookouts aloft could probably still see her sails, but from down here at deck level she had disappeared below the curvature of the earth. She was fast—faster than the *Jocasta*—and Wagstaffe would waste no time. Would he go along the north side of the chain of islands, or stay south? Either way there was no chance of the *Jocasta* catching up with her before she reached the rendezvous.

Southwick, the officer of the deck, caught his eye, obviously wanting to chat.

"The chart doesn't help us much, sir."

"It rarely does along this coast," Ramage commented sourly. "But surely the Spanish ones I gave you are better than ours?"

"They give a few more soundings, but the current is marked 'strong and variable.' This Margarita Channel—I just hope there are no shoals the chartmakers missed."

"We'll soon know. I hadn't realized that Isla de Margarita was so mountainous."

"Aye, that peak, San Juan they call it, is more than three thousand feet high. They reckon you can see it seventy-five miles away in clear weather."

Ramage nodded. "There are more mountain peaks along this coast than I thought existed!"

"It's an iron-bound coast for sure," Southwick said soberly. "This ahead might be called the Pearl Island but it's a rare old pile of rock! I wonder if they still find pearls?"

Ramage shrugged his shoulders. "I don't see why not. It depends on the oysters!"

"They've probably cleaned them all out," Southwick said gloomily.

"I'm sure the King of Spain has enough pearls in his crown by now," Ramage said vaguely, thinking of breakfast and then a few hours' sleep. "Call me as soon as we reach the Margarita Channel."

Southwick watched Ramage disappear down the companion-way and then took off his hat with all the ceremony of a bishop removing his mitre. The wind blew through his white hair and refreshed him. There were times when he felt his years. However, he felt happier now, since he was at last convinced that the Captain had given Rennick the job of capturing Castillo San Antonio only because he wanted the Master on board for the passage out of Santa Cruz.

He had been with Mr Ramage enough years now to recognize most of his moods, but he was damned if he could *understand* some of them. Just now, for example, he had been pacing the deck with a face as long as a yard of pump water, and snappy and sarcastic as a henpecked parson. Why? He should have been as cheerful as a bandmaster; he had just done the impossible—here was the *Jocasta* bowling along the coast under stunsails, and less than twelve hours ago she was moored in Santa Cruz with a Spanish Captain strutting her quarterdeck. Why the long face? Yet while going in to Santa Cruz with the *Calypso,* playing a game of bluff where the slightest mistake would have seen the frigate blown out of the water by the batteries, the Captain had had a grin on his face like a curate who had just converted the Devil.

Perhaps he was worried about chasing after this merchant ship at La Guaira. If the *Jocasta* ran up on an uncharted reef—he looked ahead nervously and then glanced at the binnacle—it would be hard to explain away to the Admiral. Would he understand how that phrase "a particular cargo" had intrigued them all?

He looked astern at the *Jocasta's* wake. The wind was freshening as the sun came up and with the sails rap full the ship would be making more than ten knots within half an hour. He eyed the stunsail booms projecting out from the ends of the yards and wondered when they were last inspected for rot. The metal fittings were rusty—he could see stained wood from down here.

Margarita was coming up fast now. He turned to Orsini, who was pacing the deck, telescope under his arm, and no doubt dreaming, like most midshipmen on a bright sunny day, of commanding his own frigate.

"Mr Orsini! You see the island of Margarita ahead of us, on the starboard bow?"

"Aye, aye, sir."

"The tall peak is Cerro San Juan, and it is 3200 feet high. Out with your quadrant, then, and take a vertical angle and tell me how far off it is. Step lively, though, we're approaching it at nearly ten knots!"

Paolo put his telescope in the binnacle drawer and hurried

down to the midshipmen's berth for his quadrant, repeating the formula to himself. But was it the right formula? He knew the height, and he could get the angle from the quadrant. The height was 2300 feet, so—wait, was it 2300 or 3200 feet?

Accidente! where was the quadrant box? He found it propping up some books at the end of a shelf and hurried back up on deck blinking in the sunlight. *Mama mia,* with stunsails set and running almost dead before the wind it was hard to see forward.

He braced himself against the pitching, checked that the quadrant was set at zero, and then carefully looked through the eyepiece. It was easy enough, he told himself; none of the business of needing to know the exact time. He moved the arm until the reflection of the peak rested on the horizon, and then looked at the scale.

"Take another one," Southwick growled. "Never rely on just one!"

Paolo wasn't sure what had happened with the first, but the second showed a difference of more than a degree. Fortunately the third agreed with the second and he hurriedly set the quadrant at zero again and took a fourth. The last three were the same.

But what was the height of San Juan, the other ingredient he needed? He could sneak into Mr Southwick's cabin and look at the chart (it was just his bad luck that it was not on top of the binnacle box; it would be later on, when the dampness had gone out of the air), but someone might think he was trying to steal something.

"Mr Orsini . . ."

The Master's voice had an odd tone.

"Sir?"

"You are sure of the angle?"

"Yes, sir: three were identical."

"What happened to the fourth?"

"I don't know, sir." There was no fooling the Master; he had sharper eyes than Uncle Nicholas.

"So now you take the angle and the height and you look it up in the tables, eh?"

"Yes, sir."

"What was the height of San Juan?"

Accidente! Paolo felt someone had put the evil eye on him this morning. Was it 3200 or 2300? Better too high than too low— or was it? He tried to picture which would give the farthest distance, but mathematics were a confusing subject which he learned by rote.

"3200 feet, sir."

"Good, it's not often you remember a figure correctly," Southwick grumbled. "Now, off with you and work it out."

Paolo hurried below, carefully wiped the quadrant with the oily rag kept in the box for the purpose—spray and even the damp salt air soon corroded the brass—and put it away. A pencil, a piece of paper and the tables . . . He turned to the back of the tables, where he had long ago written notes. "Distance off by vertical angle"—and there was the formula. Hurriedly he worked out the sum and there was the answer. Two miles. But it couldn't be! He did the sum again—just over seven miles. He did the sum a third time and the answer was still seven, and he scurried up the ladder to report to the Master.

But Mr Southwick seemed far from pleased with the news; Paolo saw that the bushy grey eyebrows were pulled down over his eyes like the portcullis of the castle at Volterra.

"Just over seven miles, Mr Orsini? When was that?"

"Well, sir, when I took the angle."

"And have you any idea how long ago that was?" Southwick tapped his watch. "A quarter of an hour ago, Mr Orsini; fifteen whole minutes."

"Yes, sir," said Paolo nervously.

"And we are making nearly ten knots, Mr Orsini," Southwick said relentlessly. "Will you favour me by telling me how far the ship has travelled in fifteen minutes?"

Paolo's mind went blank, then he groped in his memory. One knot was one mile in an hour, which was a quarter of a mile in a quarter of an hour. So ten knots was—what?

"Two miles, sir?" he said hopefully, but the Master's furious expression made him think again. A quarter of a mile at one knot. So at ten knots—why, ten quarters! So simple!

"One and a half miles, sir!"

"Mr Orsini," Southwick said firmly, "I've no doubt that you have already calculated how far the ship travels in a quarter of an hour if she is making one knot."

"Yes, sir. A quarter of a mile."

"So if you multiply a quarter by ten, you get one and a half?"

"No, sir," Paolo admitted ruefully, "two and a half."

"Thank you," Southwick said sarcastically. "Just bear in mind that an error of a mile in waters like these is more than enough to see the ship hit a shoal."

"Yes, sir. It won't happen again."

"It will, Mr Orsini, it will," Southwick said sadly. "You can knot and splice with the best o' them, but your mathematics . . ."

Just like Mr Ramage, Southwick reflected. The Captain was a fine seaman; he could handle a ship with less effort than a skilled horseman could ride a quiet nag through a gateway, but tell him that A over B equals C and ask him how to calculate what A was and his eyes went glazed. Still, one had to be fair: Southwick knew his mathematics but Bowen nearly always beat him at chess; and the Surgeon could cut off a man's leg and sew it all up, but he couldn't hold a candle to the Captain when it came to guessing how the enemy would react in a given situation. And neither Aitken nor Wagstaffe, competent enough officers though they were, could spot trouble under a distant cloud like the Captain and have the ship snugly reefed down by the time a wicked squall came out of nowhere.

"The wake looks like a snake with colic," he growled at the quartermaster. "Don't let them use so much wheel."

The big island was approaching fast now, and with the sun lifting higher he did not like the haze that was beginning to dull the outlines of the mountains, yet the glass was steady enough. That was the trouble with this damned coast; there were so many local winds. Maracaibo, another three hundred miles along the coast, was the worst; he had a note in his reference book of the *chubasco* which plagued the Gulf of Venezuela between May and August, coming up in the late afternoon and blowing a full gale and sometimes more for an hour, and then dying down and leaving you half-drowning in torrential rain. Along this stretch of the coast—more towards La Guaira, rather—the *calderetas* came screaming down from the mountains, hot, sharp blasts which could send masts by the board. His notebook mentioned just that; it was information from another master who had sailed along this coast, but there was no reference to what warning the *calderetas* gave—if any.

He looked at his watch: it wanted a few minutes to eight. Aitken would be on deck shortly to relieve him, so he picked up the slate and brought the details up to date.

Course, speed, distance run . . . Damnation, he was tired.

The Pearl Island. It sounded romantic enough, but he would be glad when it dropped over the horizon astern and the Saddle of Caracas came in sight. That was the one thing that made a landfall at La Guaira an easy task: the high ridge joining three peaks, the Silla de Caracas, stuck out like humps on camels, with one of them only three miles from La Guaira itself. What a ride those messengers must be having, galloping westwards to tell the Captain-General in Caracas that the English heretics had just stolen *La Perla* from Santa Cruz. Southwick grinned to himself as he imagined the Mayor of Santa Cruz drafting the letter.

CHAPTER NINETEEN

AT DAYBREAK the following morning the *Jocasta* was within fifteen miles of La Guaira, running along a jagged coast where mountain peak after mountain peak reared up only a few miles from the shore, the lower slopes covered with thick green forests. The coastline was a series of bold cliffs, looking like bastions defending the coastline from the constant battering of the sea, broken by occasional gaps where sandy beaches were backed by palm trees. Almost everywhere a heavy surf broke with a thunder that could be heard a mile offshore, spray erupting in white clouds as the waves surged along the rocks.

Ramage looked down at the chart spread on the binnacle box and then glanced up at the mountains. There were two ridges, the nearest with peaks rising to 4000 feet, the second which soared up to 9000 or more. And the three peaks that concerned him most were clear enough: the nearest was Izcaragua, nearly 8000 feet high; then six miles to the west was Pico de Naguata, the highest at 9000 feet, and joined by a long ridge which ran for seven miles to join Pico Avila, 7000 feet high and only three miles from La Guaira. Caracas, the capital of the province, was several miles inland, high among the mountains. There, thought Ramage, the Captain-General will soon be sitting down to his breakfast, blissfully unaware that horsemen are galloping over the mountains to warn him that La Perla has gone. Before they arrived, with luck, more horsemen would be galloping up the twisting road from La Guaira to tell him that La Perla was off the port.

La Guaira—he knew precious little about it. An open anchorage with deep water close to the shore, the port built on a narrow plain between two masses of rock . . . That could be almost anywhere. It was defended by the Trinchera Bastion on the eastern side and by El Vigia, a castle overlooking the port from a height of about four hundred feet. According to Southwick the anchorage was occasionally swept by enormous rollers from the north, coming two or three at a time; walls of water sometimes two miles long which wrenched ships from their anchors and tossed them up on the beach like driftwood.

And that, Ramage thought, is all we know about La Guaira, and entirely due to Southwick's habit of filling notebooks with details of places whenever he could find someone who had been there. It was the main port of the province of Caracas, and (in more peaceful times) fresh water could be obtained from a small reservoir which had been made some five hundred feet above the town by damming up a river. Southwick's notebook added that the main exports were cocoa, coffee, hides, dyewood and medicinal roots. A "particular cargo" comprising those mundane items and captured only by risking the Jocasta would make Admiral Davis explode with more flame and violence than had destroyed El Pilar . . .

Rennick was parading his Marines. They looked smart enough, and Ramage thought he detected a satisfied swagger in their bearing since they had blown up the forts. It would do no harm; they had a right to be proud of themselves and their officer. Although even Rennick did not know it yet, they would soon have to go below and take off their uniforms and put on sea-men's clothing. Any sharp-eyed watcher on shore with a telescope would spot those uniforms and know they were not Spanish; moreover, some of the *Jocasta's* mutineers might be living in La Guaira, only too anxious to help their Spanish masters.

The Marines to wear seamen's clothes, Ramage reflected, is about all I have decided about how we are going to cut out this mer-chant ship. Rennick has paraded his men, the gunner has been round inspecting the guns, Southwick and the bosun have checked over the tiller ropes and are now busy making sure that they missed nothing in yesterday's examination of sheets, braces and halyards. Aitken has the conn, and every one of them, from the First Lieutenant to the cook's mate, assumes that Mr Ram-age has a completely foolproof plan for cutting out the ship, just as they were now convinced that he planned the *Jocasta's* cap-ture to the last detail from the first moment he sighted the *Santa Barbara.*

His plan at the moment was to haul down that Spanish ensign as soon as possible; the sooner the *Jocasta* was sailing under her proper colours the better, although for the time being, to avoid raising the alarm, because they were now barely a mile from the shore, the red and gold flag of Spain was streaming in the wind. The frigate was still *La Perla* as far as the Spaniards were con-cerned—at least at this end of the Main.

Everyone on board was cheerful enough—except Paolo. Since the funeral services he had been taking many vertical angles of every peak that Southwick clapped eyes on and had the height noted on the chart. Ramage doubted if Paolo's book of tables had ever been used so much as it had in the past hour or two. The Master was being deliberately harsh with the boy, beginning with the way he stood as he held the quadrant. "Balance yourself as the ship rolls by swaying your body from the hips upwards," he had growled. "Don't move your buttocks; you look like a fish-wife walking down Billingsgate Hill!"

Now half a dozen seamen were hoisting up the grindstone: after the fighting across the *Jocasta's* decks there were many cutlasses with nicks in the blades which would have to be ground out, and Ramage shuddered at the thought of having to listen to the scraping once again. The cook would come up on deck soon, announcing to anyone who cared to listen that he had "to put a sharp" on his cleavers: cutting up salt tack always took the edge off them. He always appeared when the grindstone was set up; he always made the same announcement, and no one ever listened. But when they had boarded the *Jocasta*, Ramage had seen the cook join one of the boarding parties, a meat cleaver in each hand. He was a deceptive man, so thin he seemed to be starving, and normally so quiet that no one would guess he enjoyed nothing better than boarding an enemy ship.

Once again Ramage looked along the line of mountains. He had never seen a shoreline so constantly beaten by rollers; there was always a jagged line of boiling surf thundering into the foot of the cliffs, flinging up fine spray which hung as a heavy mist, blurring the slots and crevices. Yesterday he had occasionally seen small boats inshore, fishermen from the villages built wherever there was a gap in the cliffs or where a bend in the coast formed a sheltered bay and gave them a lee. They must be hardy men, working under a blazing sun with a heavy sea running most of the time. Presumably starvation faced them if a week of heavy rollers prevented them from launching their boats.

The *Jocasta* was making a fast passage: with this soldier's wind the hourly cast of the log showed she was making an effortless ten knots. During the night he had expected the stunsails to carry away at times as occasional but brief gusts came up astern without warning.

The Main was a strange and unpredictable coast, and he wished he had sailed it before. This curious light over the mountains, for instance: as the sun came up it had not washed the peaks in its usual pinkness; instead it had cast a cold, almost whitish light, bringing with it an almost frightening clarity and throwing harsh, sharp-edged shadows. Every crack and crevice, valley and distant precipice showed up in the telescope as though it was only five miles away, instead of twenty. In contrast, there had been a haze yesterday which, up in the Leeward and Windward Islands, always warned of strong winds to come. Now today there was this clearness. It could mean anything or nothing. Southwick's notebook referred to *calderetas* sweeping down from the mountains, but gave no further details. Still, if they occurred only once or twice in a year there was no reason to suppose they would bother the *Jocasta* . . .

He was getting jumpy; it was as simple as that. He had been lucky at Santa Cruz and if he had had any sense he would be on his way back to English Harbour. Instead he was bound for La Guaira, commanding—as far as any onlooker was concerned —His Most Catholic Majesty's frigate *La Perla*. Only another dozen miles to go; already Pico Avila was looming up high, towering over La Guaira just as Pico de Sante Fé stood at the back of Santa Cruz.

He looked down at his clothes. Providing he did not wear a hat, they were similar enough to the Spanish naval uniform. Southwick, with his chubby face and flowing white hair, would hardly pass for a Spaniard but, he told himself, people usually saw what they expected to see: at La Guaira they were waiting for Captain Velasquez to arrive in *La Perla* . . .

Southwick walked up to report on his inspection: "The tiller ropes are sound, sir, and so are the relieving tackles. Hardly a new rope in the ship but nothing needs changing. Just as well, since there isn't a spare coil anywhere. We might get some from the *Calypso* when we meet her."

"Very well. We'd better start getting ready for entering La Guaira."

Southwick eyed him curiously. "Aye, aye, sir. We'll be anchoring?"

"I don't know yet, but the Spaniards will be expecting us to, so we have to have everything ready."

"The men at quarters?"

"Yes, but hidden below the bulwarks. Guns loaded but not run out and boarders standing by."

Southwick obviously had many more questions to ask, but he nodded and said: "Very well, sir, I'll see to it."

Aitken, as First Lieutenant, had to know what was going on, and Ramage walked aft to where he was standing near the binnacle and gave him his instructions. "I'll take the conn," Ramage said. "We'll be there in two or three hours."

By now the grindstone was hard at work, one man working the handle, another pouring water into the trough through which the bottom of the stone turned, and a third moving the blade of a cutlass across the spinning wheel. He then sighted along the blade and, when satisfied, put it to one side, picking up another from the waiting pile.

The sun was getting hot; already the deck was uncomfortably warm and Ramage began pacing the quarterdeck. The glare from the waves as they surged past the frigate made his eyes ache and it would get worse as the sun climbed higher.

Paolo, having satisfied the Master that he could now work out the distance off by the vertical angle, was marching up and down, hands clasped behind his back, a frown on his face.

"Mr Orsini," Ramage said, "you look worried. Are sines and tangents still bothering you?"

"Oh no, sir. It's my dirk. The blade is chipped and I was hoping I could put it on the grindstone before they stow it."

"How on earth did you chip it?"

"When we boarded the *Jocasta*, sir. I was warding off a cutlass, and I think the blow made a dent in the edge."

Ramage stared at the boy. "You boarded the *Jocasta* with your dirk?" he demanded.

"Why yes, sir: it's a *very* good dirk: the best that Mr Prater had. Aunt Gianna went with me to Charing Cross—Mr Prater is the best sword cutler in London—and told him she wanted the finest dirk for me."

"I know all about Mr Prater," Ramage growled, "but that dirk is not for fighting! Why, it's only a twelve-inch blade. I've told you before, use a cutlass."

"But I had a cutlass as well, sir," Paolo protested. "I was using my dirk as a *main gauche*, but I had to ward off one Spaniard's blade with the dirk and kill him with the cutlass."

A *main gauche!* In the days when duellists paid little attention to rules, a man held a dagger in his left hand, hoping to use the sword in his right hand to swing his opponent round with a parry, leaving him wide open to a jab from the dagger. Paolo had learned duelling in Volterra; his tutor had obviously impressed on him the merits of surviving.

"Very well," Ramage said, "you can have five minutes. But let the seaman put the dirk on the stone; you'll grind away half the metal!"

Aitken was going round the deck and as he called names from a list in his hand men went obediently to collect boarding-pike, tomahawk or cutlass. Ramage noticed that the first thing a man did was to examine the point or edge and some, with obvious grunts of disapproval, went over to the grindstone.

As soon as Paolo came back to the quarterdeck, his newly

sharpened dirk slung round his waist, Ramage gave him a key: "You'll find a Spanish signal book in the second drawer of my desk. Bring it up here, and look through it. You'll find it easy enough to understand."

If anything happened to Gianna, or she died without having a son, her nephew Paolo would be the next ruler of Volterra. Well, he was getting a good training in leadership. Perhaps Gianna was shrewder than he had given her credit for when she asked him to take Paolo as a midshipman. She knew better than anyone what was needed in a ruler of that turbulent Tuscan state, where treachery was a commonplace and, once the French were driven out, revolution would probably join it. He shivered at the thought of what Gianna would face when she returned to Italy. The way things were at the moment, with the French armies victorious from the North Sea to the gates of the Holy City, it was some consolation (for him anyway) that it would be a long time before she could go back to Volterra.

He shook his head to rid himself of the thoughts. For a few moments he had been among the smoothly rounded hills of Tuscany, and it was almost a shock now to find himself staring at the sharp peaks of the Main—peaks which made him feel uneasy for reasons he could not understand but which, from long experience, he knew he should not ignore. And yet, he thought helplessly, what was it that he ought not to ignore?

Men were stowing the grindstone as Southwick bustled up, pointing to a headland just coming clear of the land on the larboard bow: "I'm sure that's Punta Caraballeda, sir. About six miles this side of La Guaira. We'll sight two smaller headlands, Cojo and Mulatos, and then we're in the anchorage."

Ramage nodded. Caraballeda was about five miles away. "We'll send the men to quarters as soon as Caraballeda is abeam. We can—"

He broke off and looked to the south. The wind was falling away and there was still a curious light over the peaks, a harsh white light as though the sun was trying to break through thin high cloud, but the only cloud in the sky was a scattering of balls of cotton. The *Jocasta* slowed perceptibly and the quartermaster looked anxiously at the dog-vanes on the hammock nettings. Each vane was made up of a number of corks with feathers stuck in them and suspended by thin line from a small staff, and they were no longer streaming out in the breeze; instead they were bobbing and jerking as the wind became fitful.

Ramage glanced aloft, then decided to follow his instincts even if it left him looking foolish. He reached for the speaking-trumpet. "We'll take in stunsails, topgallants and courses, Mr Southwick, and double-reef the topsails if we have time!"

The Master stood for a moment, obviously dumbfounded, his eyes going to the south, trying to discover the reason for the Captain's completely unexpected move. Then the habit of discipline took over as Ramage began bellowing the first of the orders.

"All the studding-sails—ready for coming in!"

Seamen stopped what they were doing and ran to their stations, a handful racing up the rigging. The suddenness of the order alerted them all that something unexpected was happening, and as Ramage continued his stream of orders the halyards were eased, tacks started and downhauls manned. Swiftly the studding-sails were lowered and the booms rigged in, slid along the yards out of the way.

Now it was the turn of the topgallants, the highest of the squaresails that the *Jocasta* was carrying.

"Man the topgallant clewlines . . . Hands stand by topgallant sheets and halyards . . . Haul taut!"

Ramage watched the men aloft struggling with the sails and was thankful the wind had eased. He glanced back to the south.

Nothing had changed; the peaks seemed to be making their own light, like phosphorescence, but the wind continued to fall away. He put the speaking-trumpet to his lips again.

"Let go the topgallant bowlines. Look alive, there! . . . In topgallants!"

So much for them. Now for the fore and main courses, the largest and lowest of the sails.

"Lower yard men furl the courses . . . Trice up . . . lay out . . ." So the stream of orders continued until the two great sails were, like the topgallants, neatly furled on the yards, and only the topsails were still set, each nearly 2000 square feet of flax, alternately bellying in a puff of wind and then hanging limp.

Ramage glanced yet again at the mountains. Aitken had hurried up to the quarterdeck, Southwick was standing at the rail, and both men were watching him. There was no expression on their faces: the Captain was giving the orders, and they and the ship's company were obeying them. Obviously they wondered why the Captain should be taking in sail in a falling wind, and Ramage realized that Southwick saw nothing strange, let alone ominous, in the light over the mountains.

Double-reef the topsails? The *Jocasta's* speed would drop to a couple of knots, the pace of a child dawdling to school. Ramage was obeying his instincts rather than the rules of seamanship, and he was liable to be ordering the topmen aloft within half an hour, setting the sails again. He looked at the mountains. Nothing had changed; nor had his instincts stopped nagging him to get the *Jocasta* jogging along under double-reefed topsails.

He raised the speaking-trumpet to his lips and soon reached the last of the orders: "Lower topsails . . . trice up and lay out . . . take in two reefs!" Now the topmen were working out on the yards, hauling at the stiff cloth of the sails and tying the reef points. "Lay in," which sent the men scrambling along the yard to the mast, was followed by "Lower booms," when the stunsail booms were dropped until they were lying along the yards; and then came "Down from aloft!"

Now there remained only the orders for the men on deck: "Man the topsail halyards . . . Haul taut . . . Tend the braces, step lively there! . . ." Finally, with a glance at the dog-vanes: "Trim the yards . . . Haul the bowlines!"

As Ramage reached out to put the speaking-trumpet back on its hook at the side of the binnacle box he saw Southwick point over the larboard side and Aitken's face suddenly freeze the moment he looked.

A long line of tumbling spray was racing over the water towards them: a great squall which must have come down the side of the mountain was now tearing up the sea. This side of the squall line the wind was little more than a breeze; beyond it there was a gale. Following it down the side of the mountains in a solid blanket were black clouds, writhing and twisting and tumbling towards the shore like lava from a volcano.

"Eight points to starboard, steer north!" Ramage snapped at the quartermaster, and snatched up the speaking-trumpet to give the orders that would brace up the yards and trim the sheets as the wind arrived. He wanted the squall to catch the *Jocasta* on the starboard quarter, giving her a chance to pick up way as the tremendous wind hit her. If it caught her on the beam it would simply lay her over; even if it did not rip her masts out she might not be able to convert the enormous pressures on her sails and masts into a forward motion, and they would capsize her, like a storm blowing down a fence.

As the men ran to the sheets and braces Ramage glanced towards La Guaira and was startled to see the whole coast hidden by the same kind of tumbling cloud pouring from the peaks, the sea already a boiling mass of water for a mile or more offshore, and the squall line moving out, slow but inexorable.

The yards were coming round, the two men at the wheel

were hauling desperately at the spokes and the quartermaster was already shouting to another two seamen to bear a hand. Ramage hurried to the binnacle and peered in at the compass, conscious that the sunlight was fading rapidly, like the beginning of a solar eclipse.

Eight points should do it, and the ship's head was beginning to swing. Over on the larboard quarter what had been a line of spray was now a steep wall of blackness, a swirling mass of rain and cloud and spray reaching up sheer like the face of a cliff.

"Must be a *caldereta*," Southwick muttered, his voice betraying awe at the sight.

"I hope the rigging is going to stand up to it," Ramage said sourly. "There's a gale of wind there . . ."

It was still nearly a mile away, advancing slowly. Again Ramage thought of lava crawling down a mountainside, or a glacier, moving slowly but with enormous strength, crushing everything in its path.

The guns were still secured, the boats lashed down. The *Jocasta* was now steering up to the north, still on the starboard tack, with a veering wind and almost directly away from the coast. There was nothing more he could do except wait and hope the wind inside that rain would be steady in direction. If it veered too fast and caught the *Jocasta* aback, the masts would go by the board. Ramage had a sudden picture of Admiral Davis's face as he tried to explain what had happened . . . but to be able to explain, he thought inconsequentially, he had to be safely back in English Harbour . . .

Three-quarters of a mile now and the wind was veering slightly. A puff of warm wind, and then another, and the black wall seemed to be speeding up. Ramage reached for the speaking-trumpet. "All hands! All hands!" he shouted. "Hold on for your lives when this squall hits us."

Aitken was watching him. "Nice range for a broadside," Ramage said.

"I'd reach it with a musket," the First Lieutenant said, and a few moments later added: "Or a pistol!"

Then it was on them; a series of ever-increasing blasts lashing them with rain and salt spray which streamed in almost horizontally, needle-sharp on the face and blinding for the eyes. The noise reached a crescendo, the wind invisible yet seeming solid, screaming into the rigging, battering at bodies, tearing at sodden clothes, whipping up ropes' ends like coachmen's whips.

Ramage, blinded even though he had held his hands over his eyes, felt the *Jocasta* slowly heeling: not the easy movement of a roll as a wave passed under the ship but a gradual inexorable tilting of the deck as the enormous force of the wind pressed against every square inch of hull, masts, yards, ropes and sails; as though she was being hove down for careening.

She was not paying off! Eight points had been too much; the ship was dead in the water and gradually going over. He managed to blink his eyes open for a moment and saw the men fighting, eyes shut, to hold the wheel, but the quartermaster had lost his footing and was struggling on his back in the lee scuppers like a stranded fish. And along the starboard side the seas, driven before this tremendous wind, were piling up like snow against a wall. Southwick was clutching the quarterdeck rail; Aitken, spreadeagled on the deck, was holding on to an eyebolt, and the whole ship was inside a cocoon of streaming rain and spray: he could barely see the end of the jib-boom. A moment before the stinging salt made him shut his eyes again he saw that the reefed maintopsail was in shreds but, by a miracle, the foretopsail was holding, a bulging, swollen grey curve straining every stitch and seam.

He realized he was now gripping the cascabel of a six-pounder gun and hard put to keep on his feet, but as he sorted out what he had just seen in his mind he knew that the *Jocasta* was on the verge of capsizing: a few more pounds of pressure, a few more degrees of heel . . . Already the water was . . . Suddenly he felt the ship recovering from being a dead mass: she seemed to give a massive shrug and the hull began to move, life slowly coming back to her as she gathered way.

The wheel! Blinking away the salt in his eyes he scrambled to the wheel. Three men were holding on to the spokes, pulling down with all their weight, but the fourth man had fallen.

"Hold her!" Ramage bellowed, seizing a couple of spokes and hauling down. "Hold her, otherwise she'll broach!"

Now, with his back to the wind and rain and spray, it was easier to see, and the ship was slowly, agonizingly slowly, coming upright as she turned to bring the wind aft: all the enormous strength was now beginning to act on the foretopsail and the transom, trying to thrust her before it instead of pressing along the starboard side, trying to lay her over on her beam ends.

"Ease her!" Ramage gasped, able to do little more than guess the wind direction, and the four of them let the wheel turn slowly, a spoke at a time. "Another couple of spokes . . . and two more . . . two more . . . that's it: hold her there!"

He staggered to the binnacle, noting that the wind-vanes had disappeared, wiped the compass glass and saw the ship was steering north by west. A moment later the quartermaster was beside him, his face streaming with blood from a cut on the brow.

"Sorry, sir, I'm all right now!"

"North by west," Ramage shouted, "hold her on that!"

He realized that the sound of gunfire was in fact the maintopsail: the torn cloths of the sail still secured to the yard were flogging violently and shaking the whole mast so that the decks trembled. But the double-reefed foretopsail was holding; it was holding and keeping the *Jocasta* running before the wind, pulling her like a terrified mare being dragged from a flooded stable.

Ramage looked round for Southwick and saw that somehow he had managed to get down to the main deck and was collecting a party of topmen to send aloft to secure the remnants of the maintopsail. But two seamen were crouched over Aitken and a moment later Ramage saw Bowen staggering across the quarterdeck towards the First Lieutenant. The Surgeon must have come up the companion-way the moment he could climb, knowing that there would be injured men needing his attention.

Southwick was dealing with the torn topsail, Bowen was attending to Aitken; what else needed doing? The quartermaster's face was a red smear as rain spread the blood. The man was white-faced and wiping his eyes with the back of his hands, but he was watching the compass and turning to give an occasional order to the men at the wheel.

Then Ramage noticed Jackson hurrying up the quarterdeck ladder and looking round anxiously. He saw Ramage and, reassured, was about to turn and go back to the main deck when Ramage waved to him and pointed to the quartermaster.

The American understood immediately and went over to tap the bloodstained man on the shoulder, but the man shook his head. Jackson pointed at Bowen and then at Ramage, and gave the man a shove away from the binnacle. With the wind still screaming it was almost impossible to talk, and Ramage went over to the binnacle to shout in Jackson's ear: "Hold her on this course unless the wind shifts!"

Jackson nodded and bellowed back: "You all right, sir?"

Ramage nodded in turn and pointed to Aitken and the quartermaster, who was now kneeling beside Bowen, more anxious to help him attend the First Lieutenant than be treated himself. "How are things on the main deck?"

"No one hurt," Jackson shouted. "All the gun tackles held. A few pikes came out of the racks, otherwise everything's all right. We were holding on tight!"

With Jackson acting as quartermaster and the fourth man back at the wheel, Ramage struggled to collect his thoughts. The foretopsail was holding, the heavy rain was easing slightly, and with the ship running off before the wind there was not so much spray—or, rather, it was coming from astern so he could look ahead without feeling that salt-tipped needles were puncturing his eyeballs. The *Jocasta* had nearly capsized—his fault entirely: he had come round eight points, and it should have been only half that, but the ship had saved herself (or, perhaps, the thanks were due to Sir Thomas Slade, the man who designed her). As far as he knew the only real damage was a blown-out maintopsail.

Was she leaking? Had these driving seas sprung a plank? More than one plank, in fact? Ramage looked round and saw that Paolo was now standing by the capstan, rubbing his head as though he had just recovered consciousness. As the boy turned Ramage beckoned to him.

"Are you all right?" he shouted.

"Yes, sir, I bumped my head."

"Very well: go down and find the carpenter. Have him sound the well and report to me."

Paolo pointed to the quarterdeck ladder: the carpenter was struggling up it, having to pull himself up against the pressure of the wind. He made his way to Ramage and saluted. "I sounded the well, sir," he bawled. "A couple of feet of water, that's all. From spray down the hatches."

"Sound every ten minutes and report to me. I'll let you have men for the pump as soon as I can. Anyone injured below?"

The carpenter shook his head and gave a wry grin. "Rare old

mess down there, sir; lots of things weren't secured!" With that he made his way to the ladder, cautiously working his way forward from gun to gun, the wind pushing him invisibly and the pitching of the ship trying to fling him.

A movement in the rigging caught Ramage's eye and he saw that men were fighting their way up the ratlines, obviously sent aloft by Southwick. They were lying flat against the rigging as they climbed, fighting the wind which was trying to wrench them off, and reminding Ramage of lizards.

Was the shrill scream of the wind gradually easing? It was hard to tell; at the moment it seemed to have been blowing for hours instead of minutes. He was thankful he had memorized the chart for this part of the coast; there was nothing ahead but Los Roques, the group of cays and reefs making a long, low barrier running from east to west, and they were still sixty miles or so to the north, another seven or eight hours' sailing.

A few minutes later the rain had stopped and the wind was certainly dropping: the topmen had reached the yard and were beginning to slash at the shreds of the topsail, careful that flogging reef-points did not cut them.

Ramage suddenly realized how cold he was: his boots were half-full of water, squelching and sucking as he walked, and his sodden clothes stuck to him like a soggy piecrust. Bowen was now standing up and helping Aitken to his feet. The First Lieutenant staggered for a moment or two, held by Bowen and the injured quartermaster; then he braced himself and made his way over to Ramage.

"I'm sorry, sir; I lost my footing."

"Are you all right now?"

"Yes, sir, just a bump on the head."

Aitken, his hair plastered down and sodden with blood, was pale. Ramage looked questioningly at Bowen, who nodded. "Very well, as you can see—" Ramage gestured aloft "—we have to get another topsail from the sailroom and bend it on. Are you up to it?"

"Yes, sir," Aitken said, his voice now firmer. "Give me half an hour and we'll have a new sail drawing!"

Ramage nodded and Aitken made his way down to the main deck. They had been very lucky, Ramage reflected, but he was resentful at losing the topsail. There was a lot of work ahead, hoisting the spare sail up on deck and then swaying it aloft in slings, securing it to the yards and fitting sheets, bowlines, clewlines, buntlines . . . there seemed to be more rope than canvas. Yet there was some 1600 square feet of canvas, a quadrilateral 36 feet along the head where it was secured to the yard, and 56 feet on the foot, and 36 feet deep.

As the rain stopped the wind eased down and began to back. Jackson was already watching the luff of the foretopsail and Ramage guessed that with luck they would be steering direct for La Guaira within half an hour.

Suddenly he thought of the *Calypso:* how far offshore did these *calderetas* extend? By now Wagstaffe should be a good sixty or seventy miles to the north, close to the chain of reefs and cays. Obviously the *calderetas* were caused by the mountains; he could only hope that they exhausted themselves within thirty miles or so. Wagstaffe was unlikely to be suspicious of the unusual light that preceded them; his first warning—if they reached that far—would be the wall of black cloud. Ramage pictured the frigate floating dismasted, utterly helpless. He cursed himself for not giving Wagstaffe definite instructions about which side of the chain of islands he was to sail: now, if the *Calypso* was not at the rendezvous, he would be hunting for a hulk somewhere in at least 250 square miles. If Wagstaffe had kept south of the islands and then lost his masts he would end up among Los Roques, stranded among rocks, coral heads, reefs, cays less than twenty feet high . . . Admiral Davis might yet end up with only one frigate.

Two and a half hours after the *caldereta* had first hit the *Jocasta*, the frigate was stretching along the coast in bright sunshine under all plain sail, the wind back in the east and steady. Punta Caraballeda was abeam to the south and Ramage could see Punta el Cojo on the larboard bow with, just beyond it, Punta Mulatos, which was only two miles short of La Guaira.

The new maintopsail was losing its creases; mercifully it had not been attacked by rats in the sailroom. The reefs had been shaken out of the foretopsail and the courses had been let fall and sheeted home. Ramage had not set the topgallants or stunsails, but apart from that the *Jocasta* showed no sign of the assault by the *caldereta*. All the men were wearing fresh clothes and the hot sun had dried out the decks. Ramage, already perspiring in the scorching sun, found it hard to believe that less than three hours ago he had been shivering with cold, his teeth chattering in a howling wind.

"Six miles to La Guaira, sir," Southwick reported.

Six miles, three-quarters of an hour's sailing. Ramage looked across to Aitken: "Beat to quarters, but don't run out the guns. Load with canister."

He turned aft, to where Paolo was crouching down, slowly turning the pages of a book in the sun. "How is that coming on?"

"Nearly dry, sir; you can turn the pages without risking tearing them. The colours have run, but I can distinguish the flags."

An hour ago Ramage had wanted to look through the Spanish signal book and he had gone to the binnacle drawer to find it still half-full of rainwater and spray, the book floating like a tiny raft. He had cursed the skill of joiners who had made a

watertight drawer, and set Paolo to work with a towel, drying
the pages with cautious dabs and then finishing off the job with
the heat of the sun. The pages were curling and the cardboard
cover had warped, but the printed words had not been affected.
Paolo handed him the book and Ramage looked through the
signals. What was the Spanish flag procedure? He had searched
through the papers on board, but there was no record that *La
Perla* had ever been given Spanish pendant numbers, the three-
figure sequence of numeral flags used in the Royal Navy to
identify ships, and which were always hoisted when going into
a harbour or anchorage.

Should he fire a salute, and if so to whom? La Guaira was
simply a port, not the capital of a province; the senior official
would be the Mayor. Again, he had no idea how many guns a
mayor rated—if any. The signal book gave him no ideas; he shut
it and gave it back to Paolo. Better to ignore salutes and
pendant numbers than to get them wrong; doing the wrong thing
was more obvious than omitting something. Better offend the
Mayor by not giving him his salute than make him suspicious
by firing the number of guns reserved for someone like the
Captain-General of the province. And anyway, Ramage thought
to himself, there should not be much time for feelings to be ruffled or suspicions aroused.

By now the Marine drummer was striding round the main
deck beating a series of ruffles. In a few moments the gunner
would be hurrying below to open up the magazine and men
were already getting ready to load the guns. Rammers, used to
drive home cartridges and shot, the sponges which would be
soaked with water to swab and cool the guns and extinguish
burning debris, and the handspikes used to train the guns, were
being unlashed ready for use.

Other men were putting two types of tubs beside the guns:

one would be filled with water for the sponges; the other would have lengths of slow match lodged in notches cut round the top edge, the burning ends hanging inside, over the water, so they could not accidentally ignite the stray grains of gunpowder which were almost inevitably scattered over the deck in the heat of action. Unless a flintlock failed to make a spark, slow matches would not be used to fire the guns; they were merely insurance.

More men were waiting for the pumps to be rigged so they could wet the decks while others stood by with buckets of sand, ready to sprinkle it on the planking to stop the guns' crews slipping. Cutlasses and tomahawks were already hung up along the inside of the bulwarks; the boarding-pikes were waiting in their racks round the masts, like Roman fasces.

Ramage, glancing up at the red and gold flag of Spain streaming out overhead, could see no reason why anyone should not think that the frigate was *La Perla*, carrying out the orders of His Excellency the Captain-General of the Province of Caracas, arriving when expected, on passage to Havana.

Punta Caraballeda was on the quarter and Punta el Cojo was on the beam when Aitken arrived on the quarterdeck to report the ship ready for action. A minute or two later Southwick, who had been busy with his quadrant measuring the horizontal angles between the three headlands, announced that they were just over a mile from the shore.

Both men stood waiting expectantly. Now, they thought, the Captain will give his instructions. Aitken was excited, anxious to know what plan the Captain had for capturing the ship with the "particular cargo;" Southwick was concerned only that he should not forget any part of the instructions. Ramage thanked them both and commented: "We should be seeing Trinchera Bastion in a few minutes. It's on the hills to the east of the port. We won't see Miguel Fort until we are almost off the town."

"No, sir," Southwick said stiffly, having made the copy of the chart Ramage had been using, and knowing that his Captain was being evasive. "And until we round Punta Mulatos we won't be able to see into the anchorage."

"Yes—tantalizing, isn't it?" Ramage remarked offhandedly, looking over the larboard bow with his telescope. "Curious that we haven't seen any fishing boats drifting after the *caldereta.* Those fellows know what to look for, and get on shore in time."

"We know—now," Southwick said crossly. "At least, I do; I think you knew already, sir."

Ramage lowered the telescope and stared at Southwick. "I've never seen a *caldereta* before in my life!"

"But you handed the sails in time," Southwick protested.

Ramage shrugged his shoulders. "Barely, but you know as well as I that any sudden change in the visibility always means a change in the weather, no matter whether you're in the Tropics or the Chops of the Channel."

"A change in the weather, yes," Southwick conceded, "but that came up like a white squall."

Ramage, unable to explain that he set more store by his own instinct than in weather lore, much of which contradicted itself, resumed his examination of the coast with the telescope and said: "There's deep water to within a musket shot of the shore along here, but I want a man ready in the chains."

Aitken hurried away to station a man with a leadline ready in case the Captain suddenly called for soundings.

Jackson, standing to one side of the binnacle, his eyes moving methodically from the compass to the luffs of the topsails, was surprised at both the First Lieutenant and the Master. There was more excuse for Mr Aitken because he had sailed with the Captain for only a few months, but Mr Southwick ought to know better. The pair of them had been quizzing Mr Ramage to know what he intended to do when they arrived at La Guaira, as though he should have a cut-and-dried plan for cutting out a ship from an anchorage he had never seen.

That showed how much they really knew about Mr Ramage. He could come up with a masterly plan at times—and usually the secret of its success was its simplicity. But where he was brilliant was in his ability to keep a completely open mind until the last moment. He would look round with that grin on his face, probably rub one of those two scars over his right eyebrow, give a few quiet orders, and that would be that.

The secret, and the American almost sighed as he recalled how many times he had tried to explain it to Stafford and Rossi, was in two things: Mr Ramage could spot an opportunity—a weakness in the enemy defences—which other men would miss; and then he was lightning-quick in deciding how to take advantage of it.

Stafford partly understood it, since Jackson had pointed out that a burglar rarely knew what he would find when he broke into a house. Usually he had only a few minutes to decide whether he would take a set of bulky silver candelabra and cutlery from the dining-room table or waste time looking for jewellery that might be hidden anywhere in the house. Staff, who freely admitted that he turned his skills as a locksmith in such directions as burglary "when times was 'ard," had chuckled then, but this morning, before the squall, he had been like everyone else in the ship's company, trying to guess the Captain's plan.

Jackson growled at the men at the wheel and they hurriedly heaved at the spokes to bring the ship back on course. The wind was following the coast, steady from the east. Curious how that squall suddenly came up from the south: a miniature gale, really, with the wind switching back the moment it cleared.

It had been a close call: some of the men reckoned the *Jocasta* heeled over so far that the ends of her lower yards had touched the water. Jackson had to admit he had not been looking; he had grabbed a ringbolt with both hands and prayed that one of the guns on the windward side would not break loose and come skidding across the deck to crush him.

He grinned happily to himself. One day he would count up how many times he had been quartermaster when Mr Ramage took a ship into action. Meanwhile he must remember to keep an eye on young Mr Orsini; if anything happened to him the Marchesa's heart would break. It was hard to know whether the lad was brave or stupid, but the way he set about those Dons in Santa Cruz—on the deck of this very ship—with a dirk in one hand and a cutlass in the other . . . He had plenty of courage, and Jackson was thankful he had been able to cut down the Don who had got behind the boy and was about to spit him with a boarding-pike. It had been all over in a second, and Mr Orsini never knew how close he had been to death.

"I can make out the Trinchera Bastion," Ramage said casually.

"You should be able to see into the anchorage in a few moments," Southwick said.

"I can already," Ramage said. "It's empty."

CHAPTER TWENTY

THE Jocasta was hove-to on the larboard tack half a mile off the landing place in front of La Guaira, her bow heading directly towards the town, which was a large cluster of white houses built on a flat ledge between the hills and sprawling down towards the water's edge.

Ramage shut his telescope with an impatient snap and South-wick gave a disgusted sniff.

"What do you think, sir? Hasn't the ship arrived yet?"

Ramage shrugged his shoulders. He thought that he had antic-ipated every possibility, ranging from finding that a Spanish ship of the line had arrived unexpectedly to discovering the "partic-ular cargo" had been unloaded and locked up somewhere on shore under a heavy guard.

Aitken coughed, his usual modest preliminary to offering a suggestion: "Perhaps they've been warned from Santa Cruz and the ship has sailed."

"No," Ramage said, "no messenger could have beaten us here, even if it was a flat road all the way—can you imagine what it's like having to cross all these mountains?"

All three men looked gloomily at the rows of peaks disap-pearing in the distance to the eastward.

"It's very strange," Southwick growled. "We know from all those Spanish letters that up to a couple of days ago Velasquez thought that damned merchant ship was waiting here."

"Aye, but anything could have happened since the last of those orders was sent from La Guaira or Caracas," Aitken said. "They're three or four days old by the time a messenger deliv-ers them in Santa Cruz."

"The place is so empty of ships that it's almost as though they're expecting an English attack," Southwick commented.

The thought had already crossed Ramage's mind: was there another British frigate cruising along this coast, sent out from Jamaica by Sir Hyde Parker?

"The ships that were here—the merchantmen we're after, and the usual droghers and sloops—would have had to go some-where to escape. They'd have come along the coast towards Santa Cruz, but we saw nothing," Ramage said.

"Not the Dons!" Southwick said scornfully. "To them, safety means getting into a harbour and relying on forts. They'd have made for Santa Cruz."

"The place is *too* empty," Ramage said, thinking aloud rather than making a comment; ominously empty. Something had happened—an order from the Port Captain or the appearance of an English frigate, perhaps—which had scattered all the usual collection of ships one would expect to find in a place like La Guaira, which was the province's main port. There should be half a dozen droghers, part of those plying between La Guaira and the villages along the coast, collecting hides and coffee, tobacco and dyewood. There should be smaller sloops, doing the same thing. And a few larger vessels bringing cargoes from places like Cartagena and Santa Marta. Even if there were few cargoes, the vessels had to be somewhere, and the most likely place for at least a few of them was here at La Guaira, the masters waiting patiently for their agents to find them something to carry. Yet there was not even a fishing boat.

Fishing boats! He was angry with himself for not having thought of that before, and opened the telescope again to look along the shore. Starting from the beach below the Trinchera Bastion he moved the telescope slowly westwards towards the landing place. There were a few rowing boats hauled well up the beach, higher than one would expect if they were being used daily. There were no buoys marking moorings, but surely they did not haul up the bigger fishing boats? And no fishing boats at the landing place.

He paused a moment. There was one boat, end on now and under oars, which had obviously left the landing place in the last few minutes. And it had passengers on board; men in uniforms, the sun glinting on gold epaulets and tassels.

"We have visitors coming out," he said. "Rig manropes on the starboard side and warn the men not to talk in front of strangers."

Aitken hurried away and Southwick said: "I can't get used to it, sir"—he gestured up at the Spanish flag. "Here we are, hove-to in a Spanish port, with Spanish officers rowing out to us!"

"Just think of the surprise *they're* going to get," Ramage said with a grin.

"You're going to let them on board? Of course, the manropes! But what if they raise the alarm, sir?"

"They can hardly do that if we have 'em on board," Ramage said mildly.

"But we'll have another handful of useless prisoners," Southwick grumbled. He was not questioning the Captain's judgement; he was so disappointed at the empty anchorage that he was looking for scapegoats.

"They're the only ones who can tell us what has been happening," Ramage pointed out. "I'm not particularly anxious to go on shore and ask the Port Captain."

"But supposing they won't tell us?"

"They will," Ramage said grimly. "They left their own beds this morning and they can probably see their houses from here. If they *think* they won't be going home tonight . . ."

Southwick nodded. "Yes, they'll tell us what happened," he said contentedly.

"They'll confirm it, anyway," Ramage said dryly.

The Master's eyebrows shot up. "Confirm what, sir?"

"That the *caldereta* hit the anchorage as hard as it hit us."

"Aye, that could be," Southwick said cautiously. "I don't know how far those things extend."

The boat took more than twenty minutes to reach the *Jocasta*, and as it came alongside the half a dozen seamen idling about along the frigate's gangway were in fact a group under Jackson with the pistols tucked in their belts hidden by loose shirts worn outside their trousers.

Ramage stood at the top of the gangway, out of sight from

the boat but where he would be seen by the first man to reach the deck.

There was a shout in Spanish from the boat and one of the *Jocasta's* seamen threw down a line to use as a painter. Another shout, and a line was thrown from aft as a sternfast. Ramage smiled to himself; he had guessed that the boat would not have long enough lines.

He waited patiently, Aitken standing behind him and Southwick waiting on the quarterdeck. The guns had not been run out, but the locks were fitted, and the trigger lines were neatly coiled and lying across the breeches. Seamen were busy on the fo'c's'le and main deck coiling ropes and polishing brass.

The first man up, fat-faced and puffing, was not in uniform. As he climbed to deck level Ramage saw that his clothes were made of expensive material and well cut. He stepped on deck and looked around crossly, obviously expecting to see Velasquez. He was followed by a painfully thin, tall man in Army uniform with the insignia of a colonel who looked blankly at Ramage, eyeing his uniform but obviously not recognizing it. The third man was clearly the Port Captain, and the trio stood staring round them as though they had just stepped out of a coach in a strange town.

Ramage stepped forward and asked in Spanish: "Can I help you?"

"Yes," the man in civilian clothes said crossly. "Where is Captain Velasquez?"

"In Santa Cruz."

"But—why is he not on board? Who are you?"

Ramage smiled politely. "He is not on board because this is a British ship and I—" he gave a slight bow "—am in command."

The three men stared blankly, but the Colonel was the first to react: his right hand swung across his body to his sword-hilt, and he had the blade half out of the scabbard before ramming it home again and letting his hand drop to his side. Jackson was standing two yards away, a pistol in his hand, and the click as he cocked it had warned the Colonel.

"Forgive me," Ramage said politely, "I must ask you to allow one of my men to look after your sword."

He gave an order to Stafford, who came up behind the Colonel, deftly unclipped the scabbard and then stepped back again.

"Now, gentlemen, let me welcome you on board his Britannic Majesty's ship *Jocasta*—" he pronounced the "j" in the Spanish way and saw that all three men recognized the name "—and if you will give your word of honour that you will behave, I suggest we dispense with guards and go down to my cabin and introduce ourselves."

The civilian nodded. "I give my word. So do these gentlemen."

Ramage looked questioningly at the Colonel. "You have my word," he said stiffly.

The third man gave his word and Ramage said: "If you are the Port Captain, please call to your boatman that they will have to wait."

As the man went to the entry port, Ramage said to Aitken, "Put the boat astern for the time being."

With that he led the way down the companion-way into the cabin. The introductions took only a few moments: the civilian was the Mayor of La Guaira, the Colonel commanded the fortress and the town garrison, and the third man was indeed the Port Captain.

Ramage sat the three of them on the settee, the Mayor in the middle. He sat at his desk, turning the chair to face the trio, and he looked at them expectantly but saying nothing. The Port Captain stared round the cabin with the concentration of a horsecoper inspecting a spavined nag before making an offer, and the Colonel examined the toes of his highly polished boots. The Mayor was, as Ramage expected, the first to break the silence.

"Where is Captain Velasquez?"

"I told you, he is in Santa Cruz." Ramage's voice was vague; clearly the topic bored him.

"But this ship—she is *La Perla*." The Mayor was truculent now.

Ramage shrugged his shoulders. "She is the *Jocasta*. You called her *La Perla*, but she is the *Jocasta* again."

"The Spanish flag—she still sails under the Spanish flag!"

Ramage yawned. "I really must change it."

"You are fighting under false colours!" the Colonel exclaimed, startling the Mayor with his vehemence.

"Hardly fighting, I assure you; just sailing. That is a legitimate *ruse de guerre*. If we were fighting, I assure you we would be doing so under our own flag."

"*La Perla,*" the Mayor persisted, obviously completely bewildered and like a man trying to break a dream. "She was in Santa Cruz. We expected her here."

"Quite so. She was in Santa Cruz and she is now here."

"You know what I mean," the Mayor said angrily, pulling a large handkerchief from his pocket and mopping his face.

"We sailed into Santa Cruz in another frigate, recaptured her and sailed her out."

"I do not believe you!"

Ramage gave a dry laugh and the Mayor flushed. "Well, I find it hard to believe," he added in a voice strangely shrill for such a fat man. "Where is the other frigate?"

"*Señor,*" Ramage said, his voice taking on a harsher note, "although I am prepared to satisfy your curiosity, you are hardly in a position to interrogate me."

"All right, I believe you," the Mayor said hurriedly. "But what is to become of us?"

"You are prisoners for the moment."

"But that is ridiculous! Why, we are close by the fortress—"

"Stop ranting," the Colonel said curtly. "You are not addressing a *junta*. No one in the fort will open fire on the frigate flying a Spanish flag, especially since they know their commanding officer is on board. And this man said we were prisoners 'for the moment.'" He looked directly at Ramage. "Do I understand you are not going to take us away?"

"I hope not," Ramage said. "You have much to do after the *caldereta*. Repairing damage to the houses, finding the ship . . ."

"The ship!" the Mayor exclaimed. "How can we search for her when we have no vessels—" He broke off, conscious that the Port Captain and the Colonel had both turned to stare at him.

"You have no need to worry," Ramage said smoothly, thankful that the Mayor had leapt into what was at best a crude trap. "She had not drifted far."

"How do you know?" the Port Captain asked warily.

"*Señor*, please!" Ramage said in an offended voice. "The *caldereta* drags her from her anchors, she drifts before the wind . . ."

"But she hasn't sailed back!"

Ramage thought quickly. "She could hardly sail back if she lost her masts and was captured by the enemy."

"*Caramba!*" the Mayor exclaimed, "we are ruined! What will the Viceroy—" Again he broke off, embarrassed that once again he had given something away.

"The fortune of war," Ramage said philosophically, seeing a clear picture of the merchant ship slowly beating her way back to La Guaira, perhaps even now in sight from the masthead.

"Well, gentlemen," he said, standing up, "I'll see you back to your boat."

"You mean we are free?" the Mayor asked excitedly. He jumped up and, forgetting how low the cabin was, cracked his head on a beam. He subsided on the settee, glassy-eyed.

The Colonel looked down at him coldly and then turned to Ramage and said: "Thank you. I do not know how you captured this ship in Santa Cruz; I would not have thought even a rowing boat could get past the forts."

"The forts are now in ruins," Ramage said quietly.

The Colonel went pale. "How many English ships made the attack?"

"One—a frigate similar to this."

"Who commanded her?"

"I did."

"Where is she now?"

"Waiting for us," Ramage said. "One of my officers is commanding her."

"Your Admiral will be pleased to see you," the Colonel said, his voice a mixture of bitterness and admiration. "The *caldereta* has made you a rich man."

C H A P T E R   T W E N T Y - O N E

THE WHITE houses of La Guaira were just dropping below the horizon as Ramage took the weights off the chart and let it roll up with a snap. He and Southwick had finally, at the end of a series of guesses, estimated the merchant ship's present position.

They had to assume that the *caldereta* had behaved in the same way at La Guaira as it had when it hit the *Jocasta*. It would have parted the merchant ship's cables and driven her northwards for about one and a half hours—providing she had not capsized. In that time she would have drifted up to eight miles. Then the wind had slowly backed, taking half to three-quarters of an hour to get round to the east. In that time the ship would have drifted another four miles or so in a north-westerly direction. After that, assuming she had not been able to set sail, she would have drifted westwards, carried by both wind and current, for four hours, covering sixteen to twenty miles. The cross on the chart showed where she should be at this moment.

Ramage had pencilled on the chart her probable track: a dog-leg about 28 miles long, setting the ship well down to the west and about ten miles offshore.

"There's a lot of 'if' and 'maybe,'" Southwick had grumbled. "*If* she hasn't capsized, *if* she drifts at this speed or that, *maybe* her masts went by the board . . ."

"It'll take us about five hours to get down to her," Ramage said. "If she can set any sail naturally we'll meet her sooner. We should sight her before it's dark."

"If she's still afloat. Do you think she's likely to have capsized, sir?"

Ramage shook his head. "No, I think she was so close in to the shore that it might have saved her when it first started blowing. It was only during the first few minutes that we nearly capsized, until we could run off before it."

"It seemed like hours," Southwick commented.

"Yes. Well, her cables couldn't take the strain and eventually they parted and she began drifting out to sea. They knew what to expect, and I think they might have been able to keep her under control. I hope so, anyway."

"I'm doubtful about our estimates of the speed at which she's drifting."

"I agree. I think she'll be slower. So we're likely to see her more to the south-west. But the visibility is good and the look-outs have telescopes."

The first hail from the mainmasthead three hours later warned that there was a small boat on the starboard bow, and the *Jocasta* bore up to find it was empty. The second hail, half an hour after that, told of three boats on the starboard bow, and they too were empty and nearly sunk.

Southwick plotted their positions and then came up to report to Ramage. "They drifted in the direction we expected, sir. A lot slower, but o' course they're half-full of water and don't have the windage of a merchant ship."

The next hail revealed a drogher drifting along, her mainsail in shreds and floating low in the water. The two men on board, taken off by one of the *Jocasta*'s boats, reported that the other three men in the crew had been washed overboard. More impor-tant, they told Ramage that while the *caldereta* was blowing they had seen the merchant ship drifting past them apparently undamaged.

This news had cheered Southwick. "We'll soon sight her beat-ing up towards us," he told Aitken, but the young Scot was gloomy: "If she could set any canvas, she'd be in sight by now. Her topsails, anyway."

The First Lieutenant was echoing Ramage's thoughts. The men from the drogher—now below under guard, thankful at having been rescued but depressed at being prisoners—had been far from sure when they had seen the merchant ship: they could not say whether it was three minutes after the wind parted their anchor cable or thirty; they explained that they had been fight-ing to stifle the mainsail, which parted the gaskets, and then busy pumping to save the vessel.

"You think she's gone?" Southwick asked Aitken.

"Aye—probably capsized just to spite us. We must have used up all our luck at Santa Cruz."

Ramage feared that Aitken's view was shared by most of the ship's company, who had been full of zest as they left La Guaira. Now, four hours later, the laughing and teasing had gone; they were cheerful enough, but no longer excited.

If he was honest, he had to admit he was losing hope; it had been something of a gamble from the start. It was satisfying to know that if the merchant ship had been in La Guaira there would have been no difficulty in capturing her and towing her out. No one could anticipate Nature playing such a trick; one which robbed both the Spanish and the British with the same savage impartiality.

"Deck there!"

The hail was from the lookout at the foremasthead, and Ramage listened as Aitken answered: "Deck here!"

"Masts, sir, looks like three masts one point on the larboard bow."

"No sails set?"

"No, sir; leastways, not uppers."

"Can you make out the hull?"

"No, sir, only the topmasts. Lying north and south, they are."

It could be her, Ramage thought. The position was about right, and apart from a neutral ship which had unluckily strayed into the path of the *caldereta*, there was no other ship it was likely to be.

Aitken was looking at him, waiting for orders.

"We'll go down to investigate her, Mr Aitken. Have the boats ready for hoisting out, and pass the word for Mr Rennick."

An hour later the *Jocasta* was hove-to a cable to windward of a small merchant ship. Ramage estimated her to be about four hundred tons. Her masts were bare; he could make out three yards lying across her decks in a tangle of ropes. Where were the others?

"At least she's not floating low," Southwick said.

"No, they're not working the pumps," Ramage confirmed, lowering the telescope.

"But there's a deal of work in getting those yards up again. She's probably sprung her masts, too," Southwick grumbled.

Ramage turned to Aitken. "We'll send two boats over. You'll take one, I'll take the other. A dozen Marines in each. Rennick can go with you."

As the First Lieutenant hurried off to the main deck, Southwick said: "Let me take a boat, sir. It's not right for you to be leading boarding parties."

"I need some exercise," Ramage said flippantly.

"But you can't trust those Dons, sir."

"Mr Southwick," Ramage said impatiently, remembering the times before when the Master had protested at being left on board, "as soon as you learn to speak Spanish you can board every Spanish ship we sight!"

"But I can bring back the Captain for you to question," the Master protested. "It's not seemly, sir."

"It may not be seemly, but it saves a lot of time." With that he went below to collect his sword.

As Jackson steered the boat across the merchant ship's stern, Ramage realized that losing her yards was not the only damage: as she pitched he saw that her rudder was smashed. The rudder-post was still there but the blade had been torn off. No wonder they were not hurrying to get the yards up again; first they needed a jury-rudder.

Now there were a dozen or more men lining the rail and

watching the approaching boats. The masts looked curiously naked, like great fir trees stripped of their branches and leaves. Yet the paintwork of the hull was in good condition and she was pierced for eight guns. And there it was—Jackson had noticed it too and grunted. Always, as you approached a Spanish or French ship from to leeward, there was the whiff of garlic.

"They look quiet enough, sir," Jackson murmured.

"Glad to see us, even though they can see from our colours it means they'll be taken prisoner. Better that than drifting all the way to the Mosquito Coast."

Jackson snapped an order to the oarsmen and a moment later the bowman had hooked on with a boat-hook and the boat was rising and falling alongside the ship. Ramage jammed his hat on his head, swung his sword round out of the way, and leapt for the rope ladder hanging down the ship's side.

The men who met him on deck were unshaven, their faces drawn with weariness and despair. Behind them the wheel spun uselessly and in several places the deck planking was stove in where yards had crashed down. On the starboard side the bulwarks were jagged, sections crushed by the weight of the falling yards.

One of the men stepped forward. He was solidly built and in better times he obviously had a cheerful face. Now his skin was grey from fatigue and his eyes rimmed with red.

"I am the master of this ship," he said nervously.

Ramage nodded and answered in Spanish. "You are now prize to his Britannic Majesty's ship *Jocasta*."

"But—well, when we first saw you we thought you were a Spanish frigate, *La Perla*."

By now the Marines had followed Ramage up the ladder and were spreading round the deck, covering the Spanish crew with their muskets. He decided to leave the Spanish master puzzled for the time being; first he wanted to find out about the "particular cargo."

"Show me the ship's papers," he said, and followed when the Spaniard pointed to the companion-way.

The cabin was comfortable; it had a good deal of mahogany panelling and the furnishings were tasteful. The master went to his desk and unlocked a drawer.

"The log and the ship's papers," he said, placing them on the desk and shutting the drawer again. Ramage saw that he was very nervous; his movements were jerky and his upper lip was beaded with perspiration. It was hot down here in the cabin, but that was the perspiration of nervousness, not heat.

"Manifests, bills of lading . . .?" Ramage asked.

"We had not completed loading."

"You are wasting my time," Ramage said impatiently. "You know what I am looking for. I can set my seamen to work searching through the holds until we find it, but unless you want to be left on board this wreck until you drift to the Mosquito Coast, I suggest you cooperate."

"*Señor,* I dare not . . ."

"The papers are in that desk. Do you want me to have you seized so that I can get them out?"

The man finally shrugged his shoulders, took another key from his pocket and unlocked the bottom drawer. Slowly he took out a sheaf of papers and put them on top of the desk. Ramage saw that he could not bring himself to push them across; that would be handing them over to the enemy. He reached over and took them.

There were two or three dozen sheets of paper and most of them had at least one large seal. He began to leaf through them, intending to look for any that came from Panama. Half of them bore the seals of the office of the Viceroy of the Indies and the rest had the seals and signatures of the Captain-General of the Province of Caracas. They referred to two separate consignments of cargo.

Then he found copies of receipts, notarized and signed by the master of the ship. They said that he had received the consignments on board, and described what they were. Ramage felt dizzy as he read the words again, and the quantities. He glanced up at the master, who was watching him like a rabbit paralysed by the eyes of a weasel.

"Where is it stowed?" he asked.

CHAPTER TWENTY-TWO

AS THE *Jocasta* glided through the entrance to English Harbour, Ramage saw the *Invincible* at anchor in Freeman's Bay with two frigates farther up towards the careening wharf. Jackson began calling out the numbers of a signal from the flagship, and Paolo was busy with the signal book.

Southwick said suddenly: "Look, sir: the *Invincible*'s men are swarming up the rigging!"

Was she about to get under way? Ramage trained his telescope on the fo'c's'le of the flagship. No, there were no men there, so she could not be weighing anchor. The men continued climbing the rigging; then some spread out along the lower yards while others carried on upwards, to go out on the topsail and topgallant yards, looking at this distance like starlings on the branches of three trees.

"They're manning the yards!" Southwick exclaimed.

280 : RAMAGE'S MUTINY

"What on earth for?" Ramage muttered anxiously, trying to
remember if it was the King's or Queen's birthday, or one of the
half a dozen other days when salutes were fired. He saw both
Aitken and Southwick staring at him.

"They might be glad to see the *Jocasta* coming back," Southwick said, barely troubling to keep the irony out of his voice.

Now Paolo was reading out the signal: the *Jocasta* was to
anchor to the north-west of the flagship—just in front of the
masked battery, Ramage noted. A moment later Jackson was
reporting another signal that had been hoisted by the flagship
with the *Calypso*'s numbers.

"Well, what is it?" Ramage asked Paolo impatiently.

"She's to anchor to the south-east of the flagship, sir."

The Admiral was gathering the frigates round him like a hen
collecting her chicks.

"The batteries, sir!" Southwick exclaimed and Ramage glanced
up to the walls of Fort Barclay, built along the top of the western arm of the entrance. Rows of red-coated soldiers were
standing to attention.

There was no more time to think about all that. "Stand by
for anchoring, Mr Southwick," he snapped, and the Master hurried to the fo'c's'le.

Ramage picked up the speaking-trumpet, gave an order to the
quartermaster and began shouting the sequence of orders for
trimming the *Jocasta*'s yards round and bringing her to the posi-
tioning for anchoring.

The ship was a hundred yards from the *Invincible* when it
started: a stentorian "Hip, hip" followed by five hundred voices
bellowing "Hurrah!"

Birds wheeled up in alarm as the cheer echoed off the hills
on either side of the anchorage and a few moments later came
a second cheer, and then a third. What on earth does one do?

Ramage could only recall the yards being manned to cheer a departing commander-in-chief, who usually stood on the quarterdeck saluting.

He glanced astern to see that the *Calypso* was through the entrance under topsails only and already bearing up to anchor south of the *Invincible*. He looked forward again to make sure the cable was ranged on deck. The anchor was clear, the topmen waiting. Aitken was beside the binnacle and calling out the bearing of the flagship. Ramage lifted the speaking-trumpet to his lips. Every man in English Harbour was watching, from the Admiral to the most heavy-footed soldier in the island's garrison; this was not the time to make a mistake in what the seamanship books referred to as "Bringing the ship to anchor."

Fifteen minutes later, with her topsails furled and riding to a single anchor, the *Jocasta* looked like any other frigate in English Harbour. The boatswain was being rowed round in one of her boats, giving signals to ensure the yards were square. A second boat had been hoisted out and Jackson was inspecting its crew, making sure their queues were neatly tied and that their shirts and trousers were clean.

Ramage came up on deck with his best uniform, his sword slung, a canvas pouch of papers under his arm. The anchor buoy had hardly hit the water before the flagship had hoisted another signal for the *Jocasta*, ordering her commanding officer to come on board. They had sharp eyes on the flagship, spotting that he was not in the *Calypso*.

The Admiral's cabin was cool, and the Admiral watched impatiently as Ramage paused to unlace the canvas pouch and take out several papers.

"Edwards," he said, "tell that steward to step lively with those rum punches. Are you sure you don't want a dash of rum in your lime juice?" he asked Ramage anxiously. "No? Well, you know best."

Clearly the Admiral regarded the drinking of lime juice without rum as a dangerous practice, liable to bring on any one of the dozen or so foul diseases which took their toll of men serving in the West Indies.

"Carry on with your report," he said impatiently. "The papers can wait. Now, what made you send that Spanish brig—what was her name, the *Santa Barbara?*—back into Santa Cruz with the prisoners? She'd have been a useful ship. I can always use a fast brig."

"There were more than two hundred prisoners, sir. I had to send some of the *Calypso's* men over to the *Jocasta.*"

"Fifty men could have brought the *Jocasta* back. That would have left you with nearly two hundred men in the *Calypso.* More than enough to guard two hundred prisoners."

Ramage had guessed he would have to face that question, and he had spent much of the time on the passage north from the rendezvous off Bonaire—where he found that Wagstaffe had not even heard of a *caldereta,* let alone experienced one—trying to think of a satisfactory answer. He had concluded that it was easier to tell the truth, which was not the same as giving a satisfactory answer, because the Admiral would also be thinking of his own share in the prize-money the brig would have fetched.

"I needed more men in the *Jocasta,* sir, so I gave Wagstaffe fifty men and put him in command of the *Calypso.*"

"Wagstaffe? Why not your First Lieutenant, that Scots fellow, Aitken?"

"I needed him on board the *Jocasta,* sir. You see—"

"No I don't. It seems to me you were very unwise in freeing two hundred prisoners. Trained seamen—just the sort of men the Spanish always need. And that brig—she's the best ship they have on the Main. You gave them the ship back and five times the number of men needed to sail her."

Edwards said quietly: "Did you sail back direct from Santa Cruz?"

"No, sir." Ramage was grateful for the interruption. "You see, sir," he told the Admiral, fighting to keep the exasperation from showing in his voice, "you want me to give you my report in the exact sequence that things happened?"

"Yes, of course, it's the only way to make a report. Can't very well begin at the end, eh?"

"After you sent the *Santa Barbara* back into port," Edwards said, "you decided you wanted four-fifths of your men in the *Jocasta*, instead of splitting them evenly between the two frigates. Why?"

"I read through the papers on board the *Jocasta* and found she was due to meet a merchant ship in La Guaira and escort her to Havana, where a convoy for Spain was forming," Ramage said hurriedly, hoping to complete the explanation before he was interrupted again, but he was unlucky.

"You understand Spanish?" the Admiral asked.

"Yes, sir. And I knew the *Jocasta* could reach La Guaira before anyone could warn the Captain-General of the province that the frigate had been recaptured."

"Why go to La Guaira?" the Admiral demanded.

"To cut out the merchant ship, sir; she—"

"What? Do you mean to say you thought of risking losing the *Jocasta* again for the sake of some damned merchant ship? Why, she'd be laden with hides and dyewood and coffee; not worth a thousand pounds in prize-money. Well, thank goodness you didn't go!"

"But I did, sir."

"You didn't get the ship, though!"

"No, sir, she wasn't there."

"There you are," the Admiral said crossly. "Just taking a needless risk. Your orders were to cut out the *Jocasta* and bring her back here. There was no mention of cruising along the coast of the Main. Bring the *Jocasta* back here; that was the important thing. Their Lordships will be pleased; you'll get all the credit, I'll see to that."

Ramage sensed that Edwards was watching him closely and sympathizing with him for the way the Admiral interrupted and jumped to conclusions after insisting Ramage told his story in a precise sequence.

"What happened at La Guaira?" Captain Edwards asked.

Ramage described the *caldereta,* minimizing the risk to the *Jocasta,* and told how he had sailed into the empty anchorage under the Spanish flag, been boarded by the Mayor, commander of the garrison and Port Captain, and learned from them that the merchant ship had drifted out to sea after parting her anchor cables in the *caldereta.*

"When I think of the *Jocasta* lying hove-to under the guns of that fort," Admiral Davis said wrathfully, "I feel like bringing you to trial. Risking the *Jocasta* just to ask dam' silly questions about a merchant ship. I'm not saying," he added, "that I don't want my captains to harass the enemy, but I did expect you to appreciate the Admiralty's interest in the *Jocasta;* she's not just another frigate."

At that moment the steward came in with a tray of drinks and hurriedly handed them round. The moment he had left the cabin Edwards said: "I get the impression that you had a particular interest in this merchant ship, Ramage."

"There were two phrases in the Captain-General's orders," Ramage explained. "One referred to 'a particular cargo' and the other referred to it as 'valuable.' The Viceroy was involved, so I thought it must be important!"

"Bah!" the Admiral exclaimed. "He or his friends had an investment in it. Safeguarding his own purse. Anyway, you finally decided to obey my orders and bring the *Jocasta* back, and I'm thankful for that!"

"Well," Ramage said cautiously, "not immediately, sir. I—"

"Don't tell me you went off and searched for this ship?"

"Yes, sir."

"But you didn't find her! I've been waiting here day after day, waiting and worrying! What a damned waste of time—"

"I think Ramage did find her," Edwards said mildly. "What was she carrying?"

"A quantity of pearls and emeralds consigned to the Spanish Crown," Ramage said in a flat voice.

The Admiral sat bolt upright. "A *quantity?*"

"Yes, sir."

"Why the devil didn't you tell me this at the beginning?" The surprise had angered the Admiral, and Ramage looked at Edwards helplessly.

"I think it was my fault, sir," Edwards said smoothly. "I kept telling him to make his report in sequence, and—"

"Yes, the poor fellow didn't get a chance. Well, don't keep on interrupting, Edwards, you confuse Ramage. Where are all these pearls and emeralds now?"

"On board the *Jocasta*, sir."

"Why didn't you bring them over with you?"

"*With* me, sir?" Ramage said, startled.

"Yes, with you. You can carry that dam' pouch of papers; surely you could have put a bag of gems in your pocket?"

The Admiral was obviously interested in his eighth share of the value and wanted to see them.

Ramage looked the Admiral straight in the eye. "There are nine crates of pearls, two years' output from the Pearl Island, and eleven crates of emeralds, two years' output from the mines of the province of Columbia, sir. The crates weigh more than a ton, complete with royal seals."

For a full minute there was complete silence in the cabin. Ramage saw the Admiral trying to put a value on them, until finally he took a deep drink and then smiled happily, suddenly comfortable in the knowledge that his share of the prize-money would make him a rich man. "Orders should never be too rigid," he said. "One must be careful not to stifle initiative. Remember that, Edwards."

Douglas Reeman Modern Naval Library

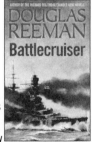